Nicola Thorne is t[...]
known novels whi[...]
The Daughters of the House, The Askham Chronicles
(*Never Such Innocence, Yesterday's Promises, Bright
Morning* and *A Place in the Sun*), *Bird of Passage,
Champagne Gold, Silk, Profit and Loss, Trophy Wife*
and *Worlds Apart*. Born in South Africa, she was
educated at the LSE. She lived for many years in
London, but has now made her home in Dorset.

The Girls
In Love
Bridie Climbing
A Woman Like Us
The Perfect Wife and Mother
The Daughters of the House
Where the Rivers Meet
Affairs of Love
The Enchantress Saga
Champagne
Pride of Place
Swift Flows the River
Bird of Passage
The Rector's Daughter
Champagne Gold
A Wind in Summer
Silk
Profit and Loss
Trophy Wife
Repossession
Worlds Apart

The Askham Chronicles

Never Such Innocence
Yesterday's Promises
Bright Morning
A Place in the Sun

NICOLA THORNE

Old Money

HarperCollins*Publishers*

HarperCollins*Publishers*
77–85 Fulham Palace Road,
Hammersmith, London W6 8JB

This paperback edition 1997
1 3 5 7 9 8 6 4 2

First published in Great Britain by
HarperCollins*Publishers* 1997

This novel is entirely a work of fiction.
The names, characters and incidents portrayed in it are
the work of the author's imagination. Any resemblance to
actual persons, living or dead, events or localities is
entirely coincidental.

ISBN 0 00 649683 0

Printed and bound in Great Britain by
Caledonian International Book Manufacturing Ltd, Glasgow

This book is dedicated
to the memory of
Dr Enid Legrange,
a much loved, admired
and most courageous woman

CONTENTS

PART I

Man of the Match: Nick

CHAPTER 1

There was always something superior about the Harveys; a feeling of class, old money.

However much Lydia Constantine tried to feel on equal terms with them, she couldn't. And, God knows, she'd tried. Tried for years.

It wasn't that the Harveys were visually smart or ostentatious. Valerie Harvey was downright shabby, seemed to delight in wearing old clothes. Old but good; the sort of thing you bought at Harrods or Harvey Nicks, or sometimes second-hand at the Oxfam shop.

Lydia shopped in little boutiques in Knightsbridge, Bond Street or Hampstead, sometimes in St John's Wood. Places where you didn't ask the price, and, my, how you would be looked down upon if you did. Lydia was sure Valerie would ask the price of everything, but this wouldn't diminish the fact that she had class; generations, maybe centuries, of breeding which enabled people to do that sort of thing, and get away with it. Lydia and her friends assumed that, if you had to ask the price of something, you couldn't afford it.

The Harveys and the Constantines sat next to one another in comfortable deck chairs on the edge of the field, their eyes on the main characters, Giles and Nick, who were fielding with the rest of the school team. It was the annual match between the school and the old boys, and Edmund Harvey was wearing whites because he might be called upon to bat. He hoped not, because he was going in at number eight and

3

didn't want to make a fool of himself and disgrace his son, because if he was called upon as late as that it would be with the object of saving the side, and he didn't think he had much of a chance.

The old boys had just come in to bat after lunch, a good lunch, during which the wine flowed, thus making the chances of beating the school, who had scored two hundred and fifty off fifty overs, practically zero. Giles had got fifty, Nick had been out for a duck. The Constantines had wriggled uncomfortably, the Harveys had been profuse in their sympathies during the lunch break.

'Bad luck, old boy.' A firm handclasp on the shoulder, a rueful shake of the head from Edmund. 'Jolly bad luck.'

Nick had smiled deprecatingly, glancing at his feet. Inwardly Lydia had seethed. Always that feeling of being patronised by the Harveys; Giles just that little bit one up on Nick.

Wasn't it always the way, especially when there was an audience, that the Constantines came off worse than the Harveys?

Bad luck every time.

Andreas Constantine was not an old boy of the school. He wore flannels, a white shirt and a blazer, a tie adorned with the crest of some club or other. Certainly it wasn't an old school tie. The sparse education he'd received in the local elementary school in Camden Town, where he'd been born the year the war ended, 1945, had been frequently interrupted by periods of truancy, indiscipline and downright rebellion, until his father hauled him into his little business at the age of fourteen, whereupon Andreas saw the light and buckled down to work.

As if to make up for his batting failure, Nick not only fielded well but got two of the old boys out for a duck. Nick seemed to shine on the field whereas Giles remained near the boundary, arms folded, with the air of a man enjoying

4

the sun, content, perhaps deliberately, to let his friend take the glory that his batting prowess had eluded.

The contrast in their styles of play was reflected in their appearances. Although close friends, they were completely unalike physically. Nick was shorter than Giles, slim, elegantly built, intense, olive skin, warm brown eyes and tightly-curled black hair.

Giles seemed the archetypal, laconic Englishman; extremely tall, straight fair hair, pale skin, deep-blue eyes, and the air of one at ease with himself, sure of himself, as if continually amused and entertained by the follies of the world.

Whatever chemistry had brought Giles and Nick together emphasised their contrasting looks as well as personalities. It was an attraction of opposites, yet they were deeply compatible. Perhaps it was their intelligence, their swiftness of mind and shared sense of humour that had not only attracted them to each other in the first place, but had maintained and strengthened their friendship through boyhood and adolescence. Each was sure that, as it had been, so it would continue for the rest of their lives.

By tea-time it looked as though Edmund would indeed be called upon to bat, and he fortified himself with a stiff gin and tonic in the refreshment tent while Valerie looked on with disapproval, nudging him in the ribs and hissing: 'You'll fall flat on your face if you're not careful!'

'Nonsense!' Edmund hissed back and, leaning over the bar, asked for a refill.

Edmund, however, acquitted himself well, scoring fifteen not out before the last batsman was despatched by Nick, who had got three wickets for forty-five runs, two catches in the field, and was declared man of the match despite his poor performance as a batsman.

Giles, as captain of the school team, received the cup from the chairman of governors, made a graceful speech of thanks, congratulated the old boys on a splendid effort, particularly his father (broad smiles and claps), and then paid tribute to his best friend Nick Constantine, deservedly man of the match.

There was applause, shuffling of feet, and as people began to move towards the bar, Giles held up his hands calling for order.

'Just one more thing, ladies and gentlemen,' he said as soon as he had their attention. 'This is the last time I shall have an opportunity to address an audience at this school, because in two weeks' time I'll be leaving it.' He paused and looked about him. 'It is a very sad occasion for me and for those like me to whom the school has come to mean such a lot, to whom it has given opportunities not only academically but in the field of sports and social activities in general. This school has a fine name, as so many of you old boys can testify.' He paused, face flustered, and looked around: 'Schools like this exist not, as some people say, as bastions of privilege but to turn out well-rounded citizens of a largely classless society, a society based on sexual and racial equality, and I shall be proud to be one of its distinguished corps of old boys.'

Giles appeared momentarily overcome by emotion, and then the Head came over to him and vigorously shook his hand. Then he held up an arm gesturing for silence.

'Ladies and gentlemen,' he began, 'this very unexpected, and gratifying, speech of Giles Harvey has left me, for once, very nearly speechless myself. As I know many of you – particularly the players – are anxious to slake your thirst, I will not detain you any longer except to thank Giles for his kind words, sentiments I strongly echo, and may I say that here,' he paused and looked at Giles, 'we have one of the finest representatives this school can produce to take its work and philosophy out into the world at large. Giles has a distinguished academic career, he has a conditional place at

6

Oxford, he has been captain of rugger and cricket. He has enjoyed enormous popularity with both staff and his fellow students and I wish him and all the sixth formers who are leaving us this term the best of success and happiness in the future.'

There was further applause, stamping of feet, followed by a rush to the bar. There Edmund Harvey was the first to procure a bottle of champagne which he opened with a flourish before proceeding to pour the contents into glasses, holding out the first two to Nick and Giles.

'Splendid speech,' he turned proudly towards his son. 'I didn't know you had it in you.'

'Well done, darling,' Giles's mother Valerie said, her clipped upper-class vowels imperceptibly raising her voice above the crowd. '*I* knew you had it in you.' She reached up to peck his cheek and Giles gave her his glass of champagne, then turned to his father for another. At that moment Andreas Constantine emerged from the crush round the bar clutching a bottle of champagne in each hand.

'I thought I'd add to the celebration,' he said, handing a bottle to Nick to uncork. 'I think we can be proud of our two boys today, Edmund. They have done us, and the school, proud. I agree that was a very good speech, Giles. I'm sure you've both got a lot to offer the world, and look,' he paused to take the other open bottle from Nick and refilled Edmund's already half-empty glass, 'can't we persuade you to spend part of the vacation on our boat? We've asked you before . . .'

Edmund pulled a wry face.

'Valerie's not a very good sailor.'

'It's *you* who doesn't want to go on the boat,' Valerie retorted indignantly. 'I think you're the one who's afraid of being seasick.'

'I am *not* afraid of being seasick,' Edmund hissed. 'I simply don't like boats.'

7

Emma Constantine, Nick's sister, slipped quietly in beside her mother.

'Sorry I'm late,' she gulped. 'Sorry I missed the match. Did we win?'

'It depends who you mean by "we",' Giles laughed.

'Well "we". You and Nick.'

'We won.' Nick turned to offer her a glass of champagne.

Little Alice Harvey, who was standing shyly beside her father, her hand tightly clenched in his, piped up.

'Daddy was *fifteen* not out.'

'Is that good?' Emma, tall and languid, dark and good looking like Nick, her twin, pretended to affect ignorance of all sport.

'It means he retired with honour.' Giles smiled at Emma and then looked across the room to where his younger brother, Paul, was tentatively edging his way towards them.

'Sorry I'm late,' he said. 'Sorry I missed the match. But I managed to hear the speeches. Did you bat, Dad?' Paul accepted a glass from Nick. 'I see we're celebrating.'

'You missed a very good match.' Edmund looked disapprovingly at his younger son. 'I suppose you'd consider it impertinent of me to ask where you've been.'

'Like me, Paul can't stand cricket.' Emma gave him a conspiratorial smile. 'Why pretend?'

'Why pretend indeed?' Nick was anxious to lower the temperature which, in this over-heated, over-crowded room, was rapidly rising. He felt nervous, strangely depressed, and he had a headache. He felt uneasy, as he always did, when his family and the Harveys were together. Dad was anxious to show off – trust him to buy two bottles of champagne – and his mother usually talked too much. Although today she'd hardly said a word. He smiled at her fondly. She looked terrific, impeccably groomed as always, beautifully dressed, elegant, her fine features just a trifle set. He knew how she felt about the Harveys.

8

'We're trying to persuade your family to join our boat in Monte Carlo for a few days in the summer.' Andreas turned to Paul. 'I'm sure you like the sea.'

'*I'd* love to come,' Paul, usually the most laid-back member of the family, replied eagerly.

'We've asked you before . . .'

'Oh, Andreas,' Lydia burst out impatiently, 'if they don't want to come, they don't want to come.'

'It isn't that we don't *want* to come,' Valerie said carefully, passing her glass to Nick for a refill. 'It's . . . well, we usually do other things in the summer.'

'I'd *love* to go,' Alice said. '*Please*, Daddy?'

'We'll have to think about it.' Edmund looked down at his youngest, then across to Andreas. 'It's very kind of you to ask.'

It was always very kind of them to ask, and they asked often. They asked them to dinner, to parties and, of course, to go on this goddamned boat. As they left the gathering the Harveys said that, of course it was *very* kind of the Constantines to ask, could they let them know later as they had so many other things to consider.

'Of course. There's no hurry. Give us a ring,' Andreas said. 'And no doubt we'll see you again before the end of term.'

The Constantines' long, sleek Rolls was parked at the end of the row in the car park. Even from a distance, it looked ostentatious. The Harveys' Volvo, a good, sensible family car, a few years old, looked indistinguishable from the rest, but there was no mistaking the pale-blue Rolls with the yellow numberplate, AND CON 1.

The two families waved goodbye, and the Constantines strolled towards the Rolls while the Harveys made their way to their car, their progress frequently interrupted as they stopped to greet numerous friends or acquaintances.

On occasions like these, Nick was assailed by a feeling of

isolation as though, when his family visited the school, they were outcasts, people who stood apart. Of course the Harveys had been associated with the school for years. Not only was Edmund Harvey an old boy, but his father had been one too. A Harvey had attended the school when it was founded in the mid-nineteenth century, well over a hundred years before.

Andreas was usually too busy to attend school functions, but Lydia was assiduous. Yet when she was in a crowd, like today, she sometimes retreated into a shell, dwarfed, as usual, by the Harveys who knew everyone. And everyone seemed to know them.

In a way, Nick knew he would be glad to leave the school.

'Thank God there will be no more "dos" like this,' he said, throwing his bags into the boot which he shut firmly.

Lydia looked sharply at him as she stood waiting for Andreas to open the door. 'I thought you enjoyed it. You seemed to.'

'And why do you always have to bring the Rolls?' he went on. 'I feel such an ass.'

Andreas had arrived late, having dropped his wife off earlier en route to a business meeting. Nick and Emma had made their way separately to the school.

'I'll drive what car I like,' Andreas said huffily, 'without advice from you, my lad. I am not ashamed to be able to afford to drive a Rolls, or own a yacht based in Monte for that matter.'

'And to buy *two* bottles of champagne,' Nick was undeterred. 'I thought you overdid it. It's so over the top.'

Lydia glanced nervously at her husband. 'Oh don't start rowing you two.' She got wearily into the car and settled in to her seat while Andreas got in beside her. Emma and Nick sat at the back.

Lydia placed a hand gingerly against her brow. 'I think I have one of my heads coming on.'

10

'What Nick *means*,' Emma said, 'is that there is something so patronising about the Harveys.'

'No, I don't know what he means.' Andreas adjusted the driving mirror, then started the engine.

'You *do* know what we mean, Dad.' Emma glanced at her father who was looking at her in the mirror. 'We never feel comfortable when we are all together, especially in the school. That's what Nick means by saying he is glad there will be no more "dos". Isn't it, Nick?'

'I don't know why you always have to invite them on the boat.' Nick gazed moodily out of the window. 'It's obvious they don't want to come.'

'Well, I shan't ask them again,' Andreas said, his pride wounded, as he slowly manoeuvred the large car out of the school car park. 'If that's how you feel.'

'Frankly,' Lydia sighed, settling back into her seat, 'I shouldn't be sorry if I never saw the Harveys again. And now that Nick is leaving, let's hope we don't have to. Except Giles,' she glanced quickly at Nick slumped in the back seat. 'I've always liked Giles. If only the rest of the family were like Giles.'

It was early evening when the Harveys arrived home. As usual, they met so many people they hadn't seen for ages, and now that Giles was about to leave it might be a long time before they met again. Paul had failed the Common Entrance exam and had been unable to follow his brother to the school which was a blow to the family pride, as well as its finances, because an expensive boarding school had to be found for him in the Home Counties.

There was an air of anticlimax after the excitement of the day. Giles went up to his room to change out of his whites while his father kept his on and went into the drawing room. After helping himself to a drink, he wandered onto the patio and sank into a lounger, watching Alice at play in the garden.

Valerie went immediately into the kitchen to prepare supper, much of which had been left ready in the fridge: cold meats and a selection of salads. She, too, helped herself to a glass of wine from an open bottle on the kitchen table.

'Shall we eat outside?' she called from the window and, receiving no answer, put her head out to discover Edmund fast asleep in the lounger, his empty glass by his side. Alice was sitting in her swing gazing thoughtfully at her father.

'Darling, come and help,' Valerie called, whereupon Alice obediently got down from her swing just as Giles appeared in the kitchen now dressed in jeans and a T-shirt.

'Where's Paul?' his mother asked, as she carefully laid slices of beef and ham on the serving plate.

'Upstairs,' Giles replied, 'in his room.'

'I do wish Paul would try and be more pleasant when he's at home. After all, he got special weekend leave for the match and then missed it.'

Giles shrugged. 'I guess it was just an excuse to get away from school. We know he doesn't like cricket.'

'But your *last* match for the school. I do think . . .'

'Mum, what is the use of thinking?' Giles began to slice bread and arrange them in a bread basket. Giles, in every way the antithesis of Paul, was helpful in the house. 'You know what Paul's like. You're always expecting him to be something he's not.'

True. Paul was the weak link in the family chain. Ten-year-old Alice was the perfect daughter: pretty, compliant, obedient yet spirited too, and Giles was almost the perfect son. Almost. Because he and his father did not entirely hit it off. Edmund, a bastion of the Tory party, didn't approve of Giles's Leftish leanings, voiced too frequently for his liking. Valerie so wished Giles would respect Edmund's views more, and keep his own opinions to himself. It made Edmund so choleric, and also contributed to his consumption of alcohol, already high enough.

'Giles, would you go and wake Daddy and tell him we're having supper on the patio? And call Paul? Alice is outside in the garden. Oh, and just take these things out for me,' and she thrust a tray into Giles's hands.

The Harvey residence was a substantial thirties building in a good part of Hampstead. It had been a gift to the young Harveys on their marriage from Valerie's parents, and was in a leafy road off Frognal. It had a small garden at the front, and a substantial one to the rear, part of which was paved to patio and the rest remained lawn. They did not number gardening among their many interests.

There was also a house in Somerset which had been in Edmund Harvey's family for several generations. It was rather dilapidated and not much visited, though they kept horses there which were looked after by a resident grooms-man whose wife acted as housekeeper. They always spent Christmas and part of the summer holidays in Somerset, and it was the excuse they always gave for not joining the Constantines on their boat.

That night as they sat eating supper on the patio, the day's events were very much in their thoughts. They kept on returning to the match, the sadness of the last days at school and, inevitably, the boat.

'I think that just once we should accept.' Valerie flung her napkin on the table and sat back. 'It's been on my mind.'

'But why?' Edmund began.

'It seems so rude to keep on saying "no". After all, it's not as though we'll be seeing all that much of them in future, as the boys will no longer be at school together. Oxford will be different.'

'*If* we get into Oxford,' Giles said.

'Oh, you'll get into Oxford, no question.' His mother seemed astonished by his remark. 'Your interview went well, didn't it? But still it's not the same. I mean there won't be all those "dos" that parents have to go to.'

13

'You didn't *have* to go.' Giles sounded peeved.

'No, darling, we wanted to. I mean it's part of one's duty to take part in school events, fund raising activities, that sort of thing. I must have seen Lydia Constantine a couple of times a month at least. Really, I *like* her. I do. She's very generous, hardworking . . .'

'Don't sound so patronising, Mum,' Paul said, pushing his chair back.

'I am *not* patronising,' Valerie said indignantly.

'You are. You know you don't really like them. You patronise them and it shows. Just because Andreas Constantine is the son of a Greek import merchant . . .'

'There is nothing wrong with being an import merchant,' Edmund said indignantly. 'Anyway, that man's a millionaire several times over. He could probably buy and sell us.'

'His father was a barrow boy or something, wasn't he?' Valerie, looking vague, fluttered her hands in the air.

'His grandfather,' Giles corrected her. 'His grandfather came from Greece and had a market stall, I think in Leather Lane in those days. It was his father who started to import wine and olives and that sort of thing. It's a multimillion pound business now. And yes I guess they *can* buy and sell us.'

'But it's breeding that counts.' Paul slyly eyed his father. 'Isn't it, Dad? The old school tie? By the way, Giles, while we're on the subject, I thought your speech was soppy and sentimental.'

'Thank *you*!' The colour slowly suffused Giles's cheeks.

'Not at all; but it's what I have against the public schools. Play up, play up and play the game. No questions asked. It's what made so many young men glad, nay eager, to lay down their lives for King and Empire. I guess the same thing would happen again if there were a war, and Giles would be the first to volunteer . . .'

14

'I don't see why I should have to put up with your cheek,' Giles retorted angrily.

'I think you should apologise to your brother.' Edmund stared sternly at Paul. 'That, or go to your room.'

'I thought *that* heavy parental attitude went out years ago.'

'Not in this house.' Edmund thumped the table with his fist. 'I'm just about sick of your lip, Paul, your iconoclasm. You're going to one of the most expensive private schools in the country, draining me in the process incidentally, just because you haven't the intelligence to get into the same school as your brother, yet you have the nerve to insult him . . .'

'Really, Dad, I don't mind.' Giles agitatedly rubbed a hand over his face. 'Let's forget it. This is getting right out of hand.'

'I apologise,' Paul said with a charming smile.

'I accept,' Giles smiled back. 'What were we talking about?'

'I was hoping to get off the subject . . .' Valerie began.

'The old school tie.' Paul seemed intent on driving his point home. 'Breeding and the Constantines, or rather the lack of it.'

'Now that sort of thing *did* go out ages ago.' Edmund speared a piece of cheese with his knife and conveyed it to his mouth. 'I've absolutely nothing against Andreas Constantine, but then I've nothing in common with him either. Nick is another matter. Nick is educated. Nick is the fortunate generation benefiting from the sacrifice of his forebears. I don't have to like Andreas Constantine to respect him, and I do. If you were to ask him, he would probably say the same thing about me.'

'I still think it would be nice to go on the yacht.' Paul got up and threw himself onto the lounger previously occupied by his father. 'I'd like it, and Giles would like it, and Alice would love it . . .'

'Oh, yes!' Alice cried, squeezing her eyes shut with rapture and clasping her hands.

'I think it would be a nice gesture,' Giles said, tight-lipped.

'Well . . .' Valerie paused and looked across at her husband. 'What do you say, Ed?'

'It appears I'm outvoted.' Edmund gave a deep sigh. 'For the sake of family harmony it seems I have to say "yes".'

CHAPTER 2

A welcoming hand reached out to help Edmund up the gangplank.

'Welcome aboard.'

'Nice to see you, Andreas.' With surprising agility Edmund Harvey jumped onto the deck.

'Call me Andy.' The hand moved to his shoulder and gave it a chummy squeeze. 'Everyone calls me Andy.'

'Nice to see you, Andy.' Valerie now seized the proffered hand and was hauled aboard. Behind her was Alice, then Paul and finally Giles who stood at the bottom of the gang-plank on the quayside talking to Nick.

Behind Andreas, also wearing nautical attire, was Lydia, and behind her was an assortment of people, one or two who were obviously crew, and another couple who were quite clearly guests. The yacht anchored in the harbour at Monte Carlo seemed huge, a seventy-two footer with lights blazing, while the sun simultaneously set across the bay, illuminating the famous castle of the Grimaldis, high on the hill.

Nick had gone to the airport in Nice to meet them in a large Range Rover which he had driven overland. At first, the idea had been that Giles should accompany him and Emma, but Edmund had insisted that the first part of the holiday should follow the hallowed family tradition of the ritual visit to Somerset where the family foregathered: various aunts, uncles, cousins and Valerie's mother and father who were still alive.

Edmund's mother had died soon after he was born, and he had been brought up in the country, largely by his grandfather and grandmother.

From the quay, Nick and Giles watched the Harvey family clamber aboard and listened to the chatter as they were introduced to the other guests who had preceded them. 'How many people have you got altogether?' Giles asked his friend.

'Just another couple, the Thompsons, plus you. We're picking up others along the way as we cruise to Majorca.'

'It's *huge*,' Giles gazed admiringly at the boat. 'I'd no idea it would be as large as this. It must be as big as Onassis's?'

Nick grinned.

'I think Dad rather hoped it would be bigger.'

'Did he know him?'

Nick shook his head. 'I don't think so. Maybe my grandfather did. Onassis was a generation older than Dad.'

'Of course.'

The conversation seemed stilted, awkward. Giles, who had been looking forward to the trip, now began slightly to regret that he'd come. Nick and he were never easy in the company of their parents, and now that they would be together for five days, close together in the restricted confines of a ship, even a vessel as large as this one. And on the last day of the holiday, the A level results were due.

'Shall we go aboard?' Nick pointed towards the gangplank and, taking his holdall, Giles sprinted along towards the hand held out to him.

'Welcome aboard, Giles. Nice to see you.'

'Thanks, Andreas.' Giles gripped the hand of his host.

'Call me Andy. Everyone calls me Andy.'

'Nice to see you, Andy.'

'And very nice to see you, Giles. Emma and my chief steward have taken your parents, and Paul and Alice to their cabins. You're sharing with Nick. Is that alright?'

18

'That's fine.' Giles smiled. 'As long as it's OK with Nick.'

'Promise not to snore?'

'Welcome aboard, Giles.' Lydia took his hand and then, drawing him towards her self-consciously, kissed his cheek. She wore a white trouser suit over a red top with a rounded neck and, with her dark hair and tanned skin, looked quite stunning. Of course they had already been here for five weeks. Giles thought that, if it were him, he'd soon get very bored entertaining various guests and spending five weeks at sea. 'Let me introduce you to your fellow guests.' Lydia indicated a couple who stood awkwardly by the gangplank. 'Frank and Sally Thompson. Frank is in the same business as Andy. Giles is Nick's best friend,' she explained. 'They're hoping to go to Oxford together.'

'How exciting.' Sally Thompson was about forty, her husband maybe five years older. She too was tanned, dressed in shorts and a sun top, and looked as though she spent a lot of time in beauty salons.

Once she had completed the introductions, Lydia studied her watch. 'We'll meet in about half an hour for drinks on deck. Did you bring a dinner jacket, Giles?'

'Oh!' Giles clapped a hand to his mouth.

Lydia looked reproachfully at her son. 'Nick should have reminded you. We always like to dress for dinner.'

'I, well . . .' Giles looked around. 'I didn't realise it would be quite as posh as this. I don't think Dad has brought a dinner jacket either.'

A shadow flitted across Lydia's face.

'Never mind,' she said. 'Tonight at least we'll dress informally.'

'Well,' Giles shuffled his feet, 'maybe tomorrow we can slip into Monte and hire something.'

Andreas looked vaguely embarrassed, while Lydia, eyebrows raised, gazed despairingly across at her guests. How like the Harveys, she seemed to be saying, to attempt to belittle their hosts even so far from home, and in their own environment.

The gentle motion of the boat on the water momentarily disoriented Giles as he woke from sleep, making him wonder where he was. The light of the water was reflected on the ceiling of the cabin and danced about as the boat swayed with the tide. The cabin was fairly large and contained not bunks, as Giles had expected, but ordinary beds bolted to the floor. There was a dressing table, a chest of drawers, two chairs and *en suite* loo and shower. His parents' room was even grander with a full size double bed and mahogany, possibly antique, furniture. It was more like a hotel than a yacht, incredibly luxurious, and must have cost a fortune.

Giles glanced over towards Nick's bed and saw that he was still fast asleep. His watch told him it was just after six, and he wished they were anchored in some remote cove where he could jump out of bed and dive into the sea for a long refreshing dip.

He felt he couldn't wait now for them to go to sea, to put some distance between the yacht and the rather oppressive atmosphere of Monte. Or was it not rather the close confines of the yacht and the oddly assorted mixture of people that were oppressive?

He thought back to the dinner party the night before: the stilted conversation, the over-indulgence of his father in drink, and his mother's disapproving looks. The fact that the women wore their finery while the men wore either blazers and flannels, or lounge suits. He didn't think his father, as ill-prepared as the rest of the family for formality, had even brought a tie, and he wore a cricket club cravat tucked into the neck of his open white shirt.

As for his mother, she had worn a shirt-waisted cotton dress that had seen better summers, inevitably a purchase from her favourite Oxfam nearly-new store. She'd thrown it in at the last minute. Was it arrogance or stupidity that had made none of his family, including himself, realise that sailing was a dressy affair, and that people like the Constantines would enjoy showing off, not only their own finery, but that of their guests?

People 'like' the Constantines. What did he mean by that? People not like us, not like the Harveys who put very little store by what people thought about them, cocooned as they were in their own innate sense of superiority?

Suddenly he hated himself and his family, and everything to do with the idea of class, epitomised so aptly by what Paul had said when he criticised his brother's speech the day of the old boys versus the school cricket match.

Giles got out of bed, and his action woke Nick who raised his head and, blinking, looked over at him.

'What's the time?'

'Six.'

'Six! Golly!' Nick turned over and thumped his pillow. 'Couldn't you sleep?'

'I thought it would be nice to go for a swim.'

'The bay is probably polluted.'

'Tomorrow, maybe. We are sailing today, aren't we?'

'About noon, Dad said.'

'It's all very exciting.' Giles perched on the side of the bed and rubbed his hands together. 'I'm looking forward to it. Do you know I've never been on a boat like this before?' As Nick remained silent he said: 'I expect it shows.'

'How do you mean?' Nick, instantly awake, looked across at him.

'Well our behaviour is rather naive.'

'*Your* behaviour naive?' Nick sat upright on the bed, leaning on his elbows. 'I thought we were the ones who were naive.'

Giles gazed at the floor. 'I don't know what you mean.'

21

'You know what I mean. I really don't know why you came. Your father said he didn't like boats.'

Giles said nothing, dismayed by the bitterness in Nick's voice.

'I suppose you felt you should,' Nick went on. 'After all, we invited you every year, and this was our last at the school. Perhaps your father, or maybe your mother, said: "Really, we better. They ask us every year and . . ."' Nick made a feeble attempt to mimic Valerie's rather high-pitched voice.

'Oh, do shut up, Nick,' Giles burst out suddenly. 'Why do you bring all this up now?'

'Because last night was so awful. Everyone was on their best behaviour.'

'My father drank too much. I thought he made a fool of himself.'

'And my mother talked too much, as if she was afraid of an awkward silence.'

It was true Lydia had gone on and on, and Giles had begun to wonder if she'd had too much to drink too. The Thompsons had remained largely silent and it was, surprisingly, Paul who kept up a spirited and intelligent conversation with Emma on his right, who also seemed absolutely oblivious to the tensions surrounding her.

In fact, Paul and Emma had been the most relaxed and normal people present.

'Look,' Giles went over to Nick's bed and sat on the side, 'let's make the best of this. We're here for almost a week. We can't go back. It would look awful. Besides, we don't want to. I think Dad and Mum genuinely wanted to come out here, but it's not the sort of thing they're used to and they don't know how to behave, or to dress. I apologise on their behalf.'

'They're more used to horsey gatherings in the country.'

'Yes, if you like, and Mum has never been much of a dresser. She has no fashion sense at all, and no interest in

22

clothes. It's nothing to do with class. It's the way she is.'

There it was, out at last, that word 'class'. They stared at each other, as if they'd committed blasphemy or a social solecism. 'That's what we're talking about, isn't it, Nick?' Giles said softly.

'I suppose it is.' Nick nodded. 'I always feel awkward when your parents are about. Always have. At one point I thought it would destroy our friendship. But somehow we always managed to steer clear of it and, besides, you were always so normal. I don't believe you're affected by class at all.'

'Except for that idiotic speech I made at the last cricket match, all about love of school and country.'

Nick grinned. 'Oh, so you did think it was idiotic?'

'Well, not at the time. Paul drew my attention to the fact that it was sentimental gush, and then I did feel ashamed. I think I must have had a rush of blood to the brain. I think that was Dad speaking, not me. Look, I honestly don't believe in class distinction, and if it does exist, I think our generation should do all it can to get rid of it.'

'My parents have got too much money,' Nick said. 'They are really the first generation to have so much, and they think it can buy them anything. Yet it can't buy them education, and it can't buy them confidence. People like your mother and father make them feel ill at ease. They want to show them that they are every bit as good as them.'

'Well, they are . . .'

'Yes, but you know the way I mean. Dad might not be admitted to the Pavilion at Lords, or Whites. He thinks to rub noses with the Harveys is a social cachet. He knows, on the other hand, that we've probably got more money than you have, and he wants to show you his Rolls and his yacht . . .' Nick put a hand over his face. 'Frankly, the whole thing makes me sick – and ashamed – because I know that in my way I'm looking down on a family who have given me everything in life, and without whom I would not be where I am today. And I love them. I love them and I'm ashamed of them. There, doesn't that make me an unworthy son?'

Giles simply didn't know what to say and, rising, went and peered out of the porthole.

'It's a lovely day,' he said. 'Let's try and make this week a good one.' And turning round he managed a smile, but Nick remained lying on his back staring at the ceiling.

'Come in,' Edmund called, and paused in the act of putting on his loafers. He looked up as the door opened, and Giles put his head round.

'Hi! Sleep well?'

'Very well, considering.'

'Considering what?'

'Considering that we are not on dry land.'

'Where's Mum?'

Edmund pointed to the shower, and that moment, a towel draped round her from her bosom to her knees, Valerie emerged, shaking her wet hair.

'Hello, darling. Did you sleep well?'

'Fine. Did you, Mum?'

'Better than I expected.'

'Because of the sea?'

'Something like that.'

'Well, we sail at noon, Nick says.'

'Good. I'm looking forward to it.' His shoes on, Edmund stood up and, going over to the dressing table, carefully examined his appearance in the mirror. Seeming pleased, he turned to his son: 'Do I look nautical enough?'

'Every inch the sailor, Dad; but I have bad news.'

'Oh!' Valerie looked up from towelling her hair, concern showing on her face.

'We have to go into town before we sail and hire monkey suits.'

'Are we going to a ball?'

'No, but they expect it.'

'But that's absurd.' Edmund's expression of self-satisfaction vanished immediately.

'Why is it absurd, Dad?' Giles perched on the bed and looked at his father.

'Because this is an informal boating holiday, at least that was what I thought.'

'Yes, but they like to dress for dinner. It's part of the form at sea. Like dressing up for a cricket match. We should have realised it. You know all those films you see about people who own large yachts. They're always in dinner jackets, swanning about.'

'But I've nothing to wear either,' Valerie wailed.

'Maybe you could buy a dress, Mum.'

'I don't see why I should. It will cost the earth.'

'I think you should out of politeness.'

'Well, if we'd been told in advance, I could have brought something.'

'I think we should have been warned,' Edmund agreed. 'Colossal expense, just for a few days.'

'Well, what do you want to do?' Giles stood up.

'I think we should have a word with, what's his name, Andy, and tell him. We were perfectly well attired last night.'

'I thought the women were overdressed.' Valerie flopped on the bed with a sigh. 'Now I know why.'

'I'm quite willing to have a word with Andy.'

'What will you say?'

'I shall apologise and point out that we know nothing about yachting. Put it down to ignorance and all that.'

'That still needn't stop us getting dinner jackets, Dad. Personally I'd like to. They've put themselves out, and I think we should show appreciation by fitting in with their customs.'

'You'd think we were talking about savages, some rare species,' Edmund grumbled.

25

'You mentioned a ball, Dad. Well, if people came to stay with us and there was a hunt ball . . .'

'Yes, but we'd tell them there was a ball, not expect them to know instinctively.'

'I feel now, with hindsight, that we should have realised they would dress for dinner on a smart yacht, and I think it would be polite and good mannered to slink off into town after breakfast and hire dinner jackets for us, and for Mum to buy a rather smarter frock.'

When the three members of the Harvey family got to the stern of the boat where a table, hovered over by an attentive, white-coated steward, was laid for breakfast, only Sally Thompson was there. Valerie looked round apologetically. 'Are we terribly late?'

'Not at all.' Sally Thompson looked up from the *Daily Mail* with a smile. 'Frank has gone with Andy to find a doctor.'

'Oh, dear!' Valerie exclaimed with concern as she sat down in the chair held out for her by the steward. 'Is someone ill?'

'Lydia has come down with some sort of bug. Apparently she was ill all night.'

'Oh, I *am* sorry.' Valerie, startled, looked at Edmund who also registered his concern.

'Andy insists we are not to let it spoil our day. His plan is still to leave by noon, if possible.'

'But only if Lydia is well enough?'

'That goes without saying.'

'Well.' Edmund, tucking his napkin into the top of his shirt, looked from one to the other as the steward handed round menus. 'We were going into Monte to hire dinner suits. Apparently dressing up for dinner is *de rigueur*.'

'I think they think it adds a holiday flavour,' Sally Thompson said diplomatically. 'I mean, it's nice to splash out occasionally.'

'Well, if we may not be sailing . . .' Edmund ignored her remark.

'Oh, I don't think it's as bad as that. Just a tummy upset. But maybe you should wait to see what the doctor says.'

There was an air of unease around the breakfast table, and conversation was desultory. Every now and then they glanced at the quay to see if there was any sign of Andreas and the doctor.

They were soon joined by Paul, Emma and Alice, who apologised for sleeping late. Emma didn't know her mother was ill and, on hearing the news and that her brother hadn't yet joined the group at the table, excused herself and disappeared below. Edmund and the younger people present ordered full English breakfasts. Valerie settled for her usual tea and toast.

'No,' she said firmly, in answer to the steward's polite enquiry, 'toast, not croissant. I'm sure you have the facility for serving toast in the English way.'

'Of course, madam.'

As Emma and Nick failed to appear, the atmosphere grew more tense. There was also no sign of Andreas and Frank.

'I say, it will be a hoot if the holiday ends before it began.' Paul poured himself orange juice from the jug in front of him.

'I don't think it will be a hoot at all.' Alice sounded distressed. 'I was *so* looking forward . . .'

'Now, no point in anticipation.' Edmund looked up in pleasure as the steward appeared bearing aloft a large tray. 'No one said anything about the holiday ending.'

'I'm sure, even if we don't sail, we'll be able to stay on board.' Sally peered out again from the pages of the *Daily Mail* which appeared engrossing. 'Andreas is *so* hospitable. We shan't be thrown out.'

At that moment there was a movement on the quay. A car drew up beside the boat and Andreas emerged, followed by Frank Thompson and a stranger who, presumably, was the doctor. Without looking at the group assembled in the stern of the boat, they hurried aboard.

The atmosphere of tension increased. Although it didn't prevent any of them from enjoying a hearty breakfast, it seemed to put a dampener on the conversation, which was sparse.

Finally, after what seemed a long time, the doctor was seen running down the gangplank, accompanied by Andreas, who paused by the side of the doctor's car for some sort of conference. He then shook the man's hand, waved him off and slowly ascended the gangplank, coming round the side of the yacht to his guests.

'I'm terribly sorry about all this,' he said before anyone could say a word. 'Lydia had a very nasty attack of sickness during the night and is not at all well. However, the doctor thinks it is nothing serious and has given her medication. There's nothing to prevent us sailing as planned.'

'Oh, but surely it's wiser to wait until Lydia has recovered?' Valerie looked at him with concern.

'No, this stuff will settle her tummy. He thinks she'll be as right as rain by tomorrow. Anyway, we won't go too far away, just in case. I'd thought of popping over to Sardinia, but maybe we'll hug the coast for a day or two. I don't intend for a moment to let this spoil your holiday. It's the last thing that Lydia wants too; but she will stay in her cabin for the time being.'

'Does Lydia get this sort of thing often?' Valerie enquired.

'Well.' Andreas scratched his head. 'Occasionally. It depends on the circumstances. She's very nervous, you know.'

Edmund looked at Valerie and then at his host.

'Andreas, before we sail we thought we should go into Monte and hire dinner jackets. Valerie would also like to buy some sort of more formal dress for evening.'

'Oh, but it's not necessary,' Andreas exclaimed. 'I *assume* you are quite happy to dress informally for the duration of the cruise?'

'No, we'd *like* to conform,' Edmund insisted. 'We had no idea you dressed for dinner. It was silly of us not to ask. You must blame our ignorance of the high life.'

Even this remark sounded patronising, Nick thought. With his sister he had appeared on deck and had stood silently listening to the conversation. Now he came forward to take his place at the table, while Emma slid into a seat next to Paul.

'We're really quite simple people,' Valerie continued, taking her cue from her husband, clearly unaware that she was making an awkward situation worse. 'Used to country life and messing around in wellies, you know the sort of thing.'

Andreas appeared abashed.

'Well, this isn't exactly the high life. We like sailing, and it's nice to have a boat and be able to keep it in a place like Monte. We like to entertain our friends and give them a good time, but that certainly doesn't mean that if they come without dinner suits or evening dresses that they have to go out and hire them. Anyway, as long as Lydia isn't well, it will be nice to remain as informal as we can.'

'Well, if you insist.' Edmund drew a cigar from the case he carried in his breast pocket.

'I do,' Andreas nodded. 'And now I'll go and give orders for the crew to get ready to sail.' He rose with the air of a weary man, pale and tired looking, obviously from the effects of a sleepless night. Beckoning the steward he said: 'Charles, I want you to look after our guests and give them a good time. See that they have everything they want.'

'Yes, sir.' The steward bowed smartly.

'Coffee, champagne, whatever they want. Lunch as usual at one. Alright?'

'Yes, sir.' The steward bowed again.

'I'll see you on deck.' He addressed the assembled company. 'By mid-afternoon we should be well out to sea, but tonight we'll anchor in some pretty little cove, maybe Antibes or Agay.'

'The bay at Agay is lovely for swimming.' Nick looked at Giles and then at his father. 'Giles said this morning that he wished he could swim.'

'Well, tomorrow you can swim all you like.' Andreas pressed Giles's shoulder. 'Be sure you enjoy yourself now.'

As she felt the engines of the yacht judder into life, aware that it was slowly leaving the safety of the quay, Lydia's insides once more started to heave and, leaning over the side of the bed, she retched into the bowl strategically placed on a table. But there was really nothing there except a thin stream of bile. For a moment she lay with her head hanging over the side, and then she righted herself, flopped back exhausted on the bed and, taking a damp cloth from the bedside table, ran it over her face, brushing back her hair.

She really wished she were dead.

The humiliation of collapsing like this just when the Harveys – the *Harveys* of all people – were aboard, was really too much, too humiliating, and Andy was furious. He had begged her to make an effort, pull herself together, even tried to tug her out of bed, but no. It had been useless. As hard as she tried, whenever she attempted to stand on her two feet she felt an overwhelming sensation of nausea, a knowledge that unless she lay down again she would fall flat on her face.

She closed her eyes and, with the gentle motion of the boat as it pulled out to sea, felt herself drifting off to sleep. Blessed sleep. If only she could never wake up again. But wake she did, and when she opened her eyes Nick was gazing down at her, eyes clouded with concern.

'How are you, Mum?'

'I . . .' Lydia put a hand on her head, looked at the clock by the bed. 'I really don't know,' she said bravely, attempting a weak smile. 'I feel pretty washed out. I'm *terribly* sorry.'

'That's absolutely alright. There's nothing to worry about . . .'

'But the *Harveys* . . .'

'The Harveys are perfectly OK, Mum. They're getting along like a house on fire with the Thompsons.'

'Oh, good.' Lydia's hand fluttered in front of her face. 'Thank God for that. I worried so much whether they'd get on. You know how difficult the Harveys are, and . . .' She paused, and looked anxiously at her son.

'And what, Mum?'

'Well, I thought the Harveys might consider the Thompsons, you know, a bit common. Well, let's face it, that's how they consider us. Jumped up working class, nouveau riche.'

'That's a horrible way to talk.' Nick nervously bit his lip, thinking how much his mother's words echoed his own thoughts.

'But you know it's true, dear. Frank and Sally Thompson are people like us, self-made, not much education. I don't think we should have asked them on the yacht with the Harveys, but frankly,' her tone of voice grew heated, 'I felt I needed some support. Another couple to take some of the load. Besides, I much *prefer* them to the Harveys. You know where you are with Frank and Sally. I shall never know where I am with Edmund and Valerie. The truth is we should never have asked them. It was just your father's desire to show off. As a matter of fact . . .' Lydia, her voice calmer now, groped under her pillow for her handkerchief and blew her nose. 'I think all this has been brought on by worry about the Harveys. I mean, we all ate the same thing last night. It's not food poisoning. Can't be.'

'You mean you think it's all due to nerves?' Nick sat on

31

the side of her bunk and tenderly stroked her hair back from her damp brow.

'Yes, I do. And so does your father. Well *he* was the one who wanted to ask them. Why, I can't think. They have always snubbed us, humiliated us and now . . .'

'Valerie is very concerned about you. Wants to come and see you.'

'Oh my God! No!' Lydia pulled her sheet up to her chin and gazed white-faced at her son. 'Please, please don't let her in here.'

'Of course I won't if you don't want me to. But she's very nice. She really is. I think you're mistaken about them. You're far too sensitive about this stupid class business. It's all in the past, Mum, and people are equal now.' As Lydia gave a derisive snort, Nick continued: 'Valerie is doing all she can to make everyone feel at ease. If she came for a friendly little chat, it might help. Maybe if you got to know her better . . .'

'My dear boy.' Lydia vigorously blew her nose again. 'I have known Mrs Harvey well, if not intimately, for at least five years, and I don't think I will ever know her better if I live until I'm ninety, seeing her every day . . .'

'Most unlikely.' Nick gave a weak laugh and, removing his hand, left his mother and stood gazing reflectively out of the porthole towards the receding shoreline.

'Quite. That woman just does something to me. I don't know what it is, or why. She's nothing to look at – in fact, she's rather plain – she has no dress sense whatsoever; but there it is.' Lydia spread her outstretched palm by the side of the bed about a foot from the level of the floor. 'She makes me feel about this high. I tell you, Nick, I don't think my tummy will ever feel right until we have seen the back of the Harveys. I just can't wait for this cruise to be over.'

CHAPTER 3

The yacht rode at anchor in the calm still waters of the bay at Agay, dominated by the tall white tower of its lighthouse. Below them in the water the children splashed about, diving from a dinghy in which the 'grown up' men of the party had been rowed ashore. Nick and Giles were making serious attempts to snorkle, but their efforts were playfully interrupted by the antics of the younger siblings abetted by Emma who had been persuaded to abandon her predilection for lying on deck, scantily clad, soaking up the sun.

Watching the proceedings from the deck were Valerie and Lydia, the latter, despite the heat, well wrapped up as though she was afraid of catching cold. In fact she seemed to be shivering all the time, but it was indiscernible from the outside and she felt it came from some primitive source, deep inside her. She had made such an effort for everything to be right for the Harveys and it was deeply humiliating for her to have spent almost the entire trip with them shut up in her cabin. The outfits and dresses she'd bought for the occasion hung unworn in her wardrobe, and fine meals she'd discussed with the chef remained uneaten, at least by her.

It was even further humiliating to realise that, despite her absence, they all in fact seem to have had a very good time, revelling in the informality, not dressing for dinner, even to the extent of remaining in the shorts or sports attire worn during the day. She'd heard sounds of revelry coming from the afterdeck and continuing until well into the night. The three men walking on the shore also seemed to be having a very good time, gusts of laughter reached her across the water. Spirals of smoke rose in the air from long, expensive cigars.

Andreas walked in the middle. He wore white shorts, a white top not tucked into the pants and espadrilles on bare feet. He was the shortest of the three, with thinning hair, not a beauty, but it was generally acknowledged that he made up for his looks by his dynamism and charm.

Andreas was a great life enhancer. People enjoyed his company. He liked parties and was a good dancer. He was considered a ruthless businessman, but what successful man in these hard days could be otherwise? He drove a tough bargain. His widowed father, Theo, had semi retired to a large house in the leafy countryside of Oxfordshire. But he kept an eye on the business which was run by his three sons, Andreas and his brothers, Tony and George, both of whom were younger than he was, so that Andreas was chairman of the company.

Both Tony and George were married with children but, except for weddings, christenings and funerals, Easter and Christmas, the family saw little of one another socially. On these occasions, after church, they all foregathered at Andreas's house and, although they'd all been born in England, except Theo, it seemed to a stranger, and at these times Lydia felt like a stranger, that they were all back in Greece again.

Since leaving school without qualifications, Andreas had educated himself. He read, he enjoyed music and opera, he kept abreast of events. His company contributed substantially to the funds of the Conservative Party because it equated conservatism with prosperity and stability.

He was extraordinarily proud of his children, particularly Nick, because Nick had got brains and used them. He was determined that Nick would go a long way. He didn't mind that Emma, although she too had brains, kept them idling at the back of her head. Both children had got their good looks from their mother, and Emma's beauty combined with her father's money, meant that she would never have to work or be financially restricted, and she could take her time about finding a suitable husband. Of the three men walking on the shore, none was handsome in the strict sense of the word, but the best looking was Edmund. He was tall and had the sort of lean, spare frame sometimes associated with members of his profession. He stooped a little, maybe because of his height, and his hairline too was receding though not to the same extent as Andreas's. He had the fine, lined features of a thoroughbred; the sort of face that, over the centuries, had looked imperiously down from family portraits lining the walls of country houses. He wore blue jeans, a blue check shirt, and an old pair of trainers on bare feet.

On the other side, Frank Thompson was of medium height, vastly overweight, blue jowled, unremarkable in every way except that he had a keen, penetrating business brain of which those who worked with him were all too aware. He supplied produce from Middle Eastern countries, including Greece, Turkey and Israel to supermarkets, and was probably nearly as wealthy as Andreas and his brothers collectively.

The one missing member of the party, his wife Sally, was sunbathing in a secluded part of the foredeck, having taken advantage of the absence of the men to remove her bikini top which allowed her taut full breasts to be exposed to the sun.

The crew were below stairs, preparing lunch.

Valerie and Lydia sipped their coffee, saying little, their attention taken either by the men walking on the shore or the younger members of the party frolicking about in the water. To her reflections Lydia added the strange fact that

35

neither the Thompsons nor the Harveys were what you might call great friends. They knew the Thompsons from business, and the Harveys from school. Andreas always considered the yacht a valuable asset for cementing useful relationships, rather than giving close friends or family a good time. It was strange, but it was a fact. Maybe he considered it a waste of money to have his yacht, with its costly upkeep, plying the Mediterranean with people he couldn't impress.

Lydia glanced guiltily across at Valerie as if wondering if she could read her thoughts, but Valerie's eyes were fixed either on the shore or on the young people having such a good time in the sea.

Surreptitiously, Lydia studied her.

Her guest had on a cotton skirt and sun top, her waist exposed, feet bare. She had the fine features of a rather faded English rose. Her hair, once blonde, was now a pepper and salt mixture that would probably remain so for many years. She had intensely blue eyes, but her face was lined and this made her seem older than her forty-two years. She had never paid much attention to her appearance and all the make-up and skincare products she used was a moisturiser at night and a trace of lipstick first thing in the morning. This had to last all day. Valerie exuded an air of self-satisfaction which many people, including Lydia Constantine, interpreted with some justification as the kind of arrogance peculiar to the upper classes.

When she had finished her coffee she put her cup and saucer down and lay full length, eyes closed, hands folded across her stomach.

'This is bliss,' she said. 'I don't feel I ever want to go home.'

Lydia started guiltily. She had just been thinking what bliss it would be, what perfect bliss, when the Harveys and the Thompsons had gone and she and her family had the boat to themselves.

36

'You must come again,' she said. 'Only I hope next time I shan't be such a poor hostess.'

'Oh, but we've had a *marvellous* time!' Valerie raised her head and, shielding her eyes from the sun, stared at her companion. 'Don't think you've spoiled it. I just feel sorry for poor old you.' She peered at her more closely. 'I must say you still look a bit peaky.'

And this was despite loads of make-up! Lydia felt rather affronted. It was true she had had little or nothing to eat for the past three days. Yesterday she'd started to drink tea, and this morning she had toast for breakfast.

'And your husband is a wonderful bridge player,' Valerie enthused. 'We beat the Thompsons hollow.'

'So I heard. Unfortunately I don't play, so poor Andy doesn't often get a game.'

Valerie was about to say that they must do something about that when they were all in London again but stopped herself just in time. After all, did she *really* want to keep up the acquaintanceship when they got back?

'Does your husband play?' Lydia enquired.

'He's not very good. He does when he has to, when we can't find a four.'

In fact the bridge and the sun and the food had made the holiday much more fun than Valerie had expected, and she realised that, in a way, the absence of Lydia had contributed to that. She guessed, if the first night had been anything to go by, that on board the yacht, her own territory, and probably in her own home as well, Lydia would be a bit of a martinet, a stickler for convention. For doing what she perceived to be the right thing, like dressing for dinner, when everyone else would much rather lounge around in their day clothes as, indeed, they were doing. There had been a general lack of organisation and an emphasis on doing one's own thing. Valerie also suspected that, without Lydia to keep an eye on him, Andy was much more fun.

37

'The children have got on so well,' Lydia murmured. 'Nick and Emma will miss them.'

'Oh, they'll hate going back. It's been wonderful for them.'

'Then couldn't you leave them here?'

Valerie stared at Lydia.

'I mean, just for a few days more, if they've nothing else to do?'

'I couldn't leave Alice,' Valerie said doubtfully.

'But why not?'

'Well, she doesn't really fit in, does she? The others are terribly good with her. Besides, Edmund would worry about her too much. He adores her. The baby you know.'

Yes, it was quite obvious how much Edmund doted on his youngest.

'Well, it's up to you. Of course they might not want to stay.'

'But are you sure?'

'Perfectly sure. I mean, if we can fix up about the flight and so on.'

'Oh, yes, there's that.'

'I'm sure Andy will be able to fix it when we get to Marseilles. Andy can fix anything.'

It had been planned that the guests would disembark at Marseilles and take the train back to Nice, where they would get their plane, while the yacht carried on round the coast and then cross to the Balearics before taking on more guests in Majorca.

'Of course we'll have to ask the children. I'm sure they'll want to stay, Giles and Paul will at least. Alice is a bit clingy. Of course Giles and Nick have loads of time before they go up to Oxford. It will be exciting for them to be together.'

'Don't the results come out soon?' Shielding her eyes, Lydia looked towards the shore where the men seemed to be signalling for the dinghy to come over and collect them. They had by now all taken off their shoes, those wearing trousers had them rolled up and were paddling in the water.

'Very soon.' Valerie, oblivious to what was happening on the shore, put her hands behind her head. 'I don't think we've got anything to worry about.'

'Oh, I don't think Nick's all that confident.' Lydia looked doubtful. If only she could have the certainty Valerie had.

'But Giles says he's sure to do well.'

'Well, if hard work merits doing well, then he should.'

'Giles spent a lot of time on the cricket field as usual.' Valerie sighed deeply. 'But everything comes so easily to him. Always has. Sometimes I think it's a bit of a disadvantage in life being an all-rounder. I mean, he doesn't know anything about struggling. Do you know what I mean?'

'I certainly do.' Lydia gave a rueful smile, then she looked intently at the woman next to her. 'Do *you* know a lot about struggling?'

'Do *I*?' Valerie appeared taken aback by the question. 'Why, I never thought about it. No I don't suppose I've had much of a struggle in life; but then it's different for a man. Don't you think? I mean, I know it sounds rather old-fashioned to say that, and Giles would have a fit if he heard me, but they still have to make their way in life much more than a woman. Oh, I know that these days women have careers and all that sort of thing, much more so even than when we were young, but it's so important for a man to make something of his life even if he has money behind him. I mean we'd hate them to be idlers, wouldn't we?'

Lydia, thinking of her daughter, nodded. There was no question of Emma struggling to pursue a career. All she wanted to do was have a good time and, her mother supposed, hang around and wait for a suitable partner to turn up.

'In many ways it makes them more of a worry,' she said slowly. 'I mean, I worry about Emma much more than Nick. Emma is so directionless.'

Valerie laughed.

'She's so pretty. She doesn't have to have a direction!'

'I still wish she were motivated to do *something*. When I was her age I learned shorthand and typing and became a secretary when I was seventeen. That's how I met Andy.'

'Oh? I wondered . . .' Valerie paused, as if she didn't like being thought nosey.

'Yes, I worked in the import department of the family firm. How did you meet Edmund?'

'Well.' Valerie cracked her knuckles one by one above her head. 'I knew him of course. The families were neighbours in Somerset. Our fathers belonged to the same hunt. You know . . .' She looked sideways at Lydia. 'It was that sort of world.'

'Privileged?' Lydia suggested.

'Yes, I suppose you could call it privileged in a way. But we had our ups and downs. Most people do.'

Old money, Lydia thought, smiling to herself. It cushioned you. You could always tell. You could even smell it. It made you so confident, so sure that things would turn out as you expected them to. Whereas she was racked by anxiety, always fearing the worst: that the business would go bust and they would be flung out of their lovely home, that Andy would die young of a heart attack, that Nick would fail his exams and Emma end up going to the bad. That was why she tried so hard always to look her best, to keep up appearances, to dress for dinner on the yacht, to show people that standards mattered. And it was this desire for perfection that always let her down, that caused the headaches, the sickness in the stomach that prevented her from fulfilling the role that she yearned for. So that on this occasion (as on others in the past) she had had to take to her bed just when she wanted to shine, to demonstrate to the Harveys, for so long a source of real pain and jealousy, that she was their equal.

In a way, Lydia Constantine was a lonely woman, lacking

close friends, people with whom she had a bond, in whom she could confide. Sometimes she felt that she and her friends, such as they were, were playing at charades, unable really to communicate to one another their true feelings, pretending that life was very different from what it actually was. Sometimes she felt that if she worried enough about something, it wouldn't happen, it was a way of prevention, a kind of charm against the unexpected. Whereas she could never imagine Valerie being beset by the doubts and anxieties, the morbidity that sometimes seemed almost to ruin her life. Valerie, with her firm base in the upper-middle classes, the county set, years, generations of privilege and tradition, seemed to have no fears at all, to be certain of her place in the world and assured that nothing would happen to disturb it.

Dripping wet, the children clambered aboard in the wake of the male party from the shore, who had been rowed back to the yacht by Giles. As the last of them, Nick, came on deck Sally Thompson appeared from the stern of the boat discreetly doing up the back of her bikini top. Suddenly the deck seemed very crowded, everyone in high good humour, especially the younger ones who had been frolicking in the water. Charles, the steward, hurried out with more deckchairs and Andy, who seemed in a particularly good mood, asked for drinks to be served. Lydia got to her feet and said she thought she'd had enough fresh air and should get back to her cabin.

'How are you feeling, my dear?' Andy asked, the expression on his face one of tender concern, although indeed he too had been beset by anxiety about the success of the holiday.

'I think I'm a little better,' Lydia said without much conviction. 'Oh, by the way, Andy, I thought it would be nice if the Harvey children – I suppose I mustn't call them children – stayed on for a few days to keep ours company.'

'What a good idea!' Andy exclaimed looking round, while Alice beamed.

'Oh, do you mean it? Oh, *may* we, Daddy?'

Lydia thought it significant that she sought her father's permission rather than that of her mother.

'Well!' Edmund had sat down and, removing his shoes, was examining the sole of one of his feet.

'Anything wrong, Ed?' Valerie enquired, looking down.

'I think I trod on something in the water,' Edmund said.

'Maybe a jellyfish,' Giles said with relish. 'I believe they're poisonous out here, Dad.'

'Thank you.' Edmund rubbed his foot and examined it again.

'Nonsense,' Andy said robustly. 'No poisonous jellyfish out here, I assure you.'

'Well . . .' Edmund went on rubbing his foot and Lydia realised that, as the announcement had taken him by surprise, he had been playing for time. 'I don't really think we should presume on the hospitality of the Constantines for much longer. No, I think we'd all better go back to London as planned the day after tomorrow.'

'Oh, *Dad*!'

There was an instant chorus of dismay during which Andreas, also looking rather perplexed, held up his hand.

'We'd *love* to have them. It's no trouble I assure you. In fact we'd love to have you all stay on. It's been such fun . . .'

'Out of the question I'm afraid.' Edmund shook his head vigorously. 'I have to be back at work on Monday.'

'We'd really *like* to stay, Dad.' Paul's tone was wheedling. 'Please.'

'Giles?' His father looked at him.

'Well, of course I'd like to stay, Dad.'

'And they've got Oxford to discuss,' Lydia added. 'It's all quite exciting.'

42

'He's got Oxford to prepare for.' Edmund looked dubiously at Valerie.

'Dad, I don't go up for over a month. There is absolutely nothing to do.'

'Well . . .' Edmund slowly began putting his shoes back on. 'I really don't know what to say. It seems an imposition and,' he glanced at his daughter, 'I am not happy about Alice staying on.'

'That's what I thought you'd say,' Valerie nodded.

'Oh, Daddy . . . Mummy . . . please!' Alice looked as though she was about to burst into tears.

'We will take very good care of her,' Sally Thompson intervened. 'I'll be sure that Alice is accompanied by someone wherever she goes.'

The Thompsons were staying on until Majorca where they were meeting their son for a villa holiday.

'Perhaps we ought to talk about it?' Valerie looked meaningfully at Edmund and indicated that they might go below deck.

'There is really nothing to talk about,' Andreas said. 'The children want to stay. We want them to stay. It's all settled.'

'But the tickets . . .'

'I'll see to all that,' Andreas said, looking at his watch. 'I'll get on to them this very moment.' And, as he abruptly left the deck Valerie shrugged and looked apologetically at Edmund as though there was really nothing left to say.

The rest of the day, as the yacht sailed towards the port of Marseilles, was spent in various activities. After lunch the children devised games on deck, and Sally resumed her sunbathing, only this time with her top on. Frank stayed in his cabin sleeping and reading. Lydia stayed in hers doing the same thing, although to this she added fretting, while Andreas went to his office, occupying himself with various business affairs including the exchange of tickets which proved to be more complicated than he anticipated because, unlike the Constantines, the Harveys had come out on a special package deal. In the end, although he didn't tell them, because he didn't want to lose face, Andreas had to pay the difference himself which amounted to several hundred pounds.

Valerie and Edmund retired to their cabin after lunch where he immediately slumped on his bed, removed his shoe and examined the sole of his foot again.

'It hurts like blazes,' he said. 'I really think I trod on something. Maybe it was a poisonous jellyfish.'

'Don't be silly.' Valerie sat down beside him and looked at the foot. It was true, it was very red and did look sore. 'We'd better ask them for something to put on it,' she said. 'They're sure to have a very extensive medical cabinet.'

'Oh, wait until we get home.' Edmund gave the foot a final rub and lay full out on the bed. 'I'm really not at all happy about the children staying here.'

'Why not?'

'Well, it's like we owe the Constantines, and I'm not sure that I want that.'

'What do you mean "owe"?'

'Well, we don't want to spend the rest of our lives being grateful.'

'Grateful for what? I think we're doing *them* a favour. If you ask me, they want company for Nick and Emma.'

'Then that doesn't mean that Alice should stay. I am very unhappy about Alice.'

'I'm not too happy about her either.'

'Then why didn't you put your foot down?'

'How could I? It was so difficult. Anyway, Sally says she'll look after her and we can telephone every day. We can't do anything about it, Edmund. Andreas has rearranged the tickets.'

'I can't understand how he did it without having to pay

44

extra. You can't change those bookings. It says so in the rules.'

'Well, don't let's worry about it.' Valerie stretched out beside him, fanning her face. 'My, it's hot today. I rather wish we were staying on.'

'Well, why don't you? You could look after Alice.'

'Too late now.'

'I don't know why we didn't think of that before.'

'You mean you go back on your own?'

'Why not?'

Valerie wriggled on the bed. 'Well it *is* too late now. No question. Anyway, Giles will make perfectly sure that Alice is looked after. He's very responsible.'

Valerie turned on her side and prepared to go to sleep. But Edmund lay with his hands beneath his head staring at the reflection of the water on the ceiling, thoughtful.

It seemed to him that they were getting a whole lot closer to the Constantines than he wanted to. Instead of saying 'Goodbye' it seemed as though, after all these years, they were saying, 'Hello and welcome'.

On the other hand, he had enjoyed himself, no question. It had been relaxed, informal and even if Frank Thompson was a bit of a bore, he realised that Andy was an intelligent and clever man. He found his views interesting if not always compatible with his own. Added to which, they were both staunch supporters of the Tory Party. Andreas was very much in favour of Europe whereas Edmund was less optimistic about the advantages of too close an association with our European allies.

Andy was a little boastful, over-anxious to please and impress, but he was also unstuffy, informative about his family's origins and not ashamed of them. Perfectly reasonable. Why should he be?

However, when all was said and done, the Constantines were rather brash, rather ostentatious. They oozed new

45

money, and their values were not quite those of the Harveys. Difficult to put into words without sounding snobbish. They were not one of us and, moreover, they never could be. Maybe their son would, eventually. With his public school and Oxford education, his accent, his polished manners in addition to the fortune he would undoubtedly inherit, he might qualify for admission to that stratum of society in which the Harveys believed themselves to inhabit: upper-middle, the criteria of which were good breeding; years of education and public service; old money.

But Nick's mother and father? Never.

That night, an air of festivity prevailed, beginning with drinks before dinner on deck. For once they all dressed, not in the clothes they'd worn during the day, but something different. The children wore jeans and clean T-shirts, the grown-up men blazers and flannels, white shirts and ties – rather similar to what they'd worn on the first night. Valerie trotted out her Oxfam dress, Sally's was an expensive black number sparkling with sequins and Lydia, making her first appearance for four days, outshone them all in a backless creation in pink and cream tulle with a low, scalloped front, by one of London's top couturiers. Lydia had spent a considerable amount of time on her appearance, although she still didn't feel completely well, in order to make up for the lost days, the dreadful days, lying in bed feeling ill, resentful and sorry for herself – a heady mixture which had done little to aid her recovery.

After dinner there was dancing on deck to music from a stereo. Lydia sat out most of the time, but Valerie and Sally both danced energetically, swapping partners with enthusiasm, and Andreas, who loved dancing, never sat out once. The evening ended with Greek dances performed by everyone with hands flung high above heads and plates sent crashing onto the decks or into the sea.

'What a lovely way to end a holiday,' Valerie said, flinging herself into a chair and gasping for breath. She felt slightly tipsy too. 'We really have had the most super time.'

'We must make this something we do every year.' Andreas flopped down beside her. 'Definitely an annual event. What do you say, Edmund?'

Andreas looked at Edmund who was leaning against the rail, glass in hand.

'Cheers!' Edmund raised his glass.

'I mean, to it happening every year?'

'A lot can happen in a year,' Edmund replied enigmatically and then, shooting his cuff back, he looked at his watch. 'We're all going to be dead tired tomorrow. Time for bed.'

Despite the lateness of the hour at which they finally turned off the light Valerie was awake early and, by the time Edmund woke up, she had finished packing. 'Wasser time?' he asked, blinking in the light.

'It's past eight. We're due in Marseilles at noon.'

'What's the hurry?'

'Well, we have to have our breakfast, say our goodbyes. Make sure the children keep in touch. Incidentally, do we know exactly when they're coming home? Don't forget Alice starts school in a couple of weeks.'

'I think he's putting them off at Barcelona. They've got some new guests coming on then.'

'But how can they fly back from Barcelona if they've tickets from Nice?'

'Oh, Andreas has arranged it all.' Edmund threw back the sheet and, drawing his foot up towards his face, began intently to examine it.

'How's your foot?'

'It's still pretty painful.' Edmund looked at it carefully. 'I'm rather glad we're going back and I can get it seen to. Look how swollen it is.' Valerie glanced at it without much concern. Her husband always took such an exaggerated interest in his health. She perched on the side of the bed.

'Do you mean to tell me Andreas has achieved all this without paying extra?'

'He told me he'd fixed it.'

'That means, don't you see, he's paid a fortune!'

'Look,' Edmund said impatiently, 'he has his pride. If he wants to pay, let him. He can afford it. I don't want to start cross-examining him. It's too infra dig. Besides, I'm damned if I want to pay extra. We've enough on our plates.'

'What do you mean?'

'We've enough expense. None of the kids is independent. I have school fees for Paul and Alice, and we've got to keep Giles through three years at least at Oxford. I haven't got a bottomless purse you know.'

'Time for breakfast!' Giles put his head round the door. 'You two arguing?'

'Just having a discussion,' Valerie replied haughtily. 'Look, how long are you staying on for?'

'I think a week. Until we get to Barcelona.'

'Well, be careful.' Valerie held up her cheek for a kiss. 'And don't dare take your eyes off Alice.'

'Mum, you worry,' Giles said fondly, and then to his father, 'Dad, how's your foot?'

'Painful,' Edmund replied. 'Glad I'm going home.'

'Well,' Giles looked at his watch, 'you've got about five minutes to get up, shower and appear in time for breakfast.'

Giles was in ebullient mood as he propelled his mother along the deck to the stern where the table was laid as usual. As usual, too, it was a lovely morning, the surface of the sea calm as the yacht ploughed towards the coast at a steady rate of knots.

Frank and Sally were already at the table, studying the menu that had been handed to them by Charles.

'Sleep well?'

48

'Fine. And you?'

'Fine.'

'We shall miss you,' Frank said, handing the menu to the steward and murmuring that he would have the usual, which was a full English breakfast complete with sausages and fried bread. 'You've been great sports.'

'Maybe we'll see you next year?' Valerie smiled sweetly.

'Better still, why don't we get together in London?' Sally suggested.

'That's a great idea.' Frank sounded enthusiastic. 'We could have a night out. Do a show.'

'I'm sure we'd love that.' Valerie's tone was lukewarm. Then she looked anxiously over at Sally. 'You will keep an eye on Alice, won't you? She's so young.'

'My dear,' Sally put a reassuring hand on Valerie's arm, 'you need have no fear about your little one. We shall all make sure she comes to no harm.'

'Mum, I'm going to be here you know.' Giles sounded aggrieved. 'I'm perfectly capable . . .' He stopped as Andreas appeared, walking slowly along the deck studying a paper in his hand. Behind him was Nick whose expression was solemn.

'Bad news? Something wrong?' Frank enquired as Andreas stopped by his chair. 'The stock market taken a dive?'

'We got the results of the A levels,' Andreas mumbled, handing the paper to Giles. 'I phoned the school.'

Giles took the paper from his hand and studied it. Then he looked up at Nick.

'Congratulations.'

Nick nodded, but said nothing. An unaccustomed stab of fear, of doubt, clutched at Valerie's heart. 'Well?' she enquired, looking at Giles.

'Not as good as expected, Mum. Nick got four straight As.' Heads turned towards Nick, yet the smiles of pleasure only seemed to hide an underlying feeling of tension that had suddenly permeated the atmosphere. Giles's eyes remained fixedly on the paper. 'I got three Bs and a C, and I think that means I can't take up the conditional offer from Oxford.'

'Conditional?' Frank looked puzzled. 'You must forgive me. Not being a university man . . .'

'Conditional on A level results,' Giles explained. 'Nick and I decided not to take the Oxbridge entrance exam, but to concentrate on A levels. A lot of people do this, but you then have to rely on your success at the interview plus the A level results. I think I did well at my interview, and I was given an offer of a place providing I got a minimum of two grades at Standard A and one at B.'

'Surely three Bs . . .' Sally's expression tried vainly to be encouraging, but Giles shook his head.

'Ain't good enough, I'm afraid.' He continued to shake his head, obviously utterly bewildered by the results. 'I can't understand it. I never thought they'd be as bad as this.'

'But, darling . . .' Valerie reached over and took the paper from him. 'Why, something must be wrong. Are you *sure*, Andreas?'

'I made them repeat it. I talked to the Head. They're as incredulous as I know Giles must be. The Head said he was one of the stars of the sixth form.'

'He can retake,' Valerie said firmly. 'Or maybe Oxford will still admit him?'

'Because he's a Harvey,' Nick intoned, and then his hand flew to his mouth. 'Sorry. Stupid attempt at humour.'

Giles appeared unoffended by the remark, a slight smile of disparagement flickering across his face. 'I'm sure even being a Harvey isn't enough to get them to admit me. But I'll telephone them. If not, it will have to be another university, if it's not too late.'

'But did you apply to any others?' His mother still looked in a state of shock as Giles shook his head.

By this time Edmund had hobbled up, followed by Paul, and they both stood behind Giles gaping over Valerie's shoulder at the paper.

'It's not the end of the world,' Edmund said finally.

'It means I may not be able to go up to Oxford with Nick. In fact, I'm sure of it. Too many good students competing for places.'

'There must be something we can do,' Andreas slumped at the table next to Valerie.

'I don't think even you can fix this, Dad.'

'No need to be rude, Nick.'

'I didn't mean to be. I just feel a bit shocked. I'm sorry. I'm saying all the wrong things this morning.'

Giles put a hand on his shoulder and gave him a sympathetic smile.

'I think I'm more shocked than you,' Nick said to him. 'I always thought we'd go to Oxford together. I don't know if I can face it without you.'

'Don't be silly. Of course you can.'

'But what will you do?'

'He'll retake,' Valerie said firmly.

'Mother, I could still not go to Oxford this year whatever I did. Also, I don't want to retake or stay on at school. I'll have to go through the clearing.'

'Whatever's that?'

'It's the system that finds places for those who failed to get into the university of their choice.'

'You'll easily get in somewhere with those grades.'

'But we don't want you to go to *any* university. We want you to go to Oxford.' Valerie sounded near to tears. 'Like Daddy and Grandpa.'

'We'll certainly have to discuss all this.' Edmund sat down heavily.

'In the meantime I'll have to come back with you, Dad. I can't stay on here on holiday.'

'Oh!' Alice, who too had silently joined the company assembled on deck with Emma, began to wail. 'Oh, *no!*'

'Well, you can stay on . . .'

'Oh, no, she can't,' Valerie said firmly. 'That is for sure. In fact, the whole family will have to go home.'

'It's a pity you rang the damn school, Andy.' Edmund cast him a reproachful glance. 'What, with this and my painful foot, it's ruined the whole damn holiday.'

Lydia, who had been listening to the drama unfold while standing unnoticed behind a pillar, quietly turned and disappeared along the deck in the direction of her cabin. She had made a special effort to pull herself together and attend breakfast in honour of the departing guests. Had put on a glamorous tracksuit and lots of make-up to conceal her pallor. She began to retch as she got to the door of her cabin, and just made it in time to the lavatory before emptying the contents of her stomach down the pan.

This was really the last straw in their Herculean effort to ingratiate themselves with the wretched Harveys, that their son should get into Oxford while Giles, to whom everything came so easily, had failed.

Then she rose from her supine position, threw water on her face and patted it dry. She felt, to her surprise, not only a whole lot better, she felt something else too: a sense of triumph which seemed to surge through her veins.

CHAPTER 4

The room was full of flowers, and among them was a particularly large arrangement of choice blooms that must have cost the earth. Edmund had wanted to throw them out or send them to a public ward, but Valerie had said how dreadful it would be if the Constantines paid a visit and there was no sign of their flowers. After all, she reasoned, it wasn't as though what had happened to him was their fault. He had stood on a poisonous jellyfish that were particularly prominent in the south of France that summer, and it had happened on the shore, and not on the yacht. No one could possibly blame the Constantines.

But Edmund did blame the Constantines. He had gone through a lot of pain and not a little fear, and he wanted to blame someone. His foot had swelled up to the size of a football, his leg came to resemble the trunk of a tree and before he was carted off to hospital with a high temperature as an emergency, he had indeed been very very afraid.

Now he was better, definitely out of danger but feeling cantankerous. His leg was still swollen, he was still in pain; but he was in no danger.

Never one at coping with illness, something of a hypochondriac, Edmund was a bad patient. Valerie had been rather glad that he was a hospital case, though of course worried and anxious at the same time, and she made up for her feelings of relief by bringing him lots of little gifts and homemade dishes of his favourite food.

Edmund was dozing in the late-afternoon sunlight that crept into his hospital room over the roofs of the adjacent complex in north London. He was of course a private patient, and had the privilege of his own comfortable room in a separate wing of the hospital. Valerie had made her visit for the day, had brought him home-made custard tarts, a great favourite, to have with his tea, and a good claret to have with his supper. Paul might or might not visit him in the evening, Giles was away, and endless hours of boredom stretched in front of him. There was a tap on the door. Edmund started from a state that was part snooze, part reverie.

'Come in,' he called and sat up expecting to see one of the nurses or doctors.

'Hello, Edmund.' The tone of voice was timid, uncertain in its welcome, and Edmund said sharply: 'Come in and close the door.' Then, when the woman had done his bidding, 'Did anyone see you coming?'

The woman didn't reply, but approached his bed as tentatively as she had entered the room, and laid a large bunch of flowers on the table next to it. She stooped and planted a kiss on his forehead, to which he gracefully submitted. Then she stepped back and gazed at him.

'You don't look too bad, Edmund. I was terribly worried.'

Edmund pointed to his leg which hung in a crane suspended from pulleys.

'And all that caused by a little jellyfish?'

Edmund extended his hands to embrace an imaginary sea creature. 'They're whoppers.'

'It's a wonder you didn't see it.'

'I was in the water wading out to the dinghy that had been sent to fetch us from the shore.'

'Didn't you *feel* it, Edmund?' Nervously the woman perched on the side of the bed.

'I felt something, but it wasn't until later that I realised my foot had swollen. Oh, really, Mary,' he reached out and put his hand over hers, 'it was a dreadful holiday . . .'

'I thought you were having a good time. You said you were on your card.'

'Well,' he shook his head ruefully, 'all the bad things happened at the end. I got this sting on my foot and we had the A level results and Giles has failed to get into Oxford.'

'Oh, but that's *terrible*.' Mary clutched his hand. 'How did that happen?'

'His grades weren't good enough. I think he took too much for granted,' Edmund said sternly. 'Didn't work hard enough, that's obvious. The worst thing was that the Constantines' son Nick got *four* As.'

'Oh, well done him!' Mary exclaimed and then stopped, faltered when she saw the expression on Edmund's face. 'But you always *liked* him, Ed, didn't you? He was Giles's best friend.'

'We liked him, of course we did and still do; but we would like our son to have got into Oxford as well.'

'Naturally.'

'Secretly the Constantines crowed. You could see it, though they tried to hide it. They made a point of announcing the results on deck so that everyone on board heard it. I'm sure it was done deliberately to humiliate Giles.'

'But why should they do that, Ed?' Mary tucked his hand firmly in hers.

'Oh, Mary, don't be so *irritating*,' Edmund said, wrenching his hand away. 'Because that's the sort of people they are. Nouveau riche. No manners and no tact.'

'I see,' Mary nodded, 'is that the definition of nouveau riche?'

Edmund looked at her suspiciously. 'You're trying to wind me up, Mary. Please don't. I haven't been well, you know. I've been very ill. I could have died.'

Mary leaned forward impulsively. 'Oh, Ed, don't you think

I've been worried sick? Not knowing anything? Not being able to find out.'

'Sorry, Mary. I couldn't let you know.'

'It made me realise the precariousness of my situation.'

'Well, Mary, you knew that some time ago,' Edmund said with the gravity of a judge delivering a verdict. 'No one tried to force you. You can't say you didn't know what you were doing. No one forced you into a relationship with me.'

Mary Rogers gazed searchingly at her long-time lover. No one forces anyone to fall in love. It was one of those inexplicable things which defied any amount of psychological or physical analysis.

Certainly, in hindsight, it seemed foolish to have fallen in love with a married man, especially one as entrenched in his marriage as Edmund, who never had the slightest intention of leaving his wife on whom he was not only dependent, but of whom he was also a little afraid.

'It never quite hit me like this, Ed. You've never been ill before. You might have died . . .' and she began to weep, as though all her pent-up worry could no longer be contained, her face buried in the bedclothes. Edmund, embarrassed and confused, put one arm round her shoulder and with his other free hand gently stroked her hair.

His relationship with Mary Rogers was more than a decade old. She had been his secretary, a highly qualified, intelligent and attractive woman. Many in the firm, in which he then worked, had thought her too intelligent and attractive to become involved with a man who clearly was only looking for something on the side.

A complicating factor, which happened two years into the affair, was that Mary became pregnant and, despite the entreaties of Edmund to abort, gave birth to a son, Adam, now eight years old.

Edmund had been too much of a gentleman to desert Mary, and after some initial resentment, he not only came to accept Adam but to love him. He was an appealing little chap, with a loveable, trusting, rather vulnerable nature.

However, Edmund felt and continued to feel, guilty about Mary, guiltier still about Adam who did not enjoy the advantages, educational and otherwise, of his legitimate sons. Adam went to the local state junior school. He was bright, but he struggled against asthma. He was also myopic. He was a dear, brave little boy whose timidity contrasted strongly with the extroversion and glamour, the good looks of the other Harvey boys.

Mary wept and Edmund patted her shoulder. But he was anxious, and kept casting furtive glances at the door. What if Paul should arrive? Well, they all knew Mary had once been his secretary. Would it seem strange that she should visit him now? There were all these questions one had to anticipate, subterfuges one had to consider, when the discovery of an illicit relationship could spell possible disaster.

Mary really was an embarrassment. He dearly wished she wasn't there, that he had never given in to the momentary temptation to slip his hand up her skirt one day when she was leaning over his desk. That had started the whole thing off. Moments of frank eroticism begun in the office culminated in a bedroom in Maida Vale where Mary still lived, supported to some extent by Edmund. She eked out his meagre allowance by working as a freelance legal typist.

'There, there,' he said, 'there, there.'

But 'there, there' wasn't enough. Edmund had never been ill before and Mary, alone in her ugly little flat in the desert that was Maida Vale, had felt lonely and cut off in a way she never had before. She'd only found out what had happened by telephoning his office from which she occasionally got legal work. It wasn't enough when you had a long term lover and a child by him.

She threw back her tear-stained face and thumped the bed with clenched fist.

'It isn't *enough*, Edmund . . .'

'What isn't enough?' He looked confused.

'All this,' she gestured wildly. 'Being out on a limb, left in ignorance of the most mundane things, having no *rights* . . . the other woman.'

'Oh, Mary,' he petulantly drew his arm away. 'This is no time to throw a tantrum. It's selfish of you. I've been very ill, *dangerously* ill . . .'

'I know that, Edmund, and don't you think I was worried sick? Hard on me. Hard on Adam.'

Yes it was hard, especially on Adam. He had a deep affection for this youngest child, flawed, illegitimate but with such a loving, trusting nature. He knew that Adam and Alice would get on well; but he also knew that it could never be. He was too established, too settled, too married, also too timid if the truth be known, to upset the applecart.

'We'll have to talk about all this when you get well, Ed.' She vigorously pushed back her hair from her face.

'Talk about what?'

'The situation. It can't go on.'

'Oh, Mary, be reasonable.'

'I *am* being reasonable.' Her lower lip started to tremble, and he thought she was going to burst into tears again. 'I've just been reasonable for too damn long. What is my life, Ed? Did you ever think of that?'

'You should have thought about it before we began, Mary,' he said, eyeing her. 'It took two of us to fall into bed, you know. You can't talk about seducers and seduced. Not in this day and age, not in a time of equality like now. You wanted an affair and you wanted Adam. You said if you didn't have him it would be too late.'

It was true. Adam's conception might have been accidental but maybe because, instinctively or not, she wasn't sure, she had wished it. But had she wished it for herself, or in the hope that it would bind Edmund more strongly to her? Did she even remotely imagine, even then, that he would abandon home, wife, family just for her?

'It's not only all this secrecy, Ed.' Mary tossed back her head, looked him boldly in the eyes. 'I don't think Adam is getting the opportunities he ought to have.'

'What opportunities?' Edmund looked alarmed and, as the pain made his foot begin to throb again, sank back on his pillows.

'*You* know what opportunities, Ed. Adam is bright but he is being held back by being at a state school.'

'It's a very good school.'

'It is not a very good school. It's an adequate school, but from there he goes on to the comp and that has not got a good reputation. I want Adam to have the same opportunities that your other children have. I want him to go to a private school too. I want the best for our son, Ed.'

'Why bring it all up now?'

'Because things have come to a head. I've had enough, enough of being cast to one side, treated like a pariah, my son a second-class citizen . . .'

'You're being over-dramatic, Mary.' Edmund began to sweat and pointed to his foot. 'Look I'm going to have to take some medication. My foot is throbbing dreadfully. I shall have to call the nurse.' His hand reached towards the bell and then halted in mid-air.

'I'm afraid you're going to have to go, Mary.'

'Why?'

'You know why . . .'

'Because I'm the mistress and you don't want people to know about me . . .'

'Don't be silly. Be sensible, please. I beg you. Look, I'm in pain. I've been very ill. I promise you that when I'm better we'll talk again, go into the whole thing . . .'

'We'd better, Ed,' Mary said, getting up. The look of desperation on her face had now been replaced by a curious amalgam of determination and spite. 'I don't want to go back to where we were. I want it all out in the open, otherwise I'm afraid I shall have to tell Valerie . . .'

'You wouldn't.'

'I would. Believe me, Ed, I would and, frankly, I think I'd enjoy seeing the supercilious, know-it-all look on her face replaced by what? Would she be surprised, Ed? Horrified?'

Helplessly, Edmund shook his head.

'I think I know Valerie, Ed. She'd divorce you. She wouldn't put up with it, to know she'd been cuckolded all these years by you, that you had a son she knew nothing about. I tell you I'm absolutely serious. This is crunch time, Ed.' She gathered up her things and made for the door, pausing just before she opened it and looking back at him. 'Think about it.'

'Manchester!' Edmund bellowed. 'What do you want to go to Manchester for?'

'Because it's a good university and they offered me a place. Also, incidentally, it's considered a trendy place to be.'

'But Manchester itself is a terrible town.'

'When were you last there, Dad?'

'Everyone knows Manchester's a terrible town.'

'Terrible in what way?'

Giles knew there would be a fuss so had determined in advance to try and keep his patience.

Edmund didn't reply. His sojourn in hospital was behind him, but his foot and leg were still swollen and he was in a fair amount of pain. The doctors had assured him the infection was cured, and now all that remained was to keep taking the tablets to complete the healing process.

Edmund fretted at the enforced inactivity. He was not a good patient. His legal practice was a one-man band, and although his clerk and secretary faxed him important material and information, he nevertheless worried.

Valerie sat by Edmund's side, her eyes cast downwards, studying her rings, her expression thoughtful. Finally she looked up at Giles.

'Manchester is very disappointing. You must see our point of view, Giles.'

'Frankly, I don't. I think you're being snobbish, just as you were with the Constantines.'

'Oh, for God's sake don't bring that up again,' Edmund roared, his nerves clearly on edge. 'I've heard enough of the bloody Constantines. Just now they seem to me responsible for all our woes.'

Giles perched on the arm of the chair opposite his parents. They were in the family living room, the scene of many such dramas in the past and, no doubt, many more to come. Although a loving and cohesive family, they were also one riven by differences largely owing to the temperament and personalities of its members. Most of the dramas in recent years had been about Paul being a disappointment; about his general attitude, his lack of ambition.

'That's a very unjust remark, Dad.'

'If we hadn't gone on that yacht, none of this would have happened.' Edmund gazed soulfully at his bandaged foot.

'You might not have stood on a jellyfish, Dad, but I would still not have got into Oxford. Nothing can help that.'

'It was the way it was announced, before *everyone* on deck. Even the steward heard.'

'Oh, *that's* what this is about?' Giles stood up and nodded his head several times. 'Wounded pride. Now I understand.'

'It certainly *wasn't* very nice,' Valerie inclined towards her husband. 'Had you both done well it would have been a different matter. It seemed to me that the Constantines were crowing.'

'I didn't think that at all. I don't think Andy really understood the implications. He didn't realise I wouldn't get into Oxford with Nick.'

'He understood the implications alright. Or if he didn't, Nick had explained them to him. They both looked extremely solemn. Remember?'

Giles remembered. It was hard not to agree that Andy must have known the effect of his announcement; but he still found it hard to think it had been made with any malice.

Not even the teeniest, weeniest desire to humiliate people who, according to Nick, always made his family feel inferior?

After the unsatisfactory conversation with his parents, Giles went up to his room, changed into a tracksuit and trainers and, putting his squash racquet and towel into his sports bag, ran back down the stairs and out of the house to the car that had been a seventeenth birthday present from his parents. It was a vintage MG and he was very proud of it. What a dash, he had thought, he would cut in Oxford roaring down the High. But it was not to be.

Instead he would be roaring up the M1 to a far less salubrious town in the north.

It was true that a great deal had been done to improve the image of northern towns since the days of L S Lowry, and his depiction of the dark Satanic mills of Salford. Manchester was a fine city with a great tradition. It was the home of a famous orchestra, the Hallé, had a magnificent library, and was a centre for the arts. Most of the important plays in London discovered the prospect of failure or success during trial runs in front of the critical audiences Manchester had to offer. But Manchester, although prestigious, with a good university, had not quite the cachet of Oxford, that city of dreaming spires, of poets, writers and many Nobel laureates.

Giles had sustained a shock which, in the circumstances, he had been at pains to conceal from his parents. It was true, the latter days of the holiday had been a disaster. The cruise, although enjoyable, had been rather too full of tension thanks also to Lydia's illness, and the feeling that somehow one ought not to be having such a good time when one's hostess was languishing on her sick bed.

Then there was the fact that, although barriers to some extent did break down, the atmosphere between his parents and Andreas was cordial rather than overtly friendly. Everyone seemed to be making too much of an effort, and then when the chance had come to relax a bit on the holiday after his parents had gone home came double disaster: his father's mishap and the results, the consequent abandonment of plans for the Harvey children to continue with their holiday. The terrible fuss and mix-up about plane tickets which Andreas somehow managed to settle.

Fortunately it wasn't until his father had got home that the extent of the damage to his foot became apparent, although it was still not too late for him to blame the Constantines.

When he got to the school Nick was waiting for him at the gates, swinging his squash racquet as though hitting the ball. As old boys they were entitled to the use of the school sports facilities and, as school had finished for the day and everyone had gone home, they almost had the place to themselves. They greeted each other, exchanging only platitudes, and after changing played a vigorous game of squash which, as usual, was won by Giles. They then took a dip in the school pool where they found a few old boys and members of staff, stopped and chatted to them before going to the dressing room to change. After that they set off as usual to the local for a beer before going, as planned, back to the Constantines for a meal. They were silent as they walked through the school grounds and out of the gates, as if self-consciously aware of their new-found status in the world. Only Giles paused for a moment and looked back.

'Very odd to think this is no longer the place where we go every day.'

'We can still come back in the hols.'

It was only a week to the beginning of the academic term.

'They were good days.' Nick put an arm loosely round Giles's shoulder. 'I shall miss you.'

'Ditto, like hell,' Giles grunted.

'Term's only eight weeks.'

'Long enough to grow apart.'

'I was thinking . . .' Nick paused again halfway up the hill to the pub and gazed at his friend. 'I wouldn't mind going to Manchester myself.'

Giles's mouth fell open.

'I'm not kidding. I'm serious. Oxford *is* very elitist. We always said it. Well now is the time to put my principles to the test.'

'But you wouldn't do this if I'd got in.'

'Maybe not. But I can't think Oxford without you will be much fun.'

'And I can't think Manchester without you will be much fun either.'

There was an air of mounting excitement between the two young men as they reached the doors of the pub.

'Let's go tell my parents,' Nick said.

'You're assuming you'll get into Manchester at this late stage?'

'I'll get in for *something*.'

'It could ruin your career.'

'Not a chance. Worth a try?'

'I dread to think what your parents will say. Look maybe I should not come back to dinner?'

'They're expecting you. Besides I need the support.'

'I think we need a half a pint to steady our nerves.' With a grin Giles pushed open the door of the pub and Nick followed him.

The Constantine house stood back from the leafy road in one of the best parts of St John's Wood. It was a low, gabled two-storey house built, maybe, towards the end of the nineteenth century and to which an extension had been added some time in the thirties. Like all the houses in the road, it had a small front garden and a path leading up to a porch and a double front door which was manned by a complex system of security devices including a camera. To one side was a garage big enough for three cars and, behind, a large garden backed onto the high wall of an embassy of an important Middle Eastern state. Unlike the Harvey house, which was casually shabby – the furniture good but old and worn by the passage of time, animals and children; the carpets best-quality Wilton or Axminster but largely thread-bare, the inevitable stains that had appeared over the years covered by equally threadbare Persian rugs – the Constantine house was sumptuous in its restrained elegance. Lydia Constantine had extremely good taste, and an abundant purse had enabled her to exercise to the full her gift for interior decoration which, every five to seven years was completely renewed: the colour schemes in the various rooms changed, the walls relined, new curtains hung and sometimes new carpets laid. Good pictures, evidence of a discriminating taste, hung on the walls; there were a few books, not many, but plenty of large coffee table tomes and glossy magazines scattered about and the impression was of a comfortable, affluent rather than an intellectual or cultured home.

Lydia was extremely fastidious and nothing escaped her. Besides, as well as the means, she had the advantage of plenty of time to indulge her passions for personal shopping, interior redecoration and the acquisition of works of art.

Recently returned from the Mediterranean, Andreas, Lydia and Emma were already in the drawing room having drinks when Nick and Giles arrived. They had not 'dressed' for dinner but they looked smart, the women in pretty dresses with jewellery, and Andreas in a business suit. Remembering the episode on the boat, Giles apologised for being in a tracksuit and offered to go home and change. Andreas replied that of course they wouldn't hear of it and told Nick, who looked uncomfortable, not to change either. Giles realised that once again an awkward situation had been set up on account of a member of his family, this time himself. In the years he and Nick had known each other, he had seldom been invited for an evening meal.

'Silly of me, I should have thought,' he said, accepting a drink from Andreas who gestured towards a chair.

'Not at all, not at all. We realised you were coming from the squash court. Who won?' He raised his glass to his lips.

'Giles won, of course.' Nick poured himself a beer. 'Always does.'

'How's your father, Giles?' Andreas spoke in a reverential tone. 'I can't tell you how bad I felt about all that.'

'It wasn't *your* fault. It was his.' Giles smiled encouragingly. 'He trod on the jellyfish.'

'Yes, but I felt in a way responsible. You can understand that, can't you? I mean the holiday hadn't exactly gone with a swing, and we so wanted you to have a good time.'

'We did have a good time. We had a marvellous time.' Giles looked apologetically at Lydia. 'I mean we were all sorry Lydia was unwell, and it took the gilt off the gingerbread, but apart from that we had a wonderful time. I assure you.'

'Oh, good!' A look of relief spread across Andreas's face. 'And he got the flowers?'

'They were magnificent. He'll be writing to you once he gets back to work.'

'No need.'

'In fact, he should have scribbled a note.'

'I expect he got so many.'

'A good few.'

Giles felt embarrassed, but wasn't that always the case? Wasn't there always that slight, almost intangible, feeling of

66

guilt, of awkwardness when it came to relations between the families?

As if to prevent further conversation on the subject, Nick turned excitedly to his father. 'Dad, we've had a brainwave . . .'

He looked so happy that Andreas's worried expression vanished, and he perched on the arm of one of the chairs as Lydia and Emma looked on expectantly.

'Sounds interesting,' he smiled encouragingly, looking from one young man to the other.

'I decided I'm going to give up the place at Oxford and apply to Manchester . . .'

Giles knew immediately that the timing was wrong and lowered his eyes to avoid seeing the reaction of the family. In the event, he didn't need to look. He could feel it. Now that the words were out, the idea immediately seemed ridiculous. He looked up at Nick and shook his head as Andreas, desperately trying to recover his composure, said: 'I don't think I'm hearing you right.'

'It was just a notion,' Giles mumbled. 'It seems rather foolish now.'

'I should think it *is* foolish,' Andreas said. 'Unless you have some very good reason, Nick, for saying what you just said.'

'We'd like to go on being together. We'd miss each other too much. We've been mates for such a long time . . .'

'And of course,' Lydia's tone was icy, 'as Giles failed to get a place at Oxford *you* would be the one to make the sacrifice.'

'It wouldn't be a sacrifice. Oxford is elitist anyway.'

'Then why did you apply to go there?'

Silence as the two younger men studied the floor.

Andreas rose, went over to the bar and shakily helped himself to another whisky.

'I'm quite unable to understand what's going on,' he said in a strangulated voice. 'What are you two telling me? You're a couple of gays or what?'

'*Daddy*!' Emma exclaimed. 'What a horrible thing to say.'

'Well, it's all the acceptable thing now, isn't it?' Andreas shrugged. 'You've got to face facts.'

'We didn't say anything about being gay, Dad.' Nick spoke very quietly. 'You can have a friendship without being homosexual.'

'Well, I think it's a very *odd* friendship, if you don't mind me saying, when two men can't bear to be separated to such an extent that one has to give up a much desired place at Oxford in order to be with the other.' He turned and looked steadily at Giles. 'Would you, Giles, for instance be prepared to make a similar sacrifice, and what do your parents make of this suggestion?'

'They don't know about it. Nick brought it up literally about an hour ago. It never occurred to me, but I guess neither of us thought it through. At the time it seemed a good idea.'

'I imagine it did. Then you wouldn't feel so bad about failing to get into Oxford. Make you feel better would it?'

Giles felt the colour rush to his face.

'That wasn't the case at all, Andreas.' He put down his glass and stood up. 'I'm sorry Nick suggested it, and I'm sorry he brought it up when he did. I didn't know he was going to so soon. It was a silly idea and I'm sorry. Look, maybe I better not stay for dinner.'

'No, stay!' Emma jumped up, a look of outrage on her face as she turned to her father. 'Dad, I don't know how you could say the things you said.'

'And I don't know how Nick could say what *he* said. He would be the first member of our family to go to any university, never mind Oxford. It's all I ever dreamed of. I feel a personal sense of outrage that after all we've done, all our sacrifices and encouragement, Nick should even entertain such an idea. Naturally I want to know what is behind it.'

'I can understand that two friends would want to be together,' Emma went on. 'I'd feel the same.'

'Well, I can't, and that's it.' Andreas turned to his son. 'I apologise, Nick, if what I said offended you.'

'I'm not offended because it's not true.'

'I've nothing against gays.'

'Except that you don't want one as your son.'

'Obviously. I think any parent would say that if they were honest. The trouble is so many of them aren't.'

'You're not discussing the issue.' Emma angrily stamped her foot. 'It's about Nick going to Manchester.'

'I can see that he won't be,' Giles said. 'And I think you're right. It was a crazy idea. Manchester may not be Oxford but it's a good university and I think all the places available will be taken up. I don't think there would be the slightest chance that he'd get a place so late now anyway. We didn't think it through. We didn't think about it at all. We simply got carried away.' He looked straight at Andreas. 'We're not gay, but we like each other. We'll miss each other. That's all.'

As Giles turned to go Lydia rose abruptly and, crossing the room, barred his way to the door.

'Giles, please stay.' She held out her hands towards him as if in a kind of supplication, but he shook his head.

'Really, I think it's better . . .'

'But we'd *like* you to stay, Giles, truly.'

'Besides, I'm not properly dressed.' He looked down at his tracksuit top.

'It really doesn't matter.'

'All the same . . .' He gave an embarrassed, deprecating smile.

Sensing defeat, and possible humiliation again, Lydia deftly stepped aside. 'I hope you'll come again soon,' she said. 'Nick will see you out.'

Silently Nick and Giles walked along the hall and out of the front door, pausing beside Giles's car which was parked

69

by the pavement. Nick ruefully scratched his head.

'I really don't know what to say . . .'

'No need to say anything.' Briefly, Giles placed a hand on Nick's shoulder. 'We both know it doesn't matter. But I really couldn't stay for dinner after that.'

'I know. I think you were right. I don't know what got into Dad.'

'If I'd thought you were going to bring it up immediately I'd have cautioned you to wait until everyone had eaten.'

'You're right. I just blurted it out. I simply didn't think.'

'*We* didn't think. Anyway the whole idea was crazy.' Giles turned towards his car, a hand upraised. 'See you.'

'See you soon.'

Watching him sadly as he drove away, Nick knew that more than a friendship had changed that night, and he wandered for some time around the garden until the chill evening air drove him inside to rejoin his family.

PART II

The Girl in the Quad: Laura

CHAPTER 5

Nick stood at the window of his room looking down into the quad. He'd seen the girl before, watched her as she emerged from the door leading to staircase F, wondering who the lucky sod was whose room she was coming from.

She walked across the quad to the gate, well wrapped up against the chill blast of the keen January wind.

He'd seen her in other places as well, caught glimpses of her through a crowd: in a pub, a coffee bar, once walking along the High with another female, deep in conversation.

It was difficult to know what attracted him to her in a city, a university, where there were so many girls to choose from. Maybe there was something about her that suggested an answer to his loneliness?

She had bronze curly hair cut slightly above shoulder length. It was an amazing colour, like molten gold. She was about five feet nine or ten, of athletic build, and she walked gracefully as though she might once have trained for the ballet before her height outstripped her. Very tall women sometimes had rather a clumsy gait, but hers was unusually graceful.

He had never been really close enough to discern her features with any certainty, but the general impression was of a rather pale face, arresting bone structure and deep-set eyes that could have been green or kingfisher blue.

She reminded him of a quattrocento painting, and he very much wanted to get to know her.

Then she disappeared off the horizon and he began to panic. He had somehow assumed that, one day, inevitably, they would meet, that theirs was a linked destiny. He spent a lot of time at his window; looking for her in the street; in various meeting places; but the girl with the green or kingfisher blue eyes failed to materialise.

He had begun to wonder whether she'd left the university, or even if she'd ever belonged to it.

Would he spend the rest of his life chasing a dream? Maybe he would be one of those people who never married because of the memory of some fruitless, unconsummated love.

Nick wondered if he was obsessed with the girl he had never met because he was so unhappy at Oxford? The row with his parents over Giles, so soon before he joined the university, had distressed him. That combined with natural nerves at the prospect of such an important change, seemed to set the tone for the first term. He had felt uneasy and unhappy. He found it difficult to form new friendships, and he spent a lot of time in his room gazing out of the window, like today, watching the girl stop by the gate for a word with the porter.

Then, suddenly, he acted. He felt exhilarated at seeing her again, and if he allowed her to disappear this time, it might be for good.

He slipped out of his room, ran down the steep winding staircase and walked swiftly across the quad, just as she had done, keeping her in sight. As he approached the gate he saw her wave to the porter and then she turned right. Nick sped after her, but as he drew abreast of the porter's lodge he heard his name.

'Mr Constantine . . .'

'I'll be back in a moment,' he said waving an arm, and as he turned the corner she was still there, about a hundred yards ahead. He felt rather like a stalker as he followed her, slowing down when she slowed down, quickening his pace when she quickened hers. It was nearly four in the afternoon and he saw her pause, consult her watch and then turn abruptly into a coffee bar.

He waited a few seconds and then followed her inside.

As she made her way to the self-service counter, he caught a glimpse of her close-up, and she was even more beautiful than he had imagined, with the most amazing grey-green eyes. He watched her as she gazed into the display cabinet as if deciding whether to have a cake and, if so, which one. Finally she selected a piece of cheesecake, put it with her coffee on a tray and sat at the only available table by the window at the far side of the shop.

Nick also had a coffee, paid for it and made as though he was looking round for somewhere to sit. Finally he approached the table by the window: 'Do you mind?'

'Not at all,' she replied, looked at him for a second, smiled and, lowering her head, went on eating her cheesecake. Nick's mouth dried up. He swallowed some coffee.

'Haven't I seen you somewhere before?' he said at last, and again she looked up with the most fleeting of smiles.

'Sounds familiar.'

'OK. It's a pick-up,' Nick grinned.

'I think we have met before,' she said. 'Laura Chase.'

'Nick Constantine.'

They shook hands across the table. Nick felt easier, more relaxed, crossed his legs and bent his head to drink his coffee. Laura finished eating and, groping in her pockets, produced a packet of cigarettes and a lighter. She held out the packet to Nick. 'Do you?'

'No, I don't.'

'I don't suppose I should either.' She clicked open the lighter and inhaled. Then exhaling she looked at him through smoke.

'I saw you at Michael Marsden's party. Are you at his college?'

'Yes, I am.'

'I know who you are. They say you're very clever.'

He felt a childish pleasure in the fact that she knew something about him.

'I don't think I'm cleverer than anyone else.'

'They say you're brilliant.'

It was thrilling to think that, somehow, she knew so much about him, maybe more than he knew about her.

'Can I get you another coffee?' he said, looking at her cup.

'Thanks.' She smiled again and held out her cup and saucer.

She had a pleasantly deep voice with a distinct northern accent. She wore no make-up except orange lipstick, and her skin glowed. As he came back with the coffees balanced on a tray he saw that she was watching him.

'Is Mike Marsden a particular friend of yours?' he asked.

'We're both doing English Lit,' she said. 'We share a tutor.'

'Is that why you go to his rooms?'

'Ah, ah!' She smiled, spooning sugar into her coffee and stirring it.

'My window faces F block. Sometimes I see you come out.'

She lit another cigarette. 'I assure you it's for the purposes of academic research. What's your subject?'

'PPE. Philosophy, politics and economics.'

'First or second year?'

'First.'

'Me, too. Are you from London?'

'Does it show?'

'No, but most people seem to come from London. I'm from Salford. That's part of Greater Manchester.'

'Oh!' Nick looked interested. 'My best friend went up to Manchester University. I'd like to have gone there too.'

'Why didn't you?'

'My parents wanted me to come to Oxford.'

'Mine, too. I was the first member of our family to go to

university so they were extremely chuffed when I got into Oxford.'

'Me, too.'

'I guess our families must be kind of similar.' She smiled. 'My father is an ex-mill worker. He was made redundant when the cotton mills started to close and he hasn't worked since. My mother's one of those downtrodden characters people make fun of.'

'I'm sure you don't make fun of her.'

'I certainly don't. In fact, I hate leaving her. Sometimes I wish I'd gone to Manchester too. Then I could have stayed at home and helped her.'

'Haven't you brothers and sisters?'

'I've got two brothers. Gordon, is fifteen and still at school. Gary is twenty-one and is a car mechanic, and my sister Sharon is twenty-three, married with two children. So I'm an auntie.'

Nick was very glad she was called Laura and not Sharon.

'Laura's a pretty name,' he mused.

'Tell me about your family.'

'Well, my father's family were Greek – hence the name Nicolas spelled without an "h". My father's grandfather, that is *my* great-grandfather, came from the Peloponnese and had a stall at a market in London.'

'Oh, so you're working class too.' Laura looked relieved. 'That's good. Somehow I thought you weren't.'

'They don't have the market stall any more,' Nick said hurriedly. 'My grandfather started to import stuff from Greece: olives, oil, wine. The business took off after the war when delicatessens began to flourish, and did well.'

'I suppose you've got a shop or something?' Laura looked up, interested.

'No, it's an import/export business with headquarters in the City, near Smithfield as a matter of fact. You know, the meat market.'

'Are you going into the business?'

Nick shook his head. 'Oh, no. I don't think so.'

'What are you going to do?'

'I'd quite like to be an academic if I do well enough.'

'Won't your Dad mind?'

'I don't think so.'

'Have you brothers and sisters?'

'One sister, Emma. She's a twin.'

'Oh, a twin.' Laura seemed to think that interesting. 'Are you alike?'

'To look at?' he smiled. 'Not very. She's much better looking than I am.'

Privately Laura thought that unlikely. To her, he seemed very dishy indeed.

'Are you close then? They always say twins are close.'

'I think we're close, but we're also very different. Emma likes a good time.' He paused nervously, not wishing to put her off. 'People *say* that I'm much more serious.'

This seemed to amuse Laura, and Nick felt a surge of relief. For a first encounter surely it was all going extremely well.

'So what does she do?'

Nick smiled. 'Nothing very much. Look, she's coming down next week. Maybe you'd like to meet her?'

Suddenly it seemed a very good way to develop the acquaintanceship.

'That would be really nice,' Laura said with her enticing, enchanting smile, and Nick thought that she was pleased at this idea of developing the relationship too.

Emma stood with her hands in the pockets of her jeans taking careful stock of Nick's room. His was one of the most ancient of Oxford colleges and, although some new buildings had been added since its foundation in the sixteenth century, Nick's room was in one of the original structures of the college. It was timbered, panelled and cosy.

It was the first time Emma had been to visit. She had recently joined up with friends to cross to North Africa and had then travelled through Africa by jeep. She'd returned feeling restless, and rather envied Nick his dedication to study. She knew that she had the capability of being almost as clever academically as Nick, but lacked the staying power.

Emma had always been very conscious of women's role in the Greek community.

It was a long time ago since her great grandfather had sailed from Corinth with a wife and a baby to seek his fortune in a strange land. There was now no longer a traditional community as such to which the Constantines belonged. They had severed their ties from the strong bonds that bound expatriates. Neither Andreas nor his children could speak any Greek. They were British, born in Britain.

Yet there were certain habits, deeply ingrained, that remained. Greek women from good families were not expected to work. They were expected to marry well, to reflect the industry and wealth of their fathers, to be a credit to the family and pass on the genes of thrift, industry and hard work.

Of course there were exceptions, but Emma was not one of them. She had grown up, assured of her place in the sun; cocooned, loved and protected. It had been a happy close-knit home; her parents were a devoted couple and it is doubtful if, despite the legendary sexual voracity of Greek males, her father had ever eyed up another woman.

Although she knew there was wealth, she and her brother were also taught the value of money. Extravagance was not encouraged; there was no showing off to school friends, being dropped at the gates in chauffeur-driven cars. They travelled like most other children, either by bus or tube.

That said, it was accepted that her father and mother liked the best of everything. They could send their children to the best schools; they could afford fine pictures, costly and elaborate furnishings, good seats at the opera, and first class restaurants. Because he thought it was the supreme example of the manufacturer's craft, Andreas could not resist adding a Rolls to his stable of cars and, eventually, acquire the yacht moored in the bay at Monte Carlo.

Although Emma was slightly bored with her life, she was not envious of Nick. She knew that she herself craved endless excitement and she would not find it in the close confines of academia. She felt flat after the African trip, felt restless and was constantly in search of a good time. Nick's room was neat, compact, with everything that he needed near at hand. It had a bed, a desk, chest of drawers, bookshelf, and a hi-fi with speakers, a stack of classical tapes by its side. It was a scholarly room, a thinker's room, one pleasant and restful to be in.

Nick was serious, purposeful. Emma was not. Yet they had so much in common. Although not identical twins, they had shared that close, confined space in their mother's womb for nine months before they were born.

Emma flopped down on Nick's neatly made bed and picked up the most recent issue of *The Economist* that lay by the side. Underneath that was a weighty tome on the politics of oppression and also, for lighter reading, a well-thumbed copy of Dostoevsky's *The Idiot*.

Nick was at a seminar. Emma had arrived in Oxford the previous evening, was staying at the Randolph and they'd dined there together. It was a happy evening, in the course of which Nick told her about Laura.

She had seldom seen the cautious, sensible Nick so excited; so transformed. Nick, as far as she knew, had never had a serious girlfriend. Over the past few months she had begun to wonder whether her father's intemperate suggestion that Nick might be gay had some foundation. What if he were? Would she have minded? As an emancipated, enlightened woman of the nineties, she liked to think she wouldn't. But, in her heart of hearts, she knew she would. And loving Nick like she did, she knew she would support him anyway. Nothing would change that.

Emma flicked through *The Economist*, found little in it to rivet her attention and, casting it aside, was about to doze off when there was a tap on the door. Thinking it was the scout or someone with a message she rose hastily, sat on the edge of the bed and called out 'come in'.

The door slowly opened and a strange face cautiously peered round it.

'Oh, sorry,' a voice said, and the person was about to withdraw when Emma hurried over and opened the door wide.

'Can I help you?'

'Well, I was wondering if Nick . . .'

'He's at a seminar.' Emma held out a hand at the same time drawing the woman into the room. 'I'm his sister, Emma.'

'I'm Laura,' the girl said.

'Come in, Laura.' Emma stood back to let her pass and then shut the door behind her. 'Do sit down,' she pointed to a chair and then once again sprawled on the bed. 'I'm awfully pleased to meet you.'

'Oh!' Laura looked relieved. 'Nick did mention me? I wasn't sure.'

Emma regarded the young woman with interest. So this was Laura. Not quite what she had expected. Not quite as beautiful as Nick's euphoric description but certainly, with an interesting, intelligent face, and she was so tall! Together they would make an arresting couple; heads would turn wherever they went.

'Nick hardly stopped talking about you,' Emma said. 'You made quite an impression.'

Laura gave a shy smile. 'He's awfully nice. It was so odd the way we met, by chance in a coffee bar.'

So he hadn't told her about his pursuit of her along

the High, of the hours he'd spent gazing out of his window waiting for her to appear. Just as well not to wear your heart on your sleeve, at least at the beginning of a relationship.

Laura, sitting comfortably back in the chair, her arms folded round her knees, was also looking at Emma with curiosity. This was the twin sister about whom Nick talked constantly: the bold adventurous, outward going Emma beside whom he seemed to consider himself rather dull. Opposites in everything, he told her. It would have been impossible, unless one knew it, to believe that they were twins.

'I hear you've been to Africa,' she said.

'Just come back.'

'It sounds very exciting.' Laura now hugged her knees. 'Do you know, I've never been abroad?'

'Really?' Emma looked interested. 'We must soon remedy that. Nick must invite you to come on our yacht. I think we're going to Greece and Turkey this year.'

'On a yacht?'

'Yes.'

'Did you say it was yours?'

'Well ours, that is the family's. It's moored at Monte Carlo. Nick didn't tell you about the yacht?' Nor the Rolls, Emma imagined.

'Nick told me very little about his family. He talked a lot about you. He told me what his father did. I told him what my father did. The usual thing.' Laura paused and looked at her solemnly. 'He didn't tell me about the yacht.'

'No particular reason why he should.' Emma was determined to sound offhand. 'Except that we haven't had it very long and it's a bit like an exciting new toy. I only mentioned it because of going abroad.'

'Of course.'

'I mean, you don't need a yacht to go abroad. I went through Africa in a jeep.'

'It must have been very exciting.' Laura sounded envious.

'It was.'

'And dangerous?'

'Not these days. Providing you've got all your jabs, all you need is your American Express card.'

Once again Laura appeared not to understand, and Emma decided that, for all her apparent sophistication, her height and good looks, she was really rather a naive young woman when it came to experience of the ways of the world. She didn't want to get on the wrong side of someone who might have an important place in Nick's life, and was just wishing he would return when the door slowly began to open and she sprang up and, rushing over to it, flung it open.

'Hi, there . . .' she began. 'Giles!' she exclaimed, and, flinging her arms round his neck, pulled him into the room. 'Giles! Nick didn't say you were coming.'

'Nick didn't know.' Giles, his arms loosely round Emma's waist, looked down at her eager face. 'I thought I'd surprise him but I didn't think I'd find you . . . and' he looked enquiringly round at Laura who had remained where she was.

'This is Laura, a friend of Nick's.'

'How do you do, Laura?' Giles reached down and shook her hand.

'Giles is Nick's best friend,' Emma began to explain but Laura nodded.

'I know. Nick told me about him. Aren't you at Manchester University?'

'Yes,' Giles said eagerly. 'Are you?'

'No, but I come from Salford. You can tell, I expect, from my accent.'

Giles smiled. 'I can't exactly distinguish a Salford accent from a Mancunian one yet, but I guessed you came from the north.'

'So Nick doesn't know you're here?' Emma looked at Giles who shook his head and then smiled apologetically in Laura's direction. 'I'm afraid I got so sick of Manchester.'

'But term's just begun . . .'

'Besides, it never stops raining.'

'It rains here too,' Laura said and stood up. 'I shall have to go. I have a tutorial. Tell Nick that, well . . . I was here.'

'I'm sure we'll meet up with you later,' Emma began to walk her to the door.

'Where are you staying?'

'The Randolph.'

'Oh!'

'I'll tell Nick to give you a ring.'

'See you.' Giles smiled as he watched her proceed to the door and, after Emma had shut it: 'Interesting girl.'

'Oh, you think so too? Nick's had a *coup de foudre*.'

'He didn't tell me.'

'It only happened in the last few days.'

'Really?'

'He followed her along the High and finally accosted her in a coffee bar. He's terribly smitten.'

'Well, I don't know.' Giles's expression was reflective. It was true that, although he himself was a bit of a flirt, Nick had never shown a serious interest in girls.

'I think he's been terribly lonely in Oxford.'

'And I've been terribly lonely in Manchester.'

'Missed each other, I guess?' Emma sounded sympathetic.

'It's ridiculous but true I suppose.' Giles sat on the edge of the bed and stared at the floor. 'I thought I could easily make friends, but I've found it hard.'

'Any particular reason?' Emma looked curiously at him.

'I think I've just known so many people well for so long, chums at school, Nick, that sort of thing. I haven't the ease with strangers I thought I would have had or, to be frank, that people seemed to expect of me. Also, I'm in digs a long way from the campus. They're mostly older students. All the freshers like me are in residential halls and I think that helps to get to know people, make friends. Because I applied so late I couldn't get a place. Digs can be very lonely. I miss the camaraderie of the school days, of London and being surrounded by people I'd known most of my life. Part of the pack.

'I shouldn't really be here now, but I thought I'd surprise Nick. Never guessed you would be here too. That's a bonus.' He looked at her fondly. She was, after all, a great mate. Perhaps more. But somehow it had always been difficult to make a pass at your best friend's sister. Difficult and, unwise too.

'How was Africa?'

'Africa was great.'

Emma sat on the floor cross-legged and began to tell him about it while they waited for Nick's return.

Later they foregathered at an Italian restaurant in the centre of the town. Laura watched the three who had known one another for so long, from whom she was excluded, inevitably, as a stranger, excitedly exchanging news in which, of course, she had no part.

Emma was the most vivacious, the most talkative, delighting in male attention. Laura was interested in her because she was closest to Nick. Yes, they were alike to look at, but it was impossible to tell that they were twins. Both were dark, handsome, but Emma's appearance was less Mediterranean than Nick's. Her skin was quite fair and with her thick, quite long, wavy black hair, dark brown eyes and full red lips, her clever but subtle use of make-up, she looked exotic, exciting; surely extremely attractive to men? She was certainly more lively than Nick who could be given to long, seemingly introspective but not unfriendly periods of silence while Emma and Giles animatedly chatted to each other. However it was easy to tell the twins were close. They had an obvious rapport. They kept on glancing at each other, exchanging looks and smiles and then they would try and draw Laura into the conversation. But it was difficult. In their company she felt shy. Besides, she had nothing to say. She had not travelled by jeep the length of Africa or shared a yachting holiday the previous summer in the Mediterranean.

But, most of all, she had not grown up with these attractive, gifted, exciting young people who not only seemed to share a common bond but, as she now knew, also had a background of wealth and privilege that most certainly excluded her.

And Giles fitted in so well. It was easy to see that he and Nick were intimates, friends, apparently, from the age of thirteen when they went to the London public day school. How many shared memories were there here? Hundreds, thousands; moments of intimacy from which she would be forever excluded.

She saw them as waves coming together, separating for a moment and then joining up again.

They deferred to her; they were nice to her but she felt strangely depressed and apart from the vast expanse of Nick's life before they had met.

Throughout the meal Laura was largely silent, watching.

It was after midnight when they saw Emma and Giles, who was also staying there, back to the Randolph. They lingered for some time in the lobby saying their goodbyes and making plans for the following day. Nick kissed Emma goodnight, Giles and Laura politely shook hands and then Giles and Emma saw them to the door waving as they descended the steps and began to walk towards Carfax.

It was very cold. Nick put his arms around her shoulders and she huddled against him.

'Enjoy the evening?' he asked, bending to look closely at her face.

'Very much.'

'I wondered . . .' he paused.

'Yes?' She looked up at him. 'What did you wonder?'

'I wondered if you felt a bit out of it?'

'Yes, I did, but don't worry. It was nice of you to ask me.'

'I'm just sorry I wasn't there when you, Emma and Giles met up.'

'It didn't matter. Seriously. I liked Emma.'

'And she liked you,' he paused. 'And Giles?'

'Oh, I liked Giles. He's *very* nice. So easy to get on with.'

'Then I'm glad.' Nick squeezed her shoulder hard. 'Those are the two people who mean most in the world to me.'

'Not your mum and dad?' She looked up at him. In the murky light from the street lamps his face looked very solemn.

'Yes, more than my mum and dad. Oh, I love them of course.'

'Is there anything between Giles and Emma?' Laura asked, as they recommenced their stroll, Nick's arm tightly round her waist.

'You mean anything romantic?'

She nodded.

'No.'

'They seem very close.'

'No, they're just good friends,' Nick laughed, 'I know it sounds trite, but in this case it's true.'

Laura appeared to ponder. She halted, detached herself from his arm and gazed at him. 'Nick?'

'Yes?'

'You didn't tell me you were rich.'

'Well!' Nick scratched his head, looked up at the night sky. 'It's not the sort of thing one talks about. It's not important anyway.'

'I mean seriously rich, with a yacht.'

'It's not my yacht. It's my dad's.'

87

'The jet-set life and all that,' she went on as though she hadn't heard him.

'Does it matter very much to you?'

'It doesn't matter to *me*, but it matters, doesn't it?'

'Why does it matter?'

'In general it matters. Class matters. My parents are working class and we live on a council estate in Salford. My father hasn't worked for over ten years. He's a bitter, frustrated man on the dole.'

'But that doesn't matter to *us*, Laura,' Nick pleaded. 'Keep it in proportion.'

'I just feel rather shocked that I am mixing with people whose father owns a yacht and who stay at the Randolph when they come to Oxford. I hadn't even been in the Randolph until tonight.'

'I don't think I have either.'

'You know what I mean, Nick.'

'No, I don't.' He began to feel rather angry. 'I don't know why you're bringing all this up, letting it interfere with our relationship which I thought was going well. I don't believe in class, don't believe it matters at all. I'm sorry you know about the yacht, but you would have found out about it sooner or later, and then you'd have said I was concealing it from you. As a matter of fact it might amuse you to know that Giles's family are very class conscious. Giles isn't, but his mother and father are. They regard my family as nouveau riche and we didn't have a particularly good time on the yacht.'

'You sounded as though you had a *very* good time.'

'Parts of it were very good. But there was a lot of tension, the end was awful and that clouded the rest. Giles's father trod on a jellyfish and got blood poisoning and Giles learned he hadn't got good enough grades to get into Oxford. We were to be separated and it made us very unhappy. It coloured the whole holiday. But the main thing is that my mother has always felt patronised by the Harveys, Giles's family, and the fact that they were on board made her ill.'

'Then why did you ask them?'

'My father wants to try and impress them, show them that he is as good as they are.'

'Are they very rich too?'

'I don't think they're badly off, but perhaps not quite as well off as my dad. And I stress it *is* my dad. The money is his. It's not mine.'

'I can't tell with you, but I can tell with Emma. The way she behaves, her self-confidence. She's the same age as me, yet she seems much older. Money has given her that particular poise.'

'No, I just think Emma's like that. Actually she's not terribly happy and I think she probably rather envies you.'

'Envies *me*?' Laura looked amazed.

'That you've got into Oxford, that you're clever enough, have a goal. Emma doesn't really know where she's going. She's restless. That's why she seems so sophisticated because she's always on the move, doing things, seeing new places, meeting new people. You see, Emma is really very insecure, and you're the lucky one.'

As if to emphasise this, Nick's arm tightened round her shoulder again, and Laura found herself slipping easily into the comfort of his embrace, feeling reassured by his words, and that already, in a way, she belonged, if not to his family, then to Nick.

CHAPTER 6

Valerie had never liked sex, although before she and Edmund were married she had seemed very keen on it indeed. When Edmund proposed, he felt that he was marrying not only a wealthy woman but a sexy one too. She was neither pretty nor plain, but had the sort of well-bred looks of women of his class, women he was used to and with whom he felt comfortable. She was uninterested in her appearance and always had been. In fact, in the years they'd been married, nothing about Valerie had changed very much except that she had gone off sex after Giles was born, and ever after that was doing him a favour.

It was no wonder he'd strayed, Edmund thought, as he eased himself off his lover and looked down at her face: eyes closed, cheeks suffused, every indication of rapture. There was even the trace of tears. Tears, after all these years. He didn't know whether it was a tribute to his prowess as a lover, or Mary's skills as a mistress.

But whether she pretended or not, Mary managed to invest their love life with something he had never had with his wife: a continual sense of excitement.

Edmund was forty-six and Mary was two years younger. When he had first known her, she was already divorced from her husband, Sam Rogers, an officer in the Merchant Navy who had abused her every time he came home on leave. He led her a wretched life, and finally she left him.

Mary had been petite, blonde, wore a lot of make-up

skilfully applied, dressed smartly and was in every way the antithesis of Valerie. And she was wonderfully sexy.

Very shortly after their affair began, Edmund decided to set up a legal practice on his own, having fallen out with his partners. Mary stayed on with his old firm until she became pregnant with Adam.

Edmund had never dreamt Mary would have the child, or that she wanted one. He had tried to persuade her with every inducement, except marriage, to have an abortion, but she refused. Edmund was too much of a gentleman to abandon her, but for a time their relationship had cooled, and he only visited out of a sense of guilt. The child was not only premature but sickly, and Mary was struggling away on her own, determined to be cheerful, keeping up appearances. It was difficult for her, but she coped.

Mary was the sort who coped, and in this she partly resembled Valerie who possessed similar traits. It seemed to go with the characteristics of a certain type of British woman. Edmund didn't love Mary now, and didn't think he ever had. He had found her very attractive, and still did. In a way, he was too calculating a man to fall in love with anyone. He could never quite abandon himself to the loss of emotional control that falling in love seemed to bring. Could never understand it in other chaps.

Parental love he did understand, and he thought that when his daughter Alice was born he had fallen in love for the first time. He simply adored her. There was nothing unpleasant or incestuous about this love, nothing unnatural. It was pure, unadulterated and he would have given his life for her. He was not certain he would have given it either for Valerie or Mary.

Mary stirred and Edmund, who had been lying on his stomach, head in his hands, turned and gazed at her.

It was a Saturday afternoon, about the only free time in the week that Edmund got. It was a toss between playing with Adam, or doing something educational with him like taking him to a film or a museum, or making love. Love won about one Saturday in three. Occasionally there was a late evening when Adam was safely in bed and asleep.

It wasn't much of a life for Mary, but she rarely complained. It was very difficult in fact to know what went on in her mind, and the outburst at the hospital had not been typical. She seldom showed her feelings, but he imagined that they were well bottled up and that sex was for her, as it was for him, a much needed release.

'Heard from Giles?' Mary said, turning over on her stomach too.

'Not for ages.'

'How's he settling down in Manchester?'

'I don't think he's very happy. He has only himself to blame.'

Edmund turned over and patted his stomach, looked at the clock by the side of the bed.

'Why is that?' Mary turned round too, aware that any moment he would say he must be off. Mary thought she would eventually get used to that kind of thing, but somehow she never did and went on wishing that he would stay because he wanted to and not because she nagged.

It wasn't much of a life and she'd often thought in the past ten years that she would have been better off on her own, but then she wouldn't have had Adam and she did adore him. It never occurred to her that she might have met someone else and had a different sort of life altogether. One that would not necessarily have excluded children. On the other hand, when she'd met Edmund she had been alone for six years and celibate for most of that time. That wasn't much of a life either.

Edmund turned his eyes from the clock to the ceiling; his fingers continued drumming on his stomach. Mary wondered if he'd heard her.

'I said, Ed . . .'

'Yes, I heard you, Mary. I was just thinking.'

'You said he only had himself to blame. Is that because he failed to get in to Oxford . . .'

'Well, we warned him Manchester wasn't much of a place.'

'I believe it's come along an awful lot since . . .'

'Yes, but it's not Oxford, or London. It's the provinces. Valerie suggested to Giles that he should retake, but he wouldn't. He was too impatient.'

'Does he still see Nick?'

'I don't really know as he hardly communicates. I know he didn't much at Christmas, if at all, because we were in Somerset and the Constantines, naturally, were in Gstaad.'

'Why do you say "naturally", Ed?'

'Because that's the sort of place people like them go to for Christmas.'

'Whereas people like you go to the country?'

He looked at her suspiciously, uncertain as to whether or not he could detect a note of sarcasm.

'And people like me stay in town,' she went on bitterly, 'because we've nowhere else to go.'

It was difficult, Edmund thought, to believe that a few moments before she'd been in tears from the emotion of their lovemaking. Women were strange creatures.

To add to the guilt Edmund felt, Mary had no close relations. She was an only child and an orphan. Well, he was an only child too, and his mother and father were also dead; but he had an extended family from Valerie's huge brood of relations, not only both parents alive but brothers and sisters, nieces and nephews, aunts, uncles and cousins galore. In Somerset the place heaved with Valerie's kith and kin, in all shapes and sizes, all invariably dressed in Barbours and green wellies, and all devoted to sport and country pursuits.

Edmund heaved himself out of bed and sat on the side,

scratching his head. He was very lean and going thin on top, and strands of hair protruded from his scalp. Mary suddenly thought he looked at the same time both lovable and oddly pathetic.

'Must go,' he said, then turning to her, 'pointless having this sort of conversation, Mary. We seem to have had it so often before. I mean, look, if you feel so discontented, break it off by all means.'

'You mean you wouldn't care?'

'Of *course* I'd care, dammit! But I don't want this continual complaining when there's nothing I can do.'

'I do not "continually" complain,' Mary said indignantly, also sitting up. 'I merely asked how Giles was.'

'And then you brought up the business of having nowhere to go for Christmas. I had the feeling you were on the verge of complaining, let's put it like that.'

Edmund began to put on his underpants and socks.

'About Adam's schooling,' Mary began.

'Oh, that's it.'

'You said you would think about it.'

No reply. Edmund went on dressing.

'I have found a school that will take him after Easter, Ed. No need to wait until September. They gave him a test and they think he's bright. The longer he stays on at a state school the more difficult it will be to get into the private system. They say it will be impossible for him to take Common Entrance if he tries from the comprehensive system. The teaching is quite different.' Mary paused. 'Ed . . .'

'Yes, I'm listening.' Edmund buttoned up his shirt. As it was the weekend he wasn't wearing a tie.

'I know you don't want to discuss it, Ed, but my mind is made up. I *told* them I was a single parent and they will accept a reduced fee. They were very nice. They know about his asthma . . .'

Edmund sat down on the edge of the bed and gazed at

94

Mary whose hands were hugging her knees, making a tent in the duvet. Her hair was scraped back, her face shiny and flushed, but this time through passion of another kind. Passion for her son, her first and last born, her only child. It was a very strong and determined passion, and Edmund knew already that he had lost.

'How much?' he asked.

'Oh, Ed, you mean you'd consider it?'

'I shall have to.'

'Fifteen hundred a term.'

Edmund whistled. 'Plus uniform, books, music lessons, games kits and extra classes for this and that.' He held up a hand. 'Oh, don't tell me, Mary. I know all about the "hidden extras". We're looking at five or six thousand a year at least. Oh, and then there are excursions; overseas holidays, cub and scout camp . . .'

'You're being pessimistic.'

'I'm being *realistic*, Mary. Believe me, I can't afford it.'

'But with Giles . . .'

'Giles only gets his fees paid. I have to pay for maintenance. I have to pay full fees for Paul and Alice. This could break me, Mary.' He tried to make his voice sound gentle, whee-dling, but inside he was boiling.

Mary's voice was steely-edged.

'But Adam is your son too, Ed.'

'Yes, but I didn't ask for him to be born. It was your decision.'

'You accepted the responsibility. You always said you would, and that you loved him.'

'Which I do.' He reached over and took her hand. 'Believe me, Mary, I do.'

'Then you will have to fork out the fees, Ed,' she said. 'I am not messing about. I've accepted a place. I have never claimed maintenance from you, Ed, never dreamt of taking you to court, you know that. I thought if a thing wasn't voluntary it wasn't worthwhile. I wanted our relationship to be based on mutual trust and affection; but now I've had enough. I really have. My mind is made up. I want Adam to be properly educated. He has not much going for him. He's illegitimate and he's not good looking. He's short-sighted and asthmatic. He's not wealthy. He's going to have to fight his way in life and I want him in there with a chance. That chance is education.'

'I'll see what I can do.' Edmund glanced at his watch and rose from the bed.

'If you haven't got the money, Ed, and I find that hard to believe, better ask Valerie. We know she's got plenty.'

When he looked at her Edmund saw a tight, mean smile on Mary's face that made it difficult for him to recall the rapture, the tears. What a fleeting thing sex was, Edmund thought, as he vowed to himself to try, oh to try so hard, never to make love to her again.

Mary stood by the window watching Edmund get into his car. She noticed his humped shoulders, the frown on his forehead, the air of weariness. She recalled how sad he'd looked, perched on the edge of her bed. He did not look a happy man, whereas she always felt exhilarated after sex and the effect took some time to wear off. But then the phrase *post coitus tristus est* was always, she believed, inferred to refer to men and not to women. Maybe it was coined in the days before women were supposed to enjoy sex at all.

After he got into the car Edmund sat there for some time as though thinking, undecided what to do or, maybe, where to go. Yet he always maintained this fiction of being a very busy man, always in a hurry. A hurry to get away after his fill of sex, because she knew he didn't get any from Valerie. A hurry maybe now to get away from her endless nagging about Adam, about the unsatisfactory nature of their relationship, away from the threats that were a recent intrusion into their life together. Yes, Mary felt exhilarated after sex, lifted onto another plane but, after a while there was a process of winding down, a sense of disillusion. She felt let down too because of the lack of follow up: the post-coital embraces, the endearments, the frolicking in and out of the bath; maybe dinner later followed by the theatre, or vice-versa. She and Edmund seldom went anywhere because he was so afraid of being seen or maybe they'd scuttle round to a local bistro and even then he spent most of his time furtively watching the door. It would have been nice, for example, to have gone to collect Adam from the friends he was with, given him the joy of seeing his mother and father arrive together. But it was never to be, maybe because Edmund was afraid even there of meeting someone he knew, some-one who would see him exposed as an adulterer.

Their affair was certainly not satisfactory; it was second or even third best, but Mary was helped by the fact that she couldn't stand Valerie: her air of swank, her patronising manner, the sheer effrontery of a rather plain, drab woman having the nerve to lord it over her.

In the days when Mary worked for Edmund, Valerie used to bray on the phone: 'May I speak to my husband, please?' without taking the trouble to announce who she was or say 'Good morning' or 'Good afternoon'. She was the sort of woman Mary instinctively disliked so she didn't mind carry-ing on with her husband. In fact she rather enjoyed it.

Maybe it was because Valerie had sensed her as a rival all those years ago that she was so rude to her? She was perfectly civil and polite to everyone else. The upper classes usually were, their hypocrisy concealed behind a display of good manners.

Mary knew she wouldn't betray Edmund to the author-ities, to his wife or to anyone else. That was just bluff; but she also enjoyed making him anxious getting, maybe, an understandable satisfaction out of seeing him suffer.

Finally Edmund leaned over the wheel, put the car into gear and shot off round the corner never once looking up to the window, from which a rather sad woman watched him. Mary turned back into the sitting room which seemed a lonely and deserted place now that he was no longer there.

Adam was spending the weekend with his friends, so Mary had lots of time to herself in which to do nothing but think. Still in her gown, she wandered aimlessly about the room, plumping up cushions, blowing imaginary specks of dust off the furniture, wondering precisely how to fill the time. In the corner by her word processor were a couple of legal documents from Edmund's old office that needed typing.

She could call a girlfriend, of whom she had a good few in similar situations; that is they were not necessarily having affairs with married men but they were either divorced or without partners.

Maida Vale was a cheerless part of London; long tree-lined streets comprising huge dreary blocks of flats or tall, once graceful Victorian family houses. Some of these bore an air of decrepitude, and were converted into bed-sitting rooms or apartments. One resembled the other, and the area seemed to attract the flotsam and jetsam of the population, those not rich enough to live in Hampstead or St John's Wood and not poor enough for the less salubrious parts of Paddington or the areas off the Edgware or Finchley roads.

There were a lot of foreigners: waiters, waitresses, students either with work permits or without, some resident, some itinerant, an awful lot of retired elderly people who had lived there all their lives and passed through various stages of fortune and misfortune. And then there were people like her, middle-aged, middle class, who had somehow become stuck in a rut without any chance of escape.

She had lived in the flat since her marriage to Sam. They'd rented it, and then, after the divorce, she had bought it with some money her mother had left her. She hadn't bought it outright of course, but there was enough for a mortgage.

It was a dreary flat then and it was a dreary flat now. It was dark because the front faced north and a line of tall trees prevented the sun ever penetrating the kitchen, the bathroom or Adam's bedroom which faced south at the back.

The mansion block, which comprised over a hundred identical flats, lined the whole side of the street, each entrance alike. Built of red brick in the thirties, and fitted out with cheap materials, it boasted a complete lack of artistic or architectural inspiration.

The entrance to Mary's flat was from a long corridor, the walls of which were painted a sickly mixture of cream and brown, the floor covered with a dull orange carpet, discoloured with age. The front door led into a small, very dark internal hall where the light was permanently switched on. From this were doors to the sitting room, the two bedrooms, one much smaller than the other, kitchen and bathroom.

It had now been Mary's home for nearly twenty years and she didn't suppose she would ever leave it. Like her elderly neighbours, she would sink quietly into genteel poverty and live there trying bravely to keep up appearances, to maintain standards either until she died or was carted off to a home for old people, or something worse.

Mary looked round at her sitting room, aware that depression was setting in. One must fight it, could fight it. She would take a bath and ring up one of her girlfriends who were always available on a Saturday night for a meal or a film in the Edgware Road or at the Odeon Swiss Cottage.

She would do that soon, but not just yet.

Laura walked along the High, happily swinging her bag stuffed with the books and papers she needed for her tutorial. She was going to be a bit late. She often was these days and, as usual, her tutor would be annoyed with her.

Laura didn't care, borne aloft as she was on the wings of

love. A romance that started in a coffee bar had become an all-consuming passion. Her first love affair, Nick's too. They were both nineteen, yet they were old enough and wise enough to know that such things were not supposed to last. It was impossible now to say that it could last forever, though they both knew it would. Nick was kind and gentle, he was also powerful and passionate, deeply satisfying as a lover.

In this profound and intimate knowledge of each other they felt completely wrapped up in themselves and lost to the world. Laura knew it showed in her work, in her attitude to her studies, to her friends. She had once enthusiastically embraced Oxford and all it had to offer. Already in her first term she had shown the promise of a future high-flyer.

And now people were saying she was throwing it all away. She had dropped out from many of the activities in which she was formerly so active, turned down a small part in her college drama production. Her friends said she was missing out, mistaking the rapture of first love for the real thing. Laura didn't care.

Laura stopped in front of the coffee bar where she and Nick had first met. She could recall with the utmost clarity every second of that first encounter. She saw him after ordering coffee from the counter, look around, come up to her table.

'Do you mind?' he'd said looking down.

'Not at all,' she'd replied, and had gone on munching her cheesecake.

'Haven't I seen you somewhere before?'

All so corny, all so enjoyable.

They'd discussed since, many times, whether there was such a thing as predestination, if people were meant for each other. They were both logical, rational people, and they still couldn't decide the answer. Since then they'd lived only to be together. It was such a short time, barely two months and yet it seemed like years.

Platitudes, all platitudes.

The woman who was sitting at the same table as Laura had been when she met Nick, looked at her rather curiously. Laura smiled at her and waved, making the expression on the face of the young woman watching her even more comical. Laura wanted to transfer her joy through the huge plate glass windows, but doubtless her youthful contemporary thought she was crazy.

Laura skipped off down the street and continued her way towards her tutor's lodgings which were in an old house tucked between Christ Church and Merton.

It was still cold, but not as bitter as it had been in January when she and Nick had met. Now it was blustery, with the promise of spring in the air. In two weeks' time, term would end and she would be back in Salford. Nick wanted her to come to London and meet his parents but she didn't think the time was right. Well, she'd see. First she felt she should see her own, convince them that an Oxford education didn't mean she was severing her roots. Soon enough to tell them that her new boyfriend was the son of a millionaire, if she bothered to tell them that at all. She couldn't yet decide.

Laura clattered up the stairs of her tutor's lodgings, paused breathlessly outside the door for a second or two and then knocked. On being told to enter she did. Her tutor was sitting by the window apparently engrossed in some document on her lap – maybe Laura's last essay – and removing her tortoiseshell glasses looked up as Laura gently closed the door behind her.

'Sorry I'm late, Maggie.'

'Late *again*, Laura.' Margaret James, lecturer in English Literature at Laura's college, emphasised the word 'again'.

'Sorry.'

Laura took off her coat, unwound her scarf and, still rather breathless, sat down in the chair opposite her tutor. Yes, the essay on her lap, heavily scored, Laura could now see, was hers. Margaret was a clever young don not much more than thirty. Everyone called her Maggie. She smoked and liked a drink and was considered a good sort. Laura had felt privileged to have her as a tutor. She was an expert in nineteenth-century English Literature which was Laura's speciality. They both adored Hardy.

Margaret watched Laura while she sat down and composed herself and, as she did, it was easy to see she was annoyed.

'Sorry,' Laura said again, producing a copy of the essay from her bag. 'Wasn't it any good?' She looked anxiously at the paper on Margaret's lap. She knew they disagreed about Hardy and women, but she didn't think that was the topic pre-eminently on Maggie's mind.

'I know I'm easy-going, Laura, but that doesn't mean you should take advantage of me.' Maggie resumed her spectacles and gazed severely at Laura over the rim.

'Oh, I don't, Maggie,' Laura assured her, grateful that she didn't have a tutor like Doctor Stokes who was rigid and set in her ways, not to say her views. She was also vindictive. Those who failed to find favour with her invariably failed their exams whereas Maggie was known to be exceptionally fair-minded, and just as good a scholar as Winifred Stokes. She was also quite pretty, not tall but with an open, good-natured freckled face and fair curly hair. She invariably wore jeans and didn't seem much interested in her appearance.

'I set great store on punctuality, Laura. Time is precious. I mean, I'm prepared to forgive the odd lapse but,' she consulted the watch on her wrist, 'you're a quarter of an hour late and I have two more tutorials after you and a lecture to deliver at two.'

'Sorry.' Laura knew she was sounding repetitive. 'I will make an effort. I really will.' She threw back her head and smiled, wishing Maggie would now get on with the purpose of the tutorial. But Maggie hadn't finished. She held up Laura's essay and brandished it at her.

'This is indicative of what I mean by your attitude, Laura. It isn't good enough. It is slapdash, slipshod. You haven't followed any of your themes through. I doubt if you even read *A Pair of Blue Eyes* critically.'

'I did.'

'Well, it doesn't show. It seems to me that you leafed through it and scribbled the first ideas that came into your head. This is worth about minus C, if that, and frankly, Laura, it is not the work of an Oxford scholar who sailed through her Oxbridge entrance.'

This time Laura stayed silent, rather staggered by Maggie's words. Maggie cleared her throat and went on.

'If I were saying this in your first term, Laura, I might have wondered about the wisdom of giving you a place. But in your first term your work was so exceptionally good that what staggers me now is how much it has deteriorated. I think we know why, don't we, Laura?'

As Maggie looked at her, Laura lowered her head. Of course, Maggie had been told all about Nick.

'It is since your affair with Nick began.'

'You can't blame *him*!'

'On the contrary, I blame you. It is perfectly possible to be in love and deliver good work. The two are not incompatible. I thought during the first few weeks it was understandable, but now it is nearly two months. Time to settle down, Laura, or I'm afraid that if you fail your exams you might find yourself being sent down.'

Laura looked at Maggie aghast.

'As bad as that?'

'As bad as that.' She handed her back her essay. 'Badly thought out, badly written. It could have been the work of a fifth-form schoolgirl.' Maggie's features softened. 'Laura, I know Doug Gentle, Nick's tutor, and Nick is not having similar difficulties. He still produces excellent work, well above average . . .'

103

Laura turned scarlet. 'I really don't think you've any business discussing me with Nick's tutor.'

'I did not discuss you with Doug. Doug brought it up. He said what a fine young man Nick was and that you were a nice couple. I agreed. I didn't mention the deterioration in your work at all, but Doug went on to enthuse about Nick saying what an excellent scholar he was and his hopes of a First and so on. I kept quiet about you, Laura.'

'Thanks.' Laura's brows knitted together.

'I can see you don't believe me. It's true.' Maggie sat back and lit a cigarette. All pretences at a tutorial had now gone. 'Frankly, I'd be ashamed to admit to anyone that your work had deteriorated. I'd think that it would reflect too much on us as females. It is true that in a love affair we tend to let it take over. "Man's love is of man's life . . ." and so on. It doesn't seem to have changed since Byron's day. Look, I've had my moments, Laura. I'm not immune to matters of the heart. I guess I've been able to call a halt if it affected my work.' She leaned forward and gazed earnestly at the by now troubled young woman sitting opposite her, the earlier euphoria having well and truly departed. 'You know I like you, Laura. I'm speaking to you as a friend, which a good tutor is meant to be: part instructor, part guide. You are supposed to come to us with any problems and I'm telling you that you have a problem, even if you don't know it, or didn't until now. Now you do and believe me, my dear, it is time to take stock before you ruin your career.'

'Does she have a man?' Nick asked.

'I don't know.' Laura snuggled up closer to him. 'She said something about Doug Gentle.'

'Doug's married.'

'Well, I don't know. I think she's quite attractive, don't you?' She looked at him, and he appeared to consider the question.

'Well, she's not my type, but she's not bad. Anyway let's not be sexist.'

'Why is it sexist?'

'It is rather, don't you think? Talking about types and all that? Whether or not a woman "has" a man?'

'Well, you brought it up.'

'I know, and I shouldn't have.'

'You're simply thinking she might be jealous? I mean, we're allowed to think that, aren't we?'

Nick grunted, as if he didn't want to commit himself.

It was three in the afternoon and they were in bed in Nick's room, whither Laura had gone after her aborted tutorial. Fled would have been a better word. Maggie's lecture had upset her, and the thought of being sent down after the first year was too awful to contemplate.

Nick took her to the pub for bread and cheese and a glass of wine and they went back to his room and made love.

It helped, but not much. It was Nick's love and support that mattered more than the physical side, at least this afternoon. Usually the physical side mattered a great deal, but today she had felt too tense to enjoy it and she let Nick come without coming herself, which upset him.

They talked again about Maggie and what she'd said, and it was then that Nick had asked if she had a man.

Laura thought that in a way Maggie was right, and the relationship between the sexes hadn't changed all that much over the centuries, long before Lord Byron and his ideas about love being a woman's whole existence. The newness and excitement about their affair had destroyed her ability to concentrate or produce good work, while Nick's work was apparently, if anything, even better.

Nick tenderly kissed her cheek and stroked her back, his fingers gently massaging her spine, his touch featherlight.

'I'm sorry about asking if Maggie had a man. By implication it *was* sexist.'

'I know what you meant. You wondered if she understood about being in love. I'm sure she does. I mean, if she hasn't got a lover at present, she did have one at some time. She told me she wasn't immune to matters of the heart. She was simply telling me she didn't let it affect her work. I can see that. She's strong. I'm weak.'

Nick kissed her back. His lips moved up to her neck. His arms closing around her, his hands cupping her breasts. She began to relax, feel desire, tremble with the need for him.

'Shall I make you come now?' he whispered, and gently lowered her onto her back.

CHAPTER 7

The dining table was beautifully laid: silver on mahogany, candles in their sconces gleaming on its highly-polished surface.

Andreas sat at one end of the long table, Lydia at the other. In the middle on one side Nick and Laura sat next to each other, their knees occasionally touching. Emma sat facing them, knowing quite well that they were playing footsie under the table.

In the end Laura, hating to be parted so soon from Nick, and for such a long time, had agreed to go with him to meet his parents. They had arrived earlier in the day, been given a warm greeting. Laura had been shown to her room which overlooked the garden at the back and which was down the hall from Nick's. Neither had said anything about the separation, but had exchanged looks while Lydia twittered, slightly uncomfortable at meeting Nick's only acknowledged girlfriend for the first time. By 'acknowledged' they meant that this was the first time Nick had openly said he had a girlfriend, who she was, what she did and all about her. Information which had been supplemented by Emma when she returned home after meeting Laura at Oxford.

Andreas was absolutely delighted to hear that his son was romantically linked with a woman. Ever since the business of Giles wanting Nick to give up Oxford for Manchester (he was quite sure that Giles was behind that idea and not vice versa, as Nick had insisted), ever since then he had nursed, however reluctantly, the idea that his son might indeed be homosexual, an idea that was abhorrent to a macho father. Thus he had welcomed Laura with open arms even if she was not quite what he expected, or would have liked.

Andreas preferred women who were openly feminine, who wore pretty dresses, lots of make-up and made themselves look attractive, and thus available to men, at all times. Andreas thought that in exchange for this you looked after women; you cocooned them, protected them and loved them. He thought it was a fair exchange which benefited both parties because marriage was essentially a partnership. In most partnerships there was a junior partner and a senior one and in marriage it was the man who predominated. Andreas didn't object to intelligent women so much as women who were overtly intellectual and Laura, as he might have feared, came into this category. Of course, being at Oxford, it was perhaps inevitable.

Lydia was the perfect stereotype of Andreas's favourite kind of woman and it was because of this, he was sure, that his marriage was so successful. Outwardly they were partners, but essentially he led and Lydia followed.

He had been greatly relieved that his individualistic and strong-minded daughter had not shone academically and had shown no inclination to follow her brother to university. Despite her stubbornness and strength of character, Emma's father was convinced that she would follow the example set by her mother: make a suitable marriage, bear children, possess a fine home, be a good hostess and lead a happy and exemplary life. It was true that Lydia worried, was over-anxious to impress, but not everyone was perfect and these deficiencies might be ironed out by her daughter with her advantages of a better education, and cushioned by wealth.

Laura had changed into a skirt and chunky sweater. It was the best she could do to look smart as she invariably wore trousers or jeans. Her only make-up was a dash of lipstick. Lydia and Emma were, as usual, impeccably turned out; Lydia in a couture dress of soft mohair, jewellery at ears, throat and wrist; Emma in a trendy purple two-piece, made of incredibly soft suede. She wore earrings and a large gold bangle, and looked as though she was dressed to go out after dinner.

Andreas wore a business suit, white shirt and silk tie. Nick was in flannels, a blue shirt, blazer and tie.

Laura had never really experienced anything like the formality of the proceedings, and for most of the meal remained tongue-tied. There was a live-in Filipino domestic called Maria, who served the dinner which had been prepared by the chef. He commuted daily from the outskirts of London. Maria's husband, Marco, did the gardening, odd jobs around the house and acted as waiter when there were large parties. Laura was completely overawed by the luxury, the style of the whole thing and wished Nick had prepared her better, though he had advised her to bring a skirt which, luckily, she possessed, having bought it as a concession for her Oxford interview the previous year.

'Nick tells me this is your first visit to London,' Andreas said, in an attempt to draw Laura into the conversation which, until then, had been largely about family matters. He had soon discovered that Laura was not much of a one for small talk.

'Yes.'

'And how do you like it?'

'Well . . .'

'We only just arrived, Dad.' Nick came to the rescue. 'I intend to show her round tomorrow.'

'Well, we hope you'll stay a few days, Laura,' Lydia said brightly. 'There's a fashion show tomorrow at Harrods. Emma and I thought of going. I wonder if you . . .'

'I don't think that's quite up Laura's street, Mum.'

'Why not?' Emma looked challengingly at her brother. 'Anything wrong with fashion shows?'

'Nothing at all.' Nick scratched his head and, turning sideways, looked at Laura. 'Interested?'

Laura shook her head. 'Though it's kind of you to ask me, I'm a traditional working-class girl,' she said with a wry smile, as though gaining confidence. 'Nick will have told you that I come from a very ordinary family, and my father's unemployed.' She looked defiantly round the table and then at Nick.

Andreas came to his rescue.

'Nick didn't tell us anything about you, Laura, except that you were a very nice girl he'd met and he'd like to bring you to meet us.' He leaned towards her. 'I'm glad he did, and believe me, we have no "side" here. My grandfather was a penniless immigrant from Greece, and we've made our money by hard work and the sweat of our brows. I don't want you to think we have any airs and graces just because we live in a nice house and can afford the best. My children have been brought up democratically, and to realise that there are many others not as fortunate as ourselves.' Andreas paused. 'All of which I may have put very awkwardly, I am not an educated man like my son. What I mean is I don't want you to feel in any way uncomfortable . . .' His flow was interrupted by the opening of the door and Maria sidled in.

'Mr Harvey is in the hall, sir.'

'Mr Harvey?' Andreas jumped up. '*Edmund* Harvey?'

'It's the young man, sir.' The girl looked over at Nick. 'Mr Nick's friend.'

'Giles!' Nick rose and, going over to the door, flung it open. 'Giles, we're in here having dinner.'

'Oh, ask him to join us!' Lydia called, and gestured to Maria to lay another place.

Giles appeared in the doorway with Nick, the customary rueful expression on his face. As usual he was clad in tracksuit and trainers and he threw his arms helplessly in the air. 'Yet again you find me in a compromising position, Lydia. I didn't expect you to be eating. I just called round to see Nick.' Then suddenly he noticed Laura and his eyes immediately lit up.

'Oh, hi, Laura! I didn't know you were here.' He crossed the room and warmly shook her hand. Then he turned to Andreas and shook his more formally, finally stooping to kiss Lydia on the cheek and give a cheery wave to Emma. 'Hi!'

'Hi!' Emma said with a smile and a similar gesture. 'Have something to eat.'

'I've eaten,' Giles said and then, in reply to Lydia's look of disbelief, 'no really. I wondered if there was any chance of you coming out afterwards Nick, but I didn't know that Laura was with you.'

'Well, we're just getting to know Laura,' Andreas said firmly. 'I think they'll be staying in this evening, but why don't you stay too and have a drink with us?'

'No, really . . .'

'Look, we've almost finished,' Andreas indicated the pudding on his plate and then the empty chair next to him. 'Why don't you take a pew? Relax, Giles. We don't mind the tracksuit.' He smiled broadly. 'Really. You seem to have got this fixation that we always dress for dinner.'

Giles slid self-consciously into his chair. 'Well, you always look very smart to me and it makes me feel a bit of a bum . . .'

'Ever since the yacht . . .'

'No, it's nothing to do with the yacht. Honestly.'

'Well, to change the subject,' Andreas leaned back magisterially in his chair. 'How's Manchester? You didn't get the chance to tell us at Christmas as we were abroad.'

'Manchester is fine.' Giles glanced at Laura.

'Like the course?'

'Yes.' His tone seemed to indicate that he wasn't too sure.

'Psychology is it you're doing?'

'Yes.'

'Laura was telling us she is from Manchester. You've met Laura already, I gather?'

'I told you, Daddy,' Emma looked sharply at her father, 'when I went to see Nick at the beginning of term. I met Laura, and Giles turned up too. We had rather a good weekend, didn't we, Giles?'

'We did.' Giles smiled.

'Tell you what,' Nick said, glancing at his watch, 'would you mind very much, Mum and Dad, if we did just pop round to the pub after dinner – Emma, Giles, Laura and I? Promise not to be late.'

After coffee, when the young people had made their exit, Lydia and Andreas sat looking at each other. For a few moments they said nothing. Andreas had a large cigar between his fingers and he frequently and absent-mindedly kept tapping the ash into a cut-glass ashtray. He gave a deep sigh and crossed one leg over the other.

'What do you think of the girl?'

Lydia pursed her lips as though she were anxious not to say the wrong thing. 'Ordinary,' she said after a while. 'Very ordinary.'

'Oh, I wouldn't have said that.'

'Not the sort of person I'd expect Nick to have chosen.'

'She's very pretty.'

'Oh, do you think so?'

'Striking.'

'Yes, but that *accent*!'

'You mustn't be so prejudiced, darling.'

'I'm not in the least prejudiced.'

'Well, I think you are.'

'Well, I'm not, Andy, I assure you. She sounds like someone in Coronation Street.'

Andreas shrugged.

'She has a regional accent, so what?'

'I just hoped that Nick would choose someone with more class. Of all the young women in Oxford, why does it have to be her?'

'I think that's a very unfortunate remark, dear, if I may say so.' Andreas had let his cigar go out and attempted to relight it. 'She's intelligent, she's most attractive. I can see why she did appeal to him. Just because she doesn't appeal to you . . .'

'I don't think I have the slightest thing in common with her. As for that speech about being working class . . . frankly, I think it was untimely and in bad taste. You can be an inverted snob you know, Andy.'

'You mean she's actually proud of being working class?'

'Exactly! And wants to ram it down our throats.'

Andreas rose, walked over to the television set and switched it on.

'I think you're taking the whole thing too seriously, Lydia. It's not as though they're going to get married. Time for the news.'

Laura snuggled up to Nick in bed. She felt cold despite the heat of his body, the warmth of the house.

'I don't think your parents like me very much,' she said.

'Nonsense.'

'I think I was silly to talk about my father being unemployed.'

'Maybe you came on a bit strong.' He kissed her cheek.

'I just wasn't prepared for all this, Nick.'

'All what?'

'The house, the style, the maid. I mean your folks are posh. This is a posh place. I felt very uneasy in my chunky sweater and my only skirt.'

'You looked very nice.'

'Your mother's dress was so gorgeous. I bet it cost a

bomb, and that suit of Emma's . . .' Laura emitted a low whistle.

Nick sat up in bed and switched on the light. They were in Laura's bed in the guest room. He had come to her because his was a single bed while Laura's was for two. It was wonderful to have the luxury of a double bed. He'd slunk along the corridor when he'd guessed his parents had turned out the light. Emma was still out, having decided to go clubbing in Soho with Giles. Nick hadn't wanted to upset his parents by being late in on Laura's first night, as the situation was fraught enough already. He had found the atmosphere at dinner almost unbearably tense, the reason why he'd wanted to go out for a breather.

Maybe bringing one's girlfriend home for the first time would be tense anyway, daunting for anyone. Everyone wanted to impress, except perhaps Laura who was determined to be herself. Nick had been a little annoyed by the vigour of her working-class speech, almost as though she relished it. In his view that had been absolutely unnecessary.

Nick put his arms round his legs and looked at Laura, so tousled and adorable beside him.

'Laura, these are the nineteen nineties. We're not living in the age of Queen Victoria.'

'So?' She looked up at him.

'I find all this talk of class and so on obnoxious.'

'I didn't mention class.'

'You said my parents were "posh". It's the same thing.'

'It isn't.'

'Well, you introduced class by talking about your home being very ordinary.'

'Well . . .' her gaze became defiant. 'It is. I am.'

'Then you're the one to introduce class. We don't. I never have.'

'For God's sake,' she exploded, 'your dad has a Rolls Royce *and* a yacht.'

'Then you wish you'd never met me?' His voice had gone very quiet.

'I never said that.'

'You're creating a barrier. I am what I am. My parents are what they are. You're class-conscious, not me, not us.'

'I still don't think your parents like me, especially your mum.'

'I think that's unfair. You've only known them a few hours.'

'You can tell. I can.'

Laura also sat up, raised her knees and, leaning her head on them looked sideways at Nick.

'Maybe it was too soon to visit your house?'

'Don't be silly,' Nick said roughly, putting his arm round her, desiring her intensely, drawing her close. But inside, he wondered if perhaps she was right.

Laura lay listening to the distant rumble of traffic as it trundled up the arterial road to and from the great conurbation that was Manchester and its environs. There was always that steady swish of traffic, day and night, and she supposed that when she was young, sharing this bedroom with her sister, she had got used to it. Certainly it had never disturbed her as it did now.

In Oxford in the spring, she awoke to the sound of birdsong coming from the college park. In winter and at other times of the year there was a profound silence, broken occasionally by the sound of a car or lorry on the Woodstock Road. But never that heavy, continuous sound of the industrial north. Although Salford no longer had the same density of huge smoking chimneys depicted by Lowry, a pall seemed to hang over it, generated by mechanisation and the industrial ghosts of the past. In those days, workers tramped in the pre-dawn along cobbled pavements to the cotton mills to begin the early morning shift.

Salford no longer possessed that historical image. But it was still, to Laura, grim despite the fact that now it had its own university, its streets were cleaner than they ever had been, and it had high-rise apartment blocks of doubtful socio-economic benefit and little or no architectural merit. Salford belonged to childhood and adolescence, and both were full of bad memories.

Maybe it was because the Chase family still lived in one of those narrow passages depicted by Lowry, where kids still played, and loose dogs roamed and housewives hung their washing out on a Monday. 'Housewife' of course was a euphemism for the women who lived on the street; hard-working wives and mothers who ran the family home and held down a job as well. People like her mother who would soon be getting up to get the boys their breakfast before she left for her own job as a tea lady in a large office block where, three nights a week, she also cleaned.

Laura turned restlessly in bed and looked at the clock. Five-thirty. She had no idea what had woken her because her mother didn't get up until six, and usually she slept well. Five-thirty, and in the tree-lined road in St John's Wood Nick would be asleep in his bed, and when he woke it would be to silence or to the sound of birds on nearby Primrose Hill.

There was something working class and industrial about being so close to a main arterial road with lorries thundering past. Something calming and civilised about Oxford or St John's Wood. Here there were no birds except a few scrawny pigeons or dusty sparrows who scavenged hopefully among the bins and black refuse sacks left out in the back passages for scraps that might have escaped the attention of the dustmen.

Maybe she'd woken because she missed Nick, missed his morning embrace, the coming together of their bodies. The exultation of making love, of loving and being loved, of living

116

all day in its memory and being transformed by this unique experience that two people shared.

Laura had never been in love before; never messed about with the fellows or hung around in clubs or on street corners as her sister and brothers had. That was how Sharon, at the age of seventeen, had managed to get herself pregnant and already, at the age of twenty-three, and with two children, had the world-wearied air of an old married woman.

Laura had been different, never fitted in, a cuckoo in the nest. She was bookish and was always to be found in a corner reading, despite the fact that there was not a single volume in the family home.

Laura's mother had been a local beauty who had also fallen for a baby when she was in her teens, the father being the man she married, the then dashing and eminently pre-sentable, indeed handsome, Albert Chase. Their children had inherited their looks. It was very odd to think that a quarter of a century ago, her now sickly and bad tempered father and overworked, dispirited mother, had known the rapture of the flesh that she had shared with Nick.

Or had they? It was almost impossible to know and, cer-tainly, to ask.

Laura was different, always had been. Yet she was not awkward or difficult, but rather shy and sweet tempered, easily put upon. The family was amazed when she got a place at Oxford, yet they were terribly proud of her but, at the same time, resentful that she had left them behind.

'Our' Laura was no longer one of us.

Laura heard the sounds of gentle tapping on the door of the room next to hers, and the quiet voice of her mother urging her brothers to get up. They were temporarily sharing the same bedroom, as she and Sharon had. Now this was Gary's room which he gave up to her when she was at home.

The familiar tapping on the door: 'Get up boys, you'll be late for work.'

Sharon had always been the last one down. She, Laura, was the first, eager in a way to be off, preferring the environment of school to home, though she would never have admitted it. Now Oxford represented freedom, and every time she came home she realised how trapped she felt and had from very early days, as though she didn't belong.

With a feeling of guilt Laura leapt out of bed, dressed quickly – she would wash later when the bathroom was free – and went downstairs where her mother was making sandwiches for the boys, and probably herself. 'Hi, Mum!' she said, but without a kiss. They were not a demonstrative ˜amily, and her mother would have thought it odd if any of her children kissed her, either good morning or good night. Kissing, Laura thought, recalling all the kissing and touching and calling of endearments that had gone on in the Constantine home, was for the middle classes.

'Did you sleep well, love?' her mother asked without looking up.

'Very well. And you?'

Laura took the slices her mother was buttering and put on the cheese spread. In the Chase household, when there were women about the men were not expected to help with any of the domestic chores, including getting their own food. Hilda Chase did everything, unless either of the girls were around, when they helped out.

Her mother nodded but said nothing. Laura thought she looked tired and gazed at her with concern.

'Mum, you are looking peaky, you know. You sure you're sleeping well?'

'Take your dad up a cup of tea, would you, Laura,' her mother glanced at the clock on the wall, 'and give the boys another knock? Oh, by the way, someone called you last night.'

'Nick?' Laura, in the act of putting on the kettle, spun round.

118

'No, someone called Giles. Said he'd ring again.'

'Giles!' Laura murmured, mystified.

'Don't you know him?'

'He's a friend of Nick's. Why should he call me?' Her mother, uncurious, shrugged her shoulders, finished her task and began to put the sandwiches in plastic boxes. In each she also placed an apple. Then she put on the lids, secured them with elastic bands and laid them on the table.

'Do you want a cup of tea, Mum?'

Hilda nodded.

'Best get that up to your father first or he'll be angry.'

Angry! Laura felt indignation mount as she climbed the stairs and knocked on the door of her parents' room. Her mother was only forty-two yet she was going grey. She looked like a woman well into her fifties.

Her father didn't reply to her knock so she opened the door and went in. The large bed practically filled the room. There was very little space for any other furniture. Her father lay with his back to the door, seemingly asleep. She shook him roughly by the shoulder.

'Here's your tea, Dad.'

He shook himself as though to say he didn't want any, pulled the eiderdown more firmly round his shoulders.

One of Dad's off days.

Laura felt the anger surge up in her, as well as a kind of despair that she should consider this behaviour in any way unusual. After all, her father had been unemployed since she was a child and she had never really known anything else. Most days he wouldn't come downstairs until about noon, and anyone who was in the house had to get him something to eat. If there was no one around he would go to the pub, have bread and cheese and a pint with his mates. He would then come home and watch television all after-noon, usually sport if there was any on, before going to the

British Legion or the working man's club where he would spend the evening playing darts.

Her father was not a great drinker. Laura had seldom seen him drunk. His normal state was one of melancholy. He was a very silent man and yet apparently he enjoyed the company of his men friends. As far as she could see, her mother and father led pretty separate lives. Hilda was close to Sharon and enjoyed her grandchildren. She had two sisters who lived nearby, and she would often visit them after work, or go round to the pub with them for a natter over a port and lemon.

Laura wondered what the Constantines would make of all this as she banged on the door of her brothers' room shouting to them to get up. It was school holidays but Gordon Chase had a job in the local supermarket. Downstairs there was breakfast on the table – bread which the boys toasted if they wanted – and cereal. Hilda was putting on her coat saying she would be late for work.

'I'll see you tonight, love,' she said, pausing at the door. 'This Giles sounded ever so posh. You must have a whole new set of friends now, Laura, love. You'll soon not be wanting to come home at all.'

'Don't be silly, Mum, I do,' Laura said, conveying her mother to the front door and wishing that they were more tactile, that she could embrace her. But she couldn't. She couldn't embrace her and she couldn't really talk to her.

Too late to break the habit of a lifetime.

'Did Giles leave a telephone number?' Laura asked as her mother prepared to leave.

'He said he'd ring again.'

'Or what he wanted?'

'Haven't a clue. Tra'aa,' her mother said, closing the door.

After the boys had gone, Laura tidied up. She wasn't going to hang around and get her father lunch. She had plenty of work to do and intended to spend the remainder of the day in the library. The rest of the vac seemed to stretch interminably in front of her, and yet she knew it was a valuable opportunity to make up for time lost because of her involvement with Nick. Maggie had given her another grim warning just before the end of term.

'Time to get a hold on yourself, Laura, or it'll be too late.'

Most of her former schoolfriends worked; one had married, one had a baby without being married and another had gone to one of the new universities, formerly a polytechnic. They were the only two in the whole school who had shone academically. The pass rate at A level had been abysmally poor.

Laura had almost been ashamed of her success. Yet she was still close enough to one or two of them, but socialising would have to wait until evening. A night out with the girls would be the order of the day on Saturday just so that she could prove going to Oxford hadn't turned her into a snob.

Laura was about to leave the house when the telephone rang. She was going to let it ring and then she thought it was a funny time for anyone to telephone, unless it was for her. Nick maybe! She rushed to pick up the phone and a voice said, rather hesitantly: 'Is that you, Laura?'

'Giles! My mother said you'd rung. Where are you?'

'I'm here. In Manchester.'

'Whatever are you doing in Manchester?'

'I'm working.'

'What, you've got a job?' Laura sounded incredulous.

'No, I'm working for my exams.'

'Me, too.'

'I say, Laura, I wondered if we could meet up.'

'That would be nice. When?'

'Today?'

'*Today*?' The question was quite unexpected. 'You mean like now?'

'Why not?'

'I thought you said you were working?'

'Well, today's a nice day. Maybe it will rain tomorrow.'

Maybe it would.

'Laura?'

'Alright. I was actually going to work, but I'll meet you if you like. Where?'

'Well, I'll pick you up. We'll go somewhere.'

'No. I'll come into Manchester to meet you.'

'OK. If you prefer. Where?'

'Outside the library.'

'Right.' Giles sounded pleased. 'When?'

'Give me an hour.'

'Fine, Laura. I'll see you then outside the Central library at about eleven.'

Laura put the telephone down and remained where she was for a few moments, head hung in thought.

It wasn't that she was ashamed of her home or of where she lived. She just didn't want Giles to meet her father.

As if able to read her mind, at that moment her father appeared, putting his head round the door of the kitchen.

'Any chance of anything to eat, love?'

'I'm just going out, Dad,' Laura said.

Her father came slowly into the kitchen and sat down heavily in a chair at the table.

'I don't feel very well today, Laura. I think it's my heart you know.'

'I thought you had your heart tested, Dad. They said there was nothing wrong with it.'

Her father shook his head. 'You can't really trust the doctors, Laura. They don't know what they're talking about.'

This was an old, familiar refrain of her father's. He had on his dressing gown and a pair of very old, scuffed slippers. A few grey hairs stuck out from the top of his open pyjama jacket, his chin was unshaven and his eyes rheumy as though

122

from lack of sleep, or maybe too much of it. The effect produced was often the same.

He looked like a tired old man and yet he was only forty-five, about the same age as Nick's father who didn't look his age either, only much younger. Andreas Constantine looked about ten years younger than Bert Chase, almost his exact contemporary.

You would have to be hard not to be moved by the plight of a man who hadn't worked for years and who had little, if any, self-esteem except in his home where he was undisputed boss. Even if he wheedled and whined to ask favours it was because he expected them to be carried out. If they weren't, he turned nasty.

Even as she was thinking about him, resenting him, Laura was hastily buttering bread, getting cheese out of the fridge and putting on the kettle.

'Where are you going, Laura?' her father asked, noting approvingly that she was doing what he wanted without argument.

'I'm meeting a friend.'

'I thought you were working, Laura?' Her father drew the chair up to the table and tackled the bread and cheese she'd laid before him.

'I was. I mean I am . . .'

'Was that who the phone call was from?'

'Yes.'

'Someone from university, I expect.'

'Yes.'

'You don't have much time these days for your old friends, do you, Laura?'

'I do have time, Dad. But they work during the day.' She put a teacup and saucer next to her father's plate and poured his tea.

'Of course,' he nodded. 'Is it a man or a woman, Laura?'

'Oh, *Dad*!'

'Just wondered. Your life's your own, you know that, and we are very proud of you. But it's bound to be that one of these days you'll draw further and further away from your family until you forget us altogether.'

Now he was getting maudlin. It was only an attempt to keep her there. He was a lonely man who, she knew, felt neglected by his family. Maybe he was frightened too. His only solace seemed to be with his male friends. But she felt now that he had gone too far along the line to be helped. He was sad, but he was despicable too, and as she tore out of the house to keep her date, the old familiar feeling of guilt raged in her heart.

She seemed to have so much and he so little.

They sat on the dry-stone wall by the side of the road looking down into the valley. It was interspersed here and there with copses, a farm and farm buildings and bisected by a stream, a tributary of the River Dove. Nearby, to the right, in a corner of the field was a gypsy caravan which someone had converted, probably, as a weekend retreat. It was surrounded by a wooden fence with a gate, and there were colourful red check curtains at the windows. Laura sighed a little enviously. The Manifold Valley was a beautiful part of Derbyshire which she knew well from camping here when she was at school, coming first with the Brownies and then the Guides.

'I'm surprised to hear you were a Guide.' Giles turned to her with amusement, surreptitiously studying her face.

'Why?' She looked curiously at him.

'Because you seem so non-conformist.'

'Oh, no. I'm very conformist. I was always very good at school. I am not a rebel.'

'You wanted to succeed?'

'Yes. I wanted to get away from my working-class environment, and I knew that education was the only way to do it.'

Giles, surprised by her candour, didn't quite know how to

reply. He expected that if he waited more information would be forthcoming, but her next remark was unexpected.

'Tell me about Nick's yacht.'

'Nick's yacht?' he asked.

'You know what I mean. His father's yacht. Where you spent the summer holidays.'

Giles was nonplussed.

'About what exactly? The size?'

'No!' Laura sounded cross. 'What it's like. He wants me to go in the summer. Is it very posh?'

'Well,' Giles paused, 'you know his mother.'

'How do you mean?'

'Well, she likes everything to be just so.'

'Was it the first time you'd visited?'

'Yes. My parents weren't keen.'

'But they enjoyed it?'

Giles remained silent, looking across the valley.

'*Did* they enjoy it, Giles?' Laura persisted.

'Oh, yeah, we had a great time. I don't know that Lydia enjoyed it much. She had a tummy bug and remained in her cabin ... Oh, and at the end, my dad trod on a jellyfish ...'

Laura burst out laughing. He thought how attractive the laughter lines made her face. He longed to put his arm around her, but he knew he mustn't. This was Nick's girl and Nick was his friend. In all his life he had never encountered a situation like it.

But was it strange after all that two friends, who had so much in common, should fall in love with the same girl?

'No, seriously,' he said, lightly putting a hand on her arm, 'he was very ill. He had to go to hospital.'

Laura clapped a hand to her mouth. 'Oh, I'm sorry.'

'Then I got the news I wouldn't be going to Oxford. All in all, the memories left by the holiday aren't good. So you see, you can't really judge it by what happened to us. I'm sure you'll have a good time.'

'Well, nothing's decided . . .' Laura ran a finger thoughtfully along the wall. 'I don't really know what his parents thought about me.'

'I'm sure they liked you.'

'I'm not so sure.' She glanced up at him. 'I think they would have liked something better for Nick.'

'Oh, come . . .'

'Seriously. His mum especially. I quite liked his dad, but you see I had no idea Nick's family had all that money. It gave me quite a shock. My family is very ordinary, working class. I'm not ashamed of it but I'm aware of it, especially since I went to Oxford. Somehow Nick doesn't strike you like that . . .'

'Like what?'

'Rich.'

'No, he doesn't. And it doesn't matter to him. It's not important. It mustn't matter to you, Laura. These days accents and all that kind of thing don't matter. In fact, it's quite fashionable to have one.'

'I know that. I'm aware of it. If it wasn't Nick's family I wouldn't care. But I care what they think about me. And how I behave with them, on a yacht and all that kind of thing, is another matter.'

Giles lowered his head. 'It really is very serious then?'

'Oh, you think it's calf love too, do you?'

'No, I don't, not at all. But it's early days. Things change. I mean you could say you scarcely know each other. I'm not saying it's not important, believe me. Anyway I wouldn't let his parents upset you.'

'Have you been in love ever, Giles?'

He paused. Then: 'I've known a few girls, but I don't think I have. Not really.'

'I hadn't either. But I do love Nick so much.'

126

'I know you do. Hey!' he said as if wishing to change the subject. 'Why don't we walk a bit? Explore the valley? They say Dovedale is very beautiful.'

'I'll show it to you.' Laura jumped off the wall and dusted her bottom. Giles jumped off too, and as he landed on the soft earth he missed his footing and leaned heavily on Laura for support. As she helped him regain his balance he put an arm round her waist and left it there. She looked at him, thought his expression strange, very direct and quizzical as he looked unfalteringly into her eyes. 'Nick's such a lucky guy,' he murmured. Then abruptly he removed his arm, leaving Laura feeling confused, suddenly anxious.

'Maybe we best be getting back?' she said.

'But it's still early,' he pleaded, looking at the sky.

'I have to see my sister tonight.' Her tone grew stubborn.

'OK.'

He knew that he'd overstepped the mark, and that Laura knew it. He felt foolish and stupid, disloyal. They went back to the car park behind the pub where they'd left the car, and Giles didn't attempt to get her to change her mind, but drove swiftly away from the valley, through Buxton and on towards Manchester saying little.

Laura guided him through the streets of Salford to her house and, as they stopped outside, he pulled on the hand-brake, switched off the ignition and looked at her.

'Sorry,' he said.

'Nothing to be sorry about.'

'It's just that I wish I'd got there first.'

Laura shrugged and gazed at the house, almost as if she hadn't heard him, seeming preoccupied. 'Look,' she said, 'do you mind if I don't ask you in? I know it's rude but . . .' she smiled at him, 'I'll explain some day.'

'It's perfectly OK. Say, maybe we can go out again? It's just that I am quite lonely up here. Nothing will happen I promise you. You're Nick's girl and Nick is my friend.'

Laura got out of the car as Giles remained where he was.

'I don't think so,' she said, peering through the window. The stubborn tone had returned again. 'But thanks, I enjoyed it. I like you too, you know, but . . .' Then, as if embarrassed by her candour, she stepped back and gave him a little wave.

'See you,' she said.

'See you,' he said, waving back, suddenly, despite her refusal to see him again, aware of a feeling of hope.

CHAPTER 8

Laura folded the letter and tucked it hurriedly between the pages of her book as the door opened and Nick put his head round.

'Hi!'

'Hi!' she said, turning to him with a smile.

'Busy?' He bent his head to kiss her and, after their kiss, she let her hand linger on his cheek drawing him down beside her.

'Pretty busy.'

'No time for . . .' he looked suggestively at her crotch and his hand wandered to the fastener of her jeans.

'You're a sexy beast,' she said playfully, smacking his hand.

'Would Hardy have approved?' Nick looked at the title of her book which had fallen to the floor. *The Life and Work of Thomas Hardy* by Michael Millgate. By now her jeans were almost off and, fully aroused, Laura lifted her T-shirt over her head.

'Hardy was quite sexy.' Laura stretched full length on the bed, jeans, T-shirt and knickers in a heap on the floor by the side. 'He liked pretty ladies, but we don't quite know whether he had affairs. Probably not.'

Nick was staring at Millgate's celebrated biography and at the letter which had fallen out of it and which now lay beside it on the floor. Laura saw his expression and, with a sudden guilty start, sat up. Too late.

'Uh, uh,' she muttered and fell back on the bed, covering her face with her hands.

'A letter from Giles?' Nick didn't seem to understand and looked at her. 'Is it for you?'

She nodded. 'I wouldn't be reading a letter meant for you.'

'No, of course not.' Still bemused, he picked it up and shook it open.

'May I read it?' His voice had gone very polite and formal, and he still had all his clothes on. Laura felt rather idiotic and she drew over herself the Indian throw she draped on the bed during the day to turn it into a sofa. Desire had swiftly ebbed at the possibility of a dramatic and damaging revelation.

She reached out and snatched the letter from him.

'I'd rather you didn't, Nick.'

'Why?' His face had a chalky whiteness, and he clenched his fists, as if digging his nails into the palms of his hands.

'It's a personal letter. I don't think you'd understand.'

She hauled herself off the bed and began to dress hurriedly. 'God, what a *stupid thing to happen*,' she added, stamping a foot on the floor in anger.

Nick stood up and, going over to the window, stood with his hands in his pockets looking out across the quad of the girls' college, a much more modern affair than his, yet built in the nineteenth century on architectural principles which emulated an earlier age and style.

'I simply don't understand what's going on, Laura.' He turned and looked at her, his face drawn with pain. 'Are you having an affair with Giles?'

'Of course I'm not!'

'Then why the letter? I mean, I think I'm entitled to an answer. He is my friend and you've only met him with me, as far as I know. Or isn't that so?'

'He looked me up in Manchester during the break.'

'I see.' Nick's tone was very quiet.

'It was completely innocent.'

'Then why didn't you tell me?'

'I should have.'

'If it was completely innocent I can't think why you didn't.'

He slumped down on the bed, head between his hands.

'Neither can I.' She sat down beside him and attempted to take his hand. He remained cold and unresponsive to her pressure.

'If he writes you a letter you don't want me to see, something is going on. Must be.'

Laura handed him the letter. 'Read it out,' she said. Nick took it from her – it was a single page – shook it open and with a deep frown of concentration on his face studied it.

'Go on. Aloud,' Laura urged.

Nick cleared his throat.

'Dear Laura,' he read.

'A word of apology for what happened that day in Longnor. I know it upset you, and in retrospect, it upset me. I wouldn't like you to think the worse of me, or for it to affect my relationship with Nick whom I love like a brother.

'The fact is that I have been very lonely and unhappy all the time I've been in Manchester. I'm usually a pretty sociable guy, yet I've been unable to make friends or to establish a relationship with someone of the opposite sex.

'I like you very much, and I guess that day I was drawn to you and went further than I should.

'I am sorry, and please don't let it affect our friendship. I know it won't affect your love for Nick.

'Incidentally, I've decided to leave the university and probably travel abroad. I'm trying to get up the courage to go and tell my parents. After that, maybe

131

I'll come to Oxford to see Nick, so please don't tell him yet.

 'I think you're a great girl,'

Here Nick paused, swallowed and glanced at Laura who was staring at the bed, listening.

 'and that Nick's a lucky lucky guy.

 'Yours ever . . .'

Nick stopped without saying Giles's name. Then he folded the letter and handed it back to Laura. 'I guess he's in love with you,' he said in an unemotional tone.

 'Don't be stupid.'

 'Seriously, that's what it looks like to me.'

 'Nick, don't be so dramatic.'

 'As a matter of fact I guessed that he fancied you. I could tell when he looked at you, especially when he arrived that night we were having dinner in London with Emma and my parents. His eyes lit up when he saw you.'

It was true. Laura had noticed it too.

 'I think it was rather despicable of him to try and chat you up in Manchester.' He paused again, as if debating whether or not to say what was on his mind. 'What happened then, Laura?'

 'Nothing happened.' Her tone was emphatic. 'He called me and asked if we could go out for the day. I was bored, fed up at home, so I agreed. I suggested that we go to a place called Longnor which is a pretty village in Derbyshire where I used to go to Brownie and Guide camp, so it had a nostalgic association for me. It's about an hour's run from Manchester. There's a nice pub there where we had a ploughman's and a pint. Then we sat on a wall looking at the valley and talked.'

 'What about?'

132

'Just this and that. Then Giles suggested we take a walk and as we got down from the wall he stumbled and put an arm round my waist and told me he thought you were lucky. I realised there was some tension there and suggested we should go back. I had to see my sister anyway, and it was getting late as we'd taken our time over lunch. He drove me home. I didn't ask him in. He didn't touch me again. He didn't try to kiss me. We said goodbye and that was that. I forgot about it and spent the next ten days in the local library. I didn't see Giles again and thought nothing more until this' – she held out the letter – 'arrived this morning. I promise. Now, it's no big deal, is it?'

'I would never have known anything about this if I hadn't come in at this moment and found this letter.'

'Probably not, and just as well too. It would be dreadful if it upset your relationship with Giles. I honestly think he's lonely and unhappy and he just wanted a friend, someone who was close to his best friend.'

'How did he get your telephone number?'

'I have no idea. Maybe in the telephone book. We're listed, Nick.' She held out a hand. 'Let's go back to when you came in.'

'You feel like it?'

'I do, and forgetting all about this.'

She tore the letter into tiny pieces and threw them into the bin.

It was not easy for Nick to forget the letter, or the fact that his best friend was attracted to his girl, because that is what it amounted to. He felt in a sense rather betrayed by Giles, and yet he knew that their friendship was too important to be broken in this manner. A certain amount of magnanimity was called for. He knew that Giles had been hurt by his failure to get into Oxford, yet he didn't think he'd retaliate by trying to take his girl away from him.

Nick believed Laura when she said that nothing had happened from her point of view. But he didn't find it hard to believe that Giles, with whom he had so much in common, was attracted to the same sort of girl as he was.

Later in the day Nick left Laura working, but he felt restless and unable to work himself. He went for a walk in the Meadows and stood for a while watching the college crews practise on the Cherwell for the Head of the River races. He had never been attracted to rowing but he knew that if Giles had gone to Oxford he may well have been selected to row for his college. He'd rowed for the school in the same way that he'd played cricket and rugby for it.

Giles, the complete all-rounder, would have revelled in life at Oxford as Nick never had. Laura, too, had enjoyed Oxford life to the full until she met him. Now she'd dropped out of everything and even her work was suffering. Her tutor kept on lecturing her about it. In many ways Laura and Giles were alike; they enjoyed the same things. They were slightly larger than life, flamboyant characters. And he, Nick, seemed to be the catalyst for change. Only he had not changed Giles and prevented him from getting into Oxford. It was Giles, the all-rounder, who had seen to that, who in his A level years had fitted in too many other activities. Meanwhile Nick had applied himself relentlessly to his work, ambitious to succeed but in a different way from Giles: to prove himself to his family, whereas Giles had no need of that, and thought he had no need until he failed to follow the distinguished line of Harvey forebears to Oxbridge.

Nick watched the sleek boats propelled by the earnest oarsmen glide swiftly through the water. He felt curiously depressed as though he had under-achieved himself. Yet why? His work he knew was good. A first in PPE would provide him with any number of promising careers: the Civil Service, the Diplomatic, maybe a Fellowship at All Souls and the chance to shine in academia. He had Laura, a wonderful girl, who loved him. He'd never had money worries, like so many fellow students, didn't know what they were. He had a close, loving family, understanding parents. What, then, made him depressed?

He went back to his room and, sitting down, wrote a letter to Giles. It took him about an hour, after which he read it through carefully several times and then tore it up, fragmenting the pieces very carefully so that they could never be reassembled, and threw them into the wastepaper basket.

He then left his room and, ignoring the telephones in the downstairs lobby in case anyone overheard him, went into the town and, slipping into a public call box, punched in Giles's telephone number.

Giles answered the phone.

'Hi!' Nick said. 'I wasn't sure you'd be in.' Giles shared a house in Didsbury, near Manchester, with some fellow students.

'Nick!' Giles's tone was equivocal, as though he wasn't sure whether or not to be glad to hear Nick's voice.

'Thought I'd call you.'

'That's great. Anything up?'

'Well,' Nick paused, 'there's a big inter-collegiate cricket match next Saturday and I wondered if you'd like to come. It would be great to see you.'

There was silence at the other end of the line. Then: 'Are you playing?'

'Yes. I think my parents and Emma will be here too. I thought we could have a kind of reunion.'

'That sounds great. Nick . . .'

'Yes?'

'I'm going to leave the university.'

Taken unawares, Nick didn't know how to respond.

'Did you hear what I said, Nick?'

'Yes, I heard you. It's a bit of a shock, isn't it?'

'Well, I don't think so. I never settled here and I think I

135

chose the wrong subject. I'm really not a psychologist.'

Giles had chosen psychology, because when he had applied, the law faculty was full.

'What are you going to do?'

'I think I'll go abroad for a year. Travel. I don't know what I want out of life. It all seems to have gone wrong. I never seemed able to settle, make friends or take an interest in my work.'

'I'm sorry. Did you tell your parents?'

'Not yet. I don't think they'll mind. I may actually decide to do law at a school and go in with my dad. I think he'd like that. You know they were never very keen on Manchester.'

Nick managed a laugh. 'Well, if you can come next week we'll talk about it.'

'Good idea. I really will try and come.' Pause. 'How's Laura?'

'Laura's fine.'

'Working hard?'

'I think so.'

'Give her my . . .' Giles seemed about to say 'love' and then changed it to 'regards.'

'I will.'

Nick thought that it was the only false note in the conversation. When he got back to his room he still felt depressed, and began to wonder why he did what he'd just done.

Was he tempting fate?

It was the kind of classic English occasion, enjoyed in perfect weather, that is the stuff of legend, of story books and nostalgia. A patch of beautifully kept sward, emerald green, elegant young men in traditional whites going about their tasks in that leisurely, unhurried way that seems to be the hallmark of cricket. The fielders lolled about, arms folded, while they waited for the batsmen to inspect the crease, consult each other with mysterious signals and then position themselves

136

before the wicket ready to receive the ball from the bowler who, bent on intimidation, endeavoured to mould his features into the resemblance of a ferocious panther preparing for the kill as he began to make his run.

For Laura, seated between Nick's parents, it was a strange ritual, one that had never attracted either of her brothers. Gary played football, even in the summer, and Gordon was bookish, myopic and not keen on sport. Laura hoped that he would be the second member of the family to follow her to university. What happened in the Test Matches was a matter of supreme indifference to the entire Chase household, none of whom could have named a single English player.

And there was Nick standing in the field, not far away from her, looking splendid in his whites, arms folded, chatting to a fellow fielder as they waited for the batsman who was just coming in to try and improve the score for his side.

Next to Lydia Constantine sat Giles, who had arrived the night before and was staying in the room of a neighbour on Nick's corridor who was away for the weekend. The Constantines, with Emma, had also arrived the night before and were staying at the Randolph. There had been a family dinner party which Laura had declined to attend, using the pretext that she was working, and also she said she felt Nick should be with his family. There would be another one tonight which she would attend.

Giles had greeted her, at first politely rather than with warmth. He paid a lot of attention to Emma whom he kissed on the cheek. He didn't attempt to kiss Laura, who hadn't replied to his letter. She hadn't been looking forward to the weekend and she wondered why Nick had invited Giles. It seemed perverse.

However, just before they wandered onto the field Giles had caught her by the arm and, unseen by the others, drew her to one side. His manner was completely different from the almost casual way he'd first greeted her. He seemed excited, conspiratorial.

'Hey,' he said, 'how are you?'

'I'm fine.' She looked at him without smiling.

'Did you get my letter?'

'Yes, thanks.'

'I thought you might have answered it.'

'I didn't know what to say. By the way, Nick saw it.'

'You showed it to *Nick*?' Giles looked aghast.

'No, he found it. I'd put it in a book and it dropped out.'

'Oh, Christ!' Giles put his hand to his mouth. 'Couldn't you have been more careful?'

'Look!' Laura felt a sense of indignation. '*I* didn't do anything.'

'Nobody did anything wrong. Two friends had a day out, that's all.'

But they both knew that it wasn't quite like that.

'Nick didn't say anything to me on the phone. I wonder why?'

'Nick doesn't like confrontation. Besides he's very fond of you.'

'Maybe he wants to talk about it this weekend?'

'I don't think so. Anyway there's nothing to talk about, is there? I explained to him that there was nothing between us. Nothing happened, but I think it's naughty of you, Giles, to complicate the situation in this way.'

'In what way?'

'You should never have telephoned me.'

'And you should never have accepted.'

He smiled at her as if to say 'touché'. Then he relented.

'OK, Laura. I'm awfully sorry. I rang you on impulse, I tried to explain about being lonely and it was true. But I am attracted to you and what I did was wrong. Nick is the best friend in the world. I never meant to hurt either of you. I tried to explain in the letter which I never knew he'd see. Somehow I thought you'd take more care of it, hide it.'

'I'd only just received it!' she said indignantly. 'Nick came in and I shoved it inside the book I was studying. Look, Giles, our relationship is difficult enough. Nick is a lovely person, couldn't be lovelier. He's also kind and good, but I've got this thing about money, about his family being so *rich*. It's a barrier. I know that.'

'You shouldn't have.'

'I know, but I have. I find his parents terribly false and I know they don't like me. I'm dreading the weekend.'

'Bear up,' Giles said, noticing Andreas and Lydia coming towards them. 'Look, if I don't have the chance to talk to you this weekend I'll call when I get back.'

'I wish you wouldn't,' Laura had replied, but she didn't think he'd heard her.

She also didn't know if she really meant it. Suddenly, Giles with his warmth, friendliness and understanding seemed a bulwark against the Constantine family.

And now here they were all together on this perfect summer's day with the sound of leather on willow, a satisfying 'plop' that seemed to happen every few seconds, punctuated or accompanied by calls of 'Well done' in gently modulated tones or a sprinkling of polite hand-clapping that echoed faintly round the ground.

Lydia Constantine smiled at Laura.

'Do you enjoy cricket?'

'I know very little about it.'

'Oh! Your father and brothers don't play?'

Laura shook her head.

'Neither does my husband, but Nick's very keen. Giles is *very good*. It's such a pity Giles didn't get to Oxford.' She shook her head sadly. 'You can't help feeling it would have done more for him than Manchester.' She glanced at Laura, murmuring sotto voce, 'You've heard he's leaving?'

Laura nodded.

'I can't think what his parents will say.' Lydia sighed and, as if disappointed at the lack of gossipy response on the part of her son's girlfriend, laid her head against the back of the chair and closed her eyes.

Lydia did not like cricket. She thought it the most boring game imaginable, but she liked the ceremony surrounding it: the whites worn by the players, the ritual of going in to bat, the breaks for lunch and tea, the possible excitement at the end if a match was close. She especially liked Lords, its aura of upper-class decadence, the distinguished elderly members with bald heads and moustaches, the elegance of the ladies who came to support the players, but who, of course, were not allowed in the Long Room, the pink and yellow ties of the members, some of whom had been on the waiting list for over half their lives, many since birth. Lydia liked the snobbery of cricket while reluctantly acknowledging the fact that it was a universal game, and that some of the best players were working-class men from disadvantaged backgrounds.

Cricket meant to Lydia what sending Nick to public school meant, what Oxford, having money and a house in St John's Wood, a Rolls in the garage and a yacht in Monte, meant: status, privilege, the chance to be above some and equal with others. Just as good as the Harveys, if not better.

And now Nick had got himself tied up with a working-class girl from a northern industrial town with an accent you could cut with a knife and whose family didn't play cricket.

The day was a success. Although Nick's college lost the match, he acquitted himself without disgrace. Lunch in the marquee for players and their families and friends was excellent: asparagus, cold beef and ham, a variety of exciting salads, excellent strawberries and cream and plenty of sparkling wines but no champagne. Andreas offered to get some but Nick, in a whisper in his ear, begged his father not to show off and was obeyed.

Tea, too, was good: more strawberries, a variety of delicious cakes, and the chance to talk with some of the parents of Nick's fellow students; most of the fathers had attended Oxford too. Lydia found it all highly satisfying, not unlike similar occasions at Nick's school, an added bonus on this occasion being that Giles's parents weren't there, even if Giles was.

More food followed later at dinner in an expensive French restaurant where, the social niceties with well-bred strangers out of the way, the talk was mainly about Giles and his decision to leave university. Lydia felt strangely excited about it, almost pleased, as if this could set Giles on the slippery slope to failure and disgrace. She realised then that she didn't really like Giles any more than she liked his family. The habit he had of always arriving half-dressed, as though appearances didn't matter, almost as if deliberately to annoy her, and the sort of casual, well-bred arrogance of his manner. There was always that air about him of 'them' and 'us', imperceptible maybe, but inevitably reminding her of his mother.

All her niceness to him over the years had really been pretence for Nick's sake. With any luck, once he went abroad, they would never see him or his family again, or at least not for a very long time.

And then to her horror she heard the word 'yacht' mentioned and there was Andy inviting Giles to join them once again *with* his family and, he hoped, looking in her direction, Laura.

'I hope your father has forgiven me for last year, Giles,' Andreas was saying when Lydia tuned in.

'Of course he has,' Giles exclaimed. 'Nothing to forgive. We had a wonderful time.'

'Giles's father trod on a jellyfish and his foot became infected,' Andreas explained to Laura.

'Yes, I heard.'

'Oh, you heard. I expect Nick told you.'

'I expect he did.'

Nick looked hard at Giles, but Giles merely smiled.

'We do hope you'll be able to come, Laura,' Lydia said graciously, 'and, of *course*, your parents are very welcome if they care to join in.'

The idea of her father on board a luxury yacht in Monte Carlo was a notion so bizarre to Laura that she burst out laughing.

'Oh, do forgive me,' she exclaimed apologetically to Lydia, seeing her expression, 'but my father has never been further south than Manchester.'

'Well, now is the time to start,' Andreas said. 'I'll write to him myself if you like.'

'What about your mother?' Emma chipped in. 'Maybe she'd enjoy it?'

'Oh, I think my mother would, but she's terribly shy.'

'*Do* try and persuade your parents,' Lydia murmured, signalling to the waiter to serve coffee. 'We'd *love* to have them.'

'I do find your parents rather insincere,' Laura said. 'They can't *possibly* want my mother and father on the boat.'

Nick stood by the college gate looking at Laura in the dim light from the lamp over the porch. He felt that the day had been farcical, full of tension, and bitterly regretted his impulse to make it a kind of family reunion, a means of reconciliation with Giles and a way for his mother, father and sister to get to know Laura better.

In fact, they knew Laura no better, or maybe they did. Maybe they now saw her in a light not as favourable as the one he would have wished. He felt she hadn't acquitted herself well. She was not the Laura he knew; clearly ill at ease, silent for the most part, yet almost aggressively defensive. But then there was also at the same time a faintly mocking air about her, as though she was observing the *dramatis personae* and finding them wanting, didn't care if they knew it. At times Laura made him angry that she made so little effort to endear herself to the people he loved.

'Say something,' Laura said, worried by his silence, aware that she'd offended him.

'I really don't know what to say. I'm quite confused. You keep on saying they don't like you, now you say because they make an effort to be nice and friendly not only to you but to your parents you find them insincere. *I* find that hurtful.'

Yes it was very hurtful, but she hadn't meant it like that. She tried to explain.

'I'm sorry. It sounded rude and I didn't mean it like that.' She stretched out a hand and touched his chest. 'I suppose I found *myself* terribly false. I mean, I feel I'm acting a part with them, was in London, too. Look, your folks are rather grand and terribly rich. I'm not used to that scene at all.'

'You're being snobbish in your own way,' Nick replied. 'My parents are being nice and you're unpleasant.' As she withdrew her hand sharply he clutched it and said, 'Sorry, I didn't mean that. I guess it was a mistake to arrange this weekend. I wanted it to be successful and it's been a disaster. We all tried too hard. I think they genuinely do want your parents on the boat. They were very keen to invite Giles's. They don't just want to show off. My father in particular likes people to be happy. He wants to give them a good time, and then he's unhappy if they don't have one. My mother is a bit of a social climber I'll admit. But basically she is a good woman full of doubts and insecurities and I love her.'

'I'm sorry.' Laura bowed her head and planted a kiss on the back of the hand which still held hers. 'We've got all mixed up this evening. Tomorrow will be better.'

Tomorrow after all, the parents were leaving in the afternoon. And so was Giles.

When Nick got back to college he found Giles lying on his bed reading. Giles put his book, page down, on his chest and looked at him.

'Nice day,' he said.

'I'm glad you think so.' Nick slumped dejectedly into a chair.

'Something wrong?'

'I think I'm trying too hard.'

'Come again?' Giles sat up, put the book on the table next to the bed and lit a cigarette.

'I want everyone to get on, love one another.'

'Don't we all?' Giles lay back again, and exhaled smoke. It rose in a cloud above his head and he tried to blow holes in it but it drifted away towards the half-open window. 'I gather you know about the letter?'

'Letter?'

'My letter to Laura.'

'Oh, that letter. Do you really think now is the time to talk about it?'

'I wondered why you asked me this weekend? In the circumstances I find it rather strange.' Giles idly examined the tip of his cigarette. He seemed perfectly relaxed and at ease with himself, whereas Nick felt in the grip of inner turmoil.

'I mean,' Giles went on, 'I found it particularly strange when Laura told me you had seen the letter.'

'I wasn't meant to.'

'So she told me. But you did.'

It seemed to Nick that somehow Giles had seized the initiative, was on top and it was all wrong. He was the guilty one and here he was acting like prosecuting counsel.

'I guess you're in love with Laura yourself,' Nick said. 'If you weren't you wouldn't have come. You wanted to see

144

her and I know how you felt because that's what I feel. I want to see her all the time. I wanted to see you because we are such old mates. We have to work it out.'

'Nothing to work out,' Giles said offhandedly. 'I'd never pinch your girl.' He looked over at Nick. 'You've got it wrong. I like and admire her but I don't think I'm in love with her. I find her very attractive, very sexy – why deny it? – but that's not love, is it? I'd be a very cynical chap if I made a play for Laura knowing how much it would hurt you.'

'I think she likes you too.'

'But that's not "love" is it? I mean one can on an impulse want to touch a girl or kiss her, and I'll admit that's what happened, which is why I wrote the letter to apologise. I didn't want her to misunderstand.'

'It certainly changed Laura.'

'In what way?'

'She's different. Our relationship is different. Something's not the same since you saw her in Manchester. I feel I'm trying to cling onto something that simply isn't there any more. It's like staring into an empty space.'

Giles was silent. The revelation that Laura apparently felt something for him was not a surprise; but he was sure it wasn't recent or connected with the episode in Derbyshire. It had been there from the time they first met. A *coup de foudre*, an attraction, and what was an attraction if it wasn't sexual? That's why he'd gone back to Manchester early in the holiday, why he'd called her and why she'd agreed to come.

More importantly, it was why he'd come down this weekend, just to be sure.

Giles sighed. There seemed little more to say on the subject that wasn't insincere.

He was conscious of violent and warring emotions, feelings he was sure he had never in his life experienced before. He had always believed himself to be a nice bloke who played

145

by the rules, a loyal, good friend who would never do anything mean or underhand: a man like his father, straightforward and honest.

Was he being honest now with his best friend, Nick? And how much did Nick believe his denials and, for that matter, how much did he?

For his sense of elation, the smell of victory overcame his scruples, and after some more casual conversation in which Laura was not referred to again, the two young men retired to their respective beds.

PART III

The Old School Tie: Giles

CHAPTER 9

Giles stood looking round the large room he had inhabited for just over eight months, the span of his short university career. It was at the back of the house overlooking the large garden of what had at one time been a prosperous Victorian mansion occupied, doubtless, by the large family of a woollen or cotton merchant, or one of the barons of the emerging industrial enterprises, which helped in that age of expansion to make Manchester great. Now it belonged to the university and had been converted into bedsits for the use of its students. In addition to the individual study bedrooms there was a common room and a large kitchen. In the summer it would be possible to sit out and work in the garden, away from the noise and bustle surrounding the university in its central location.

It was a nice room and Giles had found his fellow inmates pleasant. But he had not been happy here, because he had not been happy at the university. The reason for this was not the fault of the institution, or the course of study he was pursuing, or the city of Manchester, or the people he met, or the comfortable digs in suburban Didsbury.

Giles Harvey had simply failed to find his niche.

Until the A level results, life had been kind to Giles. He had been a good all-rounder: clever, popular, good at games, reasonably ambitious. He had a solid base in his home, and although he knew they were not wealthy in the way that the Constantines were – 'filthy rich' as his father contemptuously called them – he knew they were alright. He came from a line of solid, achieving, public-service minded, successful, landowning members of the upper-middle class. The Harvey family, past and present, had its place in the sun. No question about it. It had been presumed that Giles would ultimately follow his father into the legal profession, perhaps as a barrister rather than a solicitor. But with his late application he had found all the law faculties full, and opted instead for psychology, a subject he had never studied, knew little about and, he decided, did not really interest him.

Giles's interest in Laura had coincided with his disenchantment with university life, with the company of his fellow students and his general lack of an objective. Like his best friend, Nick, he had found her immediately attractive, compelling, interesting, different from any girl he had met before. Not to beat about the bush too much, she was certainly sexy too.

He had tried to analyse why Laura affected him like she did; to rationalise whether it was jealousy of his friend or plain concupiscence on his part, whether it was love or lust, but so far he had been unable to come up with any solution to the numerous questions he posed himself. However, on his way north from the weekend in Oxford he had realised that the situation was impossible. He would have to distance himself from Laura and Nick for some time. He would have to go abroad. Sort himself out.

Thus his dilemma made him decide to do what he had wanted to do anyway: give up psychology, say farewell to Manchester and its university, the pleasant house in Didsbury and the people he had met there.

Giles picked up his suitcase and a holdall and stole downstairs, feeling rather like a thief in the night, though it was broad daylight. Most, if not all, of the inhabitants of the house were attending lectures or classes and the place was deserted. He had not said goodbye to them, but he knew he would not be returning. He felt his parents had to be told first, and then letters would follow: to the university, to his tutor and to a guy called Henry who was on his course and lived in the same house. He knew Henry Harris better than most. He was a bit of a fish out of water too, which was maybe why they got on.

He would send Henry Harris his room and house keys, and that would be that.

No regrets? None at all. Giles closed the front door, went down the path to where his car was parked and drove off.

Edmund felt trapped by this room. It seemed in a way to typify his relationship with Mary. He felt trapped by her too, bowed down by an overwhelming sense of obligation, of guilt. What really would have suited him would have been a pretty, undemanding, not too well educated, sexy little number of about twenty-five. But he didn't think they existed nowadays. They were too conscious of their rights, about equality between the sexes, about their careers, mobile phones and getting ahead.

He was sure that when the affair had begun, Mary had marriage in mind. They had been very sexually attracted, they got on well, laughed a lot (that seemed hard to believe now), had a good time when they were together, most of it spent in bed. He thought Mary had Adam deliberately to hurry this process along, but after that she gradually changed into the rather sad, dejected, constantly whining person she was now.

Understandable really. She didn't have much fun, and he felt guilty about her.

Edmund shifted in the bed, glanced at the woman at his side and saw that she was still asleep. They had both fallen asleep after lovemaking which, for once, had occurred during the day while Adam was at school. Edmund had business in the area, and after lunch with his client had dropped in to see Mary who was working from home.

Edmund lay on his back, head propped in his hands, and looked around. Mary had taken an awful lot of trouble to try and make the bedroom into a pretty little feminine boudoir with white furniture, Laura Ashley wallpaper and matching curtains. It didn't come off. It was completely out of character with the overall gloom of the building: the dark corridors, the hideous cream and brown walls and orange carpet.

Edmund felt depressed whenever he entered it, and didn't know how Mary could continue to live there. Sometimes she talked about moving out of London and he wished she would, but they both knew she wouldn't.

'Ed,' Mary said, suddenly wide awake, as though she could read his thoughts, 'Adam's Head says he needs a lot of extra coaching.'

Edmund groaned audibly.

'I was wondering when that would come. I knew it.'

'Well, you can understand it,' she said peevishly. 'They don't get much of an education from the State. It's quite different. He's behind in Maths, English and he doesn't know any French. The Maths they do in the State schools is quite different.'

'I thought Maths was Maths anywhere,' Edmund grumbled.

'They have a different system. The Head said the State teachers made it up themselves. The system, that is. The Head has offered to coach Adam himself. He says he has a lot of innate intelligence.'

'I suppose *he* doesn't come cheap.' Edmund looked once more at the clock and swung his legs over the bed. 'How much?'

'He says he'll do it for ten pounds a lesson. Very reasonable really.'

'And how many lessons does he have to have?'

'Oh, Ed, don't be so petty.' Mary turned on her stomach and thumped the pillows. 'I find you *very* petty these days. I don't know what has got into you.'

'Worry is what has got into me, Mary. I have a lot of worries. Especially financial worries. Business is not good. People are taking to the cheap conveyancing and we're losing a lot of work. More than half my business was conveyancing and now people can do it themselves, on the cheap.'

'You should never have left Burrows,' Mary said sniffily. Burrows, Walters and Carter was the firm they had worked for when they both met.

'I have never regretted leaving Burrows.'

'That's because you're stubborn and won't admit you're wrong.'

Edmund began to dress, looking angrily at himself in the mirror while he knotted his tie. His hair was getting thinner and his wrinkles seemed to be multiplying. This was what stress did to a person. Made them old before their time. He turned to the bed and looked down at her.

'I have to go now, Mary. I've got an appointment.'

'What about the money, Ed, for the coaching? What shall I say?'

'To whom?'

'To the Head.'

Edmund flopped on the bed beside her, stretched out his hand to touch her, but she moved away.

'Can it wait a bit, Mary, until I've got some things sorted out?'

'What things?' She looked at him suspiciously.

'Some business matters. I can't be specific.'

'I would have thought your son's schooling was a matter of prime importance. Or is it because he's not like the other sons . . .'

'Don't be silly.' Edmund got up and went to the door

153

where he stopped, turning to look at her again.

'I do wish you'd try and understand,' he said.

'Ed, you make me sick, you really do.' Mary thumped the pillows hard, and when she heard the front door close she thumped them even harder, as if she was beating the life out of Ed.

Outside, Edmund stood looking up and down the road, just in case he saw anyone he knew. It was kind of instinctive and also, he realised, rather pathetic and unnecessary. After all, he could have been seeing a client. Edmund was a man whose worry and nervousness seemed to increase with the years.

Sometimes he wished he had someone to whom he could turn, but he hadn't. Neither his wife nor his mistress understood him, and his children were too young, too inexperienced, to confide in.

He got into his car, adjusted his driving mirror, scanning the tree-lined road again, and drove away. As he did, his feeling of oppression seemed to lighten, and he realised that a lot of it was due to Mary. The further he got away from her the better he felt, such was the burden of guilt he carried about her and Adam.

He wished they could cease their lovemaking and become platonic friends, but Mary would feel rejected, and he felt that some sex was, after all, better than none. It was better than doing without, looking round for another woman with more complications in an already complex life, or going to prostitutes, even decorous houses which he knew existed. The curious thing was that he and Mary still satisfied each other sexually, which gave a base to an otherwise stultifying and unsatisfactory relationship.

But what to do about increasing school fees he didn't know. And as for all his other problems ... He started to sweat. God only knew how he was going to resolve those.

Edmund didn't have another appointment. It was now five

and he thought he'd go home early and maybe take Alice to the Heath for a walk. His daughter was the one person he truly cherished and whose company he craved. She was his consolation for an altogether unhappy and troublesome life.

With Alice skipping along by his side it was possible to believe that life was simple, uncomplicated and peaceful, like her.

In a better frame of mind Edmund cast aside thoughts of his troublesome mistress, his disadvantaged natural son and his money worries, and turned off the Finchley Road and drove up the hill that wound towards his home.

Outside the house was Valerie's car and in front of it was Giles's familiar MG. It took him a second or two to wonder what Giles's car was doing there and he also felt a momentary annoyance because it occupied the place where he usually parked his car, the neighbours tacitly agreeing to leave it free out of deference to him. In expensive, high density Hampstead, few houses had garages and most of its residents had to park in the street.

Edmund parked his car further up the road, removed his briefcase and walked towards the house. If Giles had come home it would be very difficult to suggest a walk to Alice; but why should the three of them not go while Valerie got the dinner? A family outing, a rare event. He was not a very imaginative man, and he couldn't think of any reason why Giles should come home in the middle of term, but it didn't worry him.

Edmund ran up the steps of the house, put his key in the door and let himself in. It all seemed very silent. He put his briefcase down in the hall and went into the living room which was also empty. The living room led into a conservatory, and Edmund noticed that the conservatory doors were open and beyond them he could see Valerie and Giles standing under one of the poplar trees in the garden. They had their backs to the house, heads bent, deep in conversation. Of Alice there was no sign.

He stood for a while watching them, and then they turned and, seeing him, waved.

'Hi!' he said, going towards them and stretching out a hand to Giles. 'To what do we owe the unexpected pleasure?'

'Hi, Dad!' Giles awkwardly grasped his father's hand and Valerie murmured, 'I'll leave you two to talk.'

'Something wrong?' Edmund, sensing tension, was now all concern. 'Where's Alice?'

'It's nothing to do with Alice, dear,' Valerie said soothingly. 'She's having tea with her little friend, Philippa.' As Valerie prepared to cross the lawn to the house Giles held her back.

'I'd rather you stayed, Mum, really.'

'Something *is* wrong,' Edmund said with a resigned sigh. 'Let's go into the house. I could actually do with a drink.'

Now that it came to confrontation with his father, Giles felt less sure of himself. His mother seemed instinctively to understand, as he knew she would. She was not the most demonstrative of women, but she had no need to show what he knew and had always known, that she loved him.

Giles led the way into the house, back into the living room and studied the array of bottles on the drinks table.

'Usual for you, Dad? Whisky?'

'Yes, please.' Edmund slumped into a chair and ran his hands over his face.

'And for me too, please,' Valerie said, sitting next to her husband.

Giles gave his parents their drinks, said he'd have a beer and then went into the kitchen to find one. He returned to the living room and as he opened the bottle and poured the beer into a glass he realised that his hand was shaking. He hadn't for a moment thought it would be so difficult.

'Dad,' he said, still standing by the drinks table. 'Not to beat around the bush too much . . .'

'Please don't,' his father said.

'It's nothing dreadful . . .'

'Get on with it, Giles.'

'I've decided to leave university.'

Edmund took a sip from his glass and balanced it on the arm of his chair. Then he folded his hands on his lap.

'To do what?' he asked.

'I'm not quite sure.' Giles's brow puckered. 'I thought I might travel for a while.'

'Oh, I see.' Edmund's tone was sarcastic. 'A gentleman of leisure?'

'Not quite, Dad.' Giles took a chair opposite his father. 'I don't really enjoy psychology.'

'Then why did you do it?'

'Oh, *Edmund*!' Valerie exclaimed impatiently, leaning forward, hands round her knees. 'Don't make things difficult for Giles. He's finding it hard enough telling you as it is.'

'But why did he do it?' Edmund turned to her with an air of surprise. 'I mean, it's cost me a small fortune to keep him at university, and now he's telling me that he's throwing it all away to "travel". No plans, apparently, for a job or a career. Do I get my money back I ask myself? Or am I supposed to go on forking out while he bums round the world.'

'I find you very unreasonable, Ed,' Valerie said. 'Giles simply made a mistake. He didn't like Manchester much either. We said he wouldn't.'

'He should have done what you suggested and tried for higher grades. Then he could have been going to Oxford in a few months from now instead of wasting all this time.'

'I might not have got in, Dad.'

'Of course you'd have got in!' Edmund exclaimed wrathfully. 'You wouldn't have been wasting all your time on the rugger pitch and the cricket ground. You would have applied yourself to your studies and you would have got straight As. I simply can't understand you.'

157

Edmund drained his glass and, with another exclamation, rose and refilled it. Then he stood by the drinks table and glared at his son.

'And who is paying for this trip round the world? Me, I suppose?'

'I thought he could use the money your father left, Ed.' Valerie spoke placatingly. Edmund's father, who had died years before, had left the bulk of his estate to Edmund, but a small sum of money to each of his grandchildren.

'That money is invested.'

'Yes, but only shares. He can sell them.'

'Then he'll have nothing for a rainy day.'

'This is a rainy day, Dad.' Giles felt discouragement seep through him.

'It is indeed. It's a *very* rainy day. There we have Nick Constantine of whom, frankly, I never expected anything very much, covering himself with glory at Oxford, all set on a good career, whereas you who I always considered had far more ability and considerably more personality, flounder around.'

'Please don't bring Nick into this, Ed.' Valerie unfastened her hands and leaned back in her chair. 'Nick is a *very* nice boy. He worked hard and he did well but I don't think he is covering himself with glory as you suggest, and Giles is certainly not "floundering around". He has made a mistake. I think we half expected this. I'm not surprised. The only thing that does surprise me is that you are. Travel broadens the mind. I think selling the shares and using the money to travel a very good idea. Your father would have approved. If he gets short I think maybe I can help out a little. Then he can come back and go to law school. He wants to do that. Don't you, Giles?' As Giles nodded, she continued. 'He can live at home. That will save a lot of money and when he's finished he can do his articles with you and join you, which is what you've always wanted. All in all,' Valerie stood up and looked at her watch, 'I think it's a very good idea. Things may have turned out for the best.' Before she left the room she turned and gave her menfolk a bright, encouraging smile. 'You know they often do. Dinner in an hour.'

Dinner was a rather strained, silent affair, brightened by the patter of Alice who was delighted to see her elder brother at home. She was such an uncomplicated child that her presence was always a tonic. Edmund visibly relaxed and afterwards went off with her to help her with her homework.

Giles stayed in the kitchen helping his mother to fill the dishwasher and clear away.

'Thanks for your support, Mum,' he said, stooping to kiss her.

Momentarily she leaned against him and put an arm round his waist. She often wondered if Giles realised how much she depended on him. She had missed him living at home already, and knew how much worse it would be if he did go abroad.

'I do think Daddy *was* a bit unreasonable. After all, we all make mistakes and change our minds.' Valerie straightened up from the dishwasher and frowned.

'Daddy is terribly out of sorts lately. Sometimes I worry about him.'

Giles was immediately concerned.

'Is he ill?'

'Oh, no, I don't think it's anything like that. At least I don't *think* it's anything physical. It's more mental or emotional.' She paused and flopped down at the kitchen table. 'Somehow I think it's to do with money. I think he's worried about money, which is why he flew off the handle with you.'

'*Money*!' Giles also sat down and stared across the table at his mother. 'But I thought we were OK? I mean private schools, a good lifestyle. Not a yacht maybe but . . .' he laughed, 'we can't all be the Constantines.'

'No, we can't.' His mother smiled too. Then she frowned. 'I would have said we were OK. I mean he's never mentioned any difficulties to me. It's something we never talk about. Of course I have a small income of my own, you know that. I am not totally dependent on your father and never have been. Daddy has never given me an allowance or paid my dress bills, not that I have many!' She laughed self-consciously, acknowledging the fact that her family regarded her total lack of interest in clothes as an amusing and endearing eccentricity. 'I help with the housekeeping. In fact, I pay a lot of the bills, but Daddy takes care of school fees and so on, household repairs, car maintenance, holidays, Whiteboys (Whiteboys was the Somerset house), and so on. All in all, I should think our annual expenditure is quite considerable, but I would have thought we were able to meet it without much difficulty.'

'But shouldn't you talk about it, Mum?' Giles's expression was one of bewilderment.

'Yes, I suppose we should.' She nervously clasped and unclasped hands. 'But somehow we never do. I mean, I've asked him if things are alright and he said of course they are and brushed my question aside. You know how brusque, how stiff-upper-lip and all that Dad can be. However I think I'll ask him again after the outburst tonight. I mean, I can help quite a bit if necessary. I just wanted my money to go to you children. After I've gone there will be quite a lot, especially if my parents go before me which I suppose they will.'

Giles rose to get a beer out of the fridge and, breaking open the can, put it to his lips, his expression thoughtful.

'Maybe I should have a chat with Dad?'

'Oh, no, please don't! He wouldn't like that at all. He'll get over this and we'll work something out. He just doesn't like surprises. But he would be very upset if he thought I'd brought up the subject of money.'

'But,' Giles insisted, 'he brought up the subject of money. He made quite a meal of it, asking if I expected him to pay.'

'I know he did; but still he would be very upset if you asked him if things were OK financially. I know he would. Now, darling,' she looked at the clock on the kitchen wall and began to remove her apron, 'it's nearly time for the nine o'clock news. I hope Daddy has made sure that Alice is in bed.'

Edmund sat by the bedside of his daughter for a long time after she'd gone to sleep listening to the gentle sound of her breathing. He recalled the time he used to read to her every night when she was small, the rapt expression on her face as he turned the pages, sometimes the tears when a well-loved story reached the end. Those intimate moments between father and daughter had been very precious to him, still were, though now he had to drag her away from the television set or fetch her from some school friend with whom she had been having tea. Alice was now eleven and Edmund reflected, rather sadly, on how quickly children grew up and matured, how swiftly the years of childhood seemed to vanish behind them.

He leaned forward and, putting out the light by the side of her bed, tiptoed away. As soon as he closed the door his sense of peace and euphoria vanished and the worry, the feeling of dread, returned. He crept along the hall to his study and shut the door, leaning against it for a moment, trying to subdue the mounting panic that sometimes threatened to overwhelm him. At these dark moments he would see the collapse of his life; his work, his home; everything in ruins.

Edmund took a few deep breaths and then, hurrying to his desk, unlocked a drawer and drew from it a notebook which he considered for several seconds, flicking over the pages.

Finally he scribbled a number on his blotter, drew the

telephone towards him and tapped the keys, keeping the handset close to his ear as he heard the ringing tone at the other end.

No one there. He let it ring for several seconds and was about to replace the handset when a voice at the other end said: 'Hello?'

Edmund cleared his throat. 'Hello! Mr Davies?'

'Jeremy Davies speaking.'

'Mr Davies, my name is Edmund Harvey. You don't know me, but your name has been given to me by a mutual acquaintance.'

'May I ask who?'

'Philip Petersen.'

'Oh, yes.' The tone of voice, which had been cautious, even suspicious, relaxed. 'How is Philip?'

'Very well when I saw him which was at lunch today. I understand,' Edmund cleared his throat again, 'that is, he *gave* me to understand you might be looking for some capital to expand your business, a high risk investment which I understand the banks are reluctant to accommodate.'

'May I ask the nature of your interest, Mr Harvey?' The tone was brusque and unfriendly again.

'Certainly. I have funds at my disposal which I invest on behalf of clients who are prepared to take a risk in exchange for high profits. Naturally I would much prefer to discuss this in person rather than over the telephone.'

'There's nothing funny about it, is there?' Mr Davies demanded suspiciously.

'On the contrary,' Edmund replied haughtily. 'I am a lawyer with an international reputation and with over twenty years' experience, largely in commercial affairs. I can call on considerable sums of money available, surprisingly, at substantially lower rates than you might expect in today's climate. The service is also completely confidential, and if we do not come to an arrangement all documentation is

162

destroyed and the matter forgotten. It is absolutely bona fide. I only deal through personal recommendation, and between my clients and myself there is an atmosphere of complete trust.'

'Do you mind if I check you out with Petersen?'

'Not at all.' The receiver was beginning to slip from Edmund's clammy hand, and he transferred it to the other side, wiping his hand on his knee. 'Check it out and call me back. Not tonight as it's getting late. I'll give you my office number.'

'Good of you to get in touch with me, Mr Harvey. I appreciate it.' The tone of voice had now mollified.

'Not at all. I hope we can do business.'

'I hope so.'

Edmund gave Davies his office number, there were more expressions of cordiality and then he replaced the receiver and sat where he was for several minutes, his head bent, his hands shaking.

Valerie finished clearing up in the kitchen, to which she had returned after watching the news with Giles and having a chat. He then decided to go to the pub to see if any of his friends were about, and Valerie went back to the kitchen to remove the dishes from the dishwasher, put them away and lay the table for breakfast which the family usually had together. After doing her chores Valerie sat for a few minutes at the kitchen table reading the *Evening Standard*. After glancing at the clock and seeing it was after ten, she decided to go to bed. Edmund often worked in his study at night, sometimes until quite late. Valerie put out all the downstairs lights and slowly climbed the stairs. She was in a thoughtful and not altogether happy mood. She had tried to make light of Giles's news, but it was really a matter of putting on a brave front. She was no less unhappy about it than her husband, but she was more expert at concealing her feelings.

Valerie was a conventional woman, with conventional ideas, and thought it was the role of the woman to mend relationships in families, and where possible, keep things on an even keel. She reached the first-floor landing and paused at the door of Alice's room. She gently turned the handle and peeped inside. Alice always slept with the window open and the curtains drawn back, and it was possible to see her still form in the bed.

Hopefully, with life ahead of her, her dreams were the happy, untroubled ones of youth.

Valerie closed the door as gently as she had opened it and continued walking along the corridor. Then, seeing a light under the door, she paused outside Edmund's study. She was about to turn the handle when she heard his voice, a low murmur, then silence, then he started to speak in hushed tones again. She turned the handle gently so as not to disturb him, but the door was locked. This rather shocked her and she stood back looking fixedly at the door. She wondered why he was talking so quietly, as though he didn't want to be heard but, above all, why the door was locked in a house where there were few secrets, or had been until now. Valerie climbed the stairs to the second floor where there were the boys' bedrooms, hers and Edmund's and the guest room.

Still thoughtful, she got undressed, washed and did her teeth, cleansed her face, ran a comb through her hair – Valerie's routine at night, like the morning, was brief and basic.

She climbed into her bed, took her book from the bedside table and donned her reading glasses. But she was still preoccupied and the words seemed to blur on the page. Suddenly the house seemed a house of secrets, of discord, possible disaster. The comfortable certainty of years past seemed no longer there. The order and routine she was used to had gone. It was not the first time she'd paused outside Ed's study and heard him speaking quietly on the phone as if he had a hand over his mouth to prevent himself being heard. But it was the first time she'd tried the door – because she had wanted to talk to him about Giles – and found it locked. Maybe he always locked it? That was a thought.

After several attempts to restart her book, Valerie gave up and turned to put out the light. She and Edmund had slept in twin beds for years, so when he came to bed he wouldn't disturb her. She lay for a few moments but realised that she was still too wide awake, too nervous, to contemplate sleep. She put on the light again and was about to pick up the book when Edmund came in and seemed surprised to see her still awake. He turned and closed the door and was about to go into the bathroom when she called out to him: 'Ed, come over here for a minute.' She patted the bed and Edmund, looking very weary and beginning to unfasten his tie, came over to her.

'Yes, dear?' he said, looking down at her.

'Ed, is there anything the matter?'

'The matter?' Edmund appeared nonplussed by her question and shook his head.

'I mean,' Valerie went on, 'is there anything wrong? Be honest, Ed.'

'How do you mean, Valerie?' He perched on the side of her bed, his tie in his hand.

'What do you do in your office, murmuring away on the phone so late at night?'

'My dear, you know I have a lot of business to do at home.'

'Why lock the door?'

'So that I'm not disturbed.'

'Why?'

'Because,' he made as if to get up, clearly irritated, but she put out a hand and held on to his arm.

'Are you worried about anything, Ed?'

'No.' He was clearly getting annoyed and tried to get up again.

'You can tell me you know, confide in me. I'm your wife

and if there is anything wrong I want to know. Maybe I can help?'

'There is nothing wrong,' he insisted, this time succeeding in dragging himself away, and got to his feet. Then he appeared to relent. 'Well, alright, if you like I *am* worried about Giles.'

'But you've only just heard about Giles, and you have been like this for weeks, maybe months. Preoccupied, as if you're worried or unhappy. Also, I know you don't sleep. You're very restless. Is everything alright at the office, Ed? Is it money? If it is I have a bit put by, you know, and perhaps I can help.'

'Look, Valerie,' Edmund said wearily, 'I do appreciate your concern, but there is *nothing* wrong, *nothing* you can do. And if it was money, which it isn't, you know I would never touch your money. I've told you that before. Look, it's very late. I'm tired and you look tired. So let's talk about Giles tomorrow, eh?'

He smiled at her and, suddenly, as if on impulse, bent down and kissed her on the brow.

As an expression of husbandly tenderness, that was as far as he had gone for quite some time.

CHAPTER 10

Laura, white-faced, sat with bowed head trying to hide the tears, the bitter tears of chagrin and failure.

'I'm terribly sorry, Laura,' Maggie said, finding it hard to hide her own feeling of disappointment at the failure of a promising student, but angry at the same time that Laura was responsible for her own predicament, 'but I feel you have only yourself to blame. You admit that you did very little work, and that showed in the exam results. However,' she leaned back in her chair and lit a cigarette, 'the College Head has agreed to take you back if, after a year away, you can satisfy us that you have recovered your ability to work by passing next year's exams. Maybe a year away from Nick will be a good thing to bring you to your senses.'

'Nick had absolutely nothing to do with it,' Laura retorted, eyes smarting.

'Well, Nick's results were alright, I hear,' she said, adding sarcastically, 'obviously he was able to put passion on one side and concentrate on work.'

'That's a horrible thing to say!' Laura leapt from her chair.

'Nevertheless it's true, isn't it, Laura?' Maggie's tone became gentle, more understanding. 'We talked about this before, if you remember. "Man's love is of man's life a thing apart . . ." It's awful to have to quote it in the nineteen-nineties, when it was written over a hundred and fifty years ago, but in many ways it still remains true, at least among some of my students. Not all of them, thank heaven.' She looked up with a smile. 'Some of them are sensible enough to balance their work with their love life. I hope that when you return to us, Laura, and I'm sure you will, that this is a valuable lesson you've learned, and one that will stand you in good stead for the rest of your life.'

Maggie rose and put a hand on her student's shoulder. 'I'm sure this year off will be of inestimable benefit to you, Laura. I know that you won't like me saying this, but in many ways you are immature. I think that's why your first love affair knocked you sideways. Some of my more experienced students were able to cope . . .'

'I suppose because they came from better families,' Laura burst out. 'Most people from Oxford do.'

Maggie paused by the door.

'I think that's rather a silly thing to say. Wherever they came from – and not all were by any means well off – they had a sense of priority which you unfortunately lacked. It has nothing to do with money or class. Just plain common sense.' She gave Laura a final tap on the shoulder and opened the door. 'Come and see me before you go. You've a first-class brain and I want you to use it in the year ahead.'

Nick stood at the room window looking out into the quad, waiting for that girl to appear again, swinging across in easy strides just as he used to observe her before he fell in love with her. Maybe he was in love with her then: love at first sight? It had been a tremendous experience, their love affair. Mind blowing, staggering, all the usual adjectives, yet none of them sufficiently adequate to express what he and Laura meant to each other.

But now he was rather frightened. Laura had been summoned by Maggie and she had been away a long time. Laura had been anxious about her results and so had he about his; but he got through, no sweat. There had been a mild ticking off from his tutor because, though good, the results were not of a sufficiently high standard for a first. No chance of an All Souls Fellowship unless he improved on these.

Nick thought if she'd done well she'd have charged back. But it was impossible to think that she'd failed.

He paced restlessly round the room, tried to read, and he was about to set off and look for her, starting with the tutor's lodgings when, glancing out of the window, he saw that familiar, beloved figure hurrying across the quad. He bounded to the door and, racing down the stairs, greeted her at the entrance. She looked up at him and her stark expression told him the worst. He folded her in his arms and helped her up the stairs.

Laura threw herself onto the bed and stared at the ceiling. She still hadn't said a word, catatonic shock. Nick began to worry about her.

'I'll make tea,' he said, finally getting up from the side of the bed where he'd been sitting holding her hand.

Laura spoke at last. 'A drink would be nice. I failed, Nick. I'm to be sent down.' Nick stood in front of the kettle, not quite taking it in. He plugged it in, then went to a cupboard where there was a bottle of brandy and poured her a good measure. She sat up as he approached and took the proffered glass with the ghost of a smile.

'Sorry. I'm being an ass.'

Nick sat down again and took her free hand.

'They can't send you down.'

'They can, and I am. They need the place for someone else, someone who is prepared to work and benefit from being at this great university.' Laura rolled her eyes to the ceiling and finished the brandy in her glass in a gulp.

'It's my fault,' Nick said.

'No, it isn't. It's mine. You managed to be in love and work. I didn't.'

'I thought you knew your Hardy and your Eliot inside out?'

169

'I thought I did too, but not with sufficient "maturity" to satisfy the examiners, that is Maggie. She said my scholarship, such as it was, was too shallow, no depth. I suppose I could say she is a frustrated old bitch, but I shan't. I think she's right.' Laura sat up on the bed, put down her glass and linked her hands round her knees.

'You know what the worst part is? Having to tell my family that I failed. Got into Oxford and got chucked out.'

'Can't you say you're having a year off?' Even as he said it, Nick knew the excuse sounded rather lame.

Laura went on as though she hadn't heard him. 'We're a family of failures, low achievers, and I thought I was different.'

'You're not a low achiever, you're not a failure.'

Laura continued regardless. 'Maggie said some of her students managed to combine love with success in exams. I cheapened the whole thing by dragging in class, rather as I did that night we had dinner with your folks. I guess I have a lot to learn, Nick. Stop blaming others, for a start.'

Nick poured hot water onto his tea bag, stirred it in his mug and then added milk.

It would mean Oxford without her, not seeing her every day, not making love to her at every opportunity. And that he supposed was the truth of the matter: what had inspired and fired him had drained her. That was the only explanation he could think of. It was a disaster.

'You could stay on in Oxford,' he said. 'I mean in town. Living in Oxford. We could share a house. I don't mind leaving college. It is a bit like being in a boarding school. We . . .' He began to get excited.

'And what would I use for money? The dole would hardly pay the rent.'

'Laura,' Nick paused, then went on diffidently. 'You know money is no problem. I could keep you. You can get all the benefits you're entitled to and I'll take care of the rest.'

170

'What *would* your mum and dad say?' Laura's tone was heavy with sarcasm.

Nick shrugged.

'Given that they don't like me very much,' Laura continued.

'That's your idea.'

'It's true. Then if at the end you don't get your fellowship they'll blame me.'

'They won't. Look, if you like, we needn't even tell them. I mean that you've been sent down. We can just say we're sharing a house. No need for them to know.'

'They'll find out. Emma will tell them. Giles will tell them. Hey!' Laura paused and looked thoughtfully at Nick. 'Now Giles and I are in the same situation. Isn't that a coincidence?'

By the look on Nick's face she realised she'd made a mistake even mentioning it.

In the age of corporate identity: large multiple stores and chains dominating the high streets, Boothroyds the Chemists was, if not unique, an increasingly rare sight to behold. Round the corner from the Chase household, it occupied a central position in a modest road, which also had a greengrocer, a butcher, a paper shop and a small supermarket where Gordon worked during the holidays.

Laura had worked for Boothroyds since the age of thirteen or so, on Saturdays and during the school holidays. Mr and Mrs Boothroyd, who lived in a flat over the shop, had become almost as close as her own family. Even so, she couldn't tell them that she had been rusticated from Oxford because they had shared the pride of the family and school when she had got a place. 'Our' Laura had been the toast of everyone. Mr Boothroyd was pleased, if a little surprised, to see Laura asking for her old job during the long vacation. Mrs Boothroyd was a lady who literally enjoyed bad health, made the most of her many complaints, and was in and out of the doctor's surgery and hospital out-patients clinics as fast as they could accommodate her. Maybe it was marriage to a pharmacist that had made her so concerned about her health, and she was forever trying out the free samples of this medicine and that with which her husband was deluged from the drug companies.

Mr Boothroyd was a gentle, patient man, tolerant of his wife's hypochondria, and Laura was devoted to him, more devoted, if the truth be told, than she was to her own father. She enjoyed being back in the shop, behind the counter in her white coat while Mr Boothroyd remained in the dispensary and Mrs Boothroyd, relieved of her duties in the shop, found more time for her trips to the many clinics she could persuade to take an interest in her health problems.

Laura had left Oxford early and had been working at the shop for about a month during which time Mr Boothroyd had gradually come to the conclusion that all was not well with his favourite. Laura had always been a bright, effervescent girl and now she was strangely silent and withdrawn; she had always been of a confiding nature and now she was secretive, buttoned up. Mr Boothroyd tried to get her to talk, but it was useless. He decided that when she had something to say she would tell him, in her own good time.

Laura finished serving the last customer, advising her on the best colour of lipstick from the variety on offer, saw her to the door, changed the 'Open' sign to 'Closed', locked the door and took the keys to Mr Boothroyd who was busy cashing up.

'Quite a good day, Laura,' he said with a smile, and she agreed, smiling back. It was so nice to see her joyful expression that he ventured to comment further. 'Laura, I haven't seen you smile very much these days. Is there anything the matter?' Laura shook her head and he could sense her clamming up. 'Maybe the work at Oxford is harder than you realised, Laura?' Mr Boothroyd suggested, following

172

Laura to the back of the shop where she removed her white coat and collected her cardigan from a hook and her shopping bag from a chair. Laura turned to him and shook her head.

'Nothing's wrong at all, Mr Boothroyd, thanks. I'll see you tomorrow.'

'Right, Laura.' Mr Boothroyd smiled philosophically and saw her to the door, which he unlocked to allow her out and then relocked again.

Laura thought that if Mr Boothroyd continued to be so nosey she would leave and get a job elsewhere. Somewhere no one knew her, where they were not so curious. She knew he only meant it kindly, but she resented this intrusion in her private life. Laura was grieving and she wanted to keep herself to herself. She was grieving for her ruined career at Oxford and the shame she would have brought on her family if they'd known. She was grieving for her relationship with Nick and for the hurt she'd caused him by leaving Oxford without telling him. She was grieving for all the missed chances, for being nearly twenty and, in a short time, having lost so much.

Laura got home and, to her surprise, found her mother already in the kitchen preparing the tea. Thursday was usually the day Hilda stayed at the office to clean, and Laura took over the maternal role and prepared tea for her father and brothers. Today she'd bought mince at the butcher's and was going to make hamburgers and chips, a favourite of the boys, naturally.

'Hello, Mum,' Laura said, closing the door and putting her shopping on the table. 'Didn't expect to see you. I bought some mince to make hamburgers for tea.' Laura began to get her parcels from her bag and looked up to see her mother staring at her. 'Is there anything wrong, Mum?'

'Well,' Hilda put down the bread knife with which she'd been slicing bread and sat down heavily on a nearby chair. 'I arranged to work tomorrow because I wanted to talk to

173

you, Laura. I want to tell you before I tell the boys, and they'll both be late in this evening. Sharon knows already.'

'Mum, are you ill?' Laura said with concern, aware that suddenly the misery she'd felt about herself had been transferred to something else. She sat down opposite her mother, scrutinising every nuance of expression on her face.

'I'm not ill, Laura.' Hilda flicked away a lock of hair that had fallen over her eye. Laura noticed that her eyes were very bright. Her face was also flushed and there was an air of agitation about her which was unusual. Usually her mother was the embodiment of stoicism and calm.

'Laura, I'm going to leave your father!' Hilda raised her head and looked her daughter boldly in the eyes. 'It hasn't been an easy decision, but I've been thinking about it for a long time. I've told your dad, of course, discussed it with him. He won't take me seriously, but I am serious.'

'Mum! Is there someone else?'

Hilda laughed, raised her eyes to the ceiling. 'How nice it would be if there was, love. No there's no one else. I just can't stomach your father any more, his loutishness, his selfish ways. There's absolutely nothing *wrong* with him, you know.'

'Like Mrs Boothroyd,' Laura murmured and, in reply to her mother's unspoken question, 'there's nothing wrong with her either.'

'Your father's a lazy useless old bugger and I am just sick to death of slaving away all day and having to look after him.'

'But, Mum, where will you go?' As the implication of her mother's words began to sink in, Laura felt aghast.

'Well, I shall go to our Sharon's to start off with, or to my sister Marjorie. Then I'm applying for a council flat, to be rehoused. I know my rights. I've been planning this for a long time. I wanted to see you settled and on the way to a career. The boys can stay with their father. They'll be alright.

They'll cope. I'm so proud that you got into Oxford, Laura.'

Laura sat studying her clenched hands on her lap.

'This is a terrible shock, Mum. You can't think how much.'

Hilda looked surprised.

'But had you no idea, love, how I felt about your father?'

'Well, I knew you weren't very happy, but I never thought you'd leave him.' Laura looked round. 'Where is he tonight, by the way?'

'He's gone to his sister's to have a moan, no doubt. I told him I was going to tell you of my decision and he could stop away as long as he liked. I'm going to Sharon's tonight. I'm not sleeping in this house again. I know it's a shock, but my mind is made up. It's best to make the break, and make it quick, and while you're here you can help your father and brothers get accustomed to the situation. By the time you go back to Oxford they'll be used to it.'

As soon as Laura came into the shop the following morning, Mr Boothroyd knew that something had happened. She was always in good time, but this morning she was particularly early. He had hardly started work himself, Mrs Boothroyd having already left to keep an appointment at the hospital.

Mr Boothroyd, shrugging on his white coat as he let Laura in, said: 'You're early, Laura. Couldn't sleep?' It was meant as a joke, but Laura nodded as she took off her cardigan and hung it on its hook.

'I've had some terrible news, Mr Boothroyd.' As she turned to him tears sprang to her eyes. 'My mum is leaving my dad.'

'Oh, dear, Laura, I'm *very* sorry to hear that.' Mr Boothroyd's expression was immediately one of sympathy, and he put an avuncular hand on her arm. 'Whatever made her decide to do that?'

'They never got on, Mr Boothroyd.' Laura sank into the

chair under the clothes peg. 'My father, as you know, hasn't worked for years, is not in the best of health, though my mum thinks he puts a lot of it on.' She glanced fleetingly at Mr Boothroyd, but his expression didn't change.

'It's a very big step to take, Laura.' Mr Boothroyd sighed. 'Though perhaps, in this day and age, sadly, not all that uncommon. One must expect it. There isn't another . . .' he paused delicately. Laura shook her head.

'Oh, no, no one else. My mum's not like that. She just wants her independence. She's going to stop with my sister or my Auntie Marjorie until the council get her a flat. She's got it all worked out. She's been planning it for months, maybe years. In fact, last night she didn't sleep at home.'

'She's gone just like that?' Mr Boothroyd looked surprised.

'Just like that. Thought it was best. She'd already taken most of her things to Sharon's. It was a very strange feeling when my father and brothers came home. For a while no one mentioned it. My father can't believe it. My brother Gary is probably going to move in with his girlfriend anyway. They've been thinking of it for some time.'

'Good thing they've got you, Laura,' Mr Boothroyd said and then gazed at her. 'Is that what you've had on your mind recently?'

Laura shook her head but remained silent.

'There has been something, hasn't there?'

'It's not that Mr Boothroyd . . .' Laura had entwined the fingers of both hands and sat there twisting them. 'It came as a complete surprise to me. I could never see my Mum leaving the family. No, what . . . what has been the matter,' her voice faltered then went on with a rush, 'I've been sent down from Oxford. I failed my exams and I've had to leave the university.'

'Oh, Laura!' Mr Boothroyd grasped her shoulder so hard that she almost winced, jumped in pain. 'Oh, Laura, I am so sorry . . .'

176

'I can go back,' she hurried on, 'if I pass next year. But I haven't been able to tell the family. I couldn't tell anyone. I felt so ashamed after all they, and people like you, expected of me.'

'But, Laura, how did it happen? You were so bright. Didn't you work?'

'Not hard enough . . . I fell in love, Mr Boothroyd. There was, is, a man, Nick.'

'Ah!' Mr Boothroyd assumed the tactful, sagacious expression he kept for customers who sought his advice on the intricacies of various methods of contraception. 'Is he still about?'

'Oh, yes! And it wasn't his fault. It was mine. He didn't fail his exams. I think it was all just too much for me. I was very silly. Very weak. My tutor had warned me my work wasn't good enough, but I thought I had it in me to make up.' She shook her head. 'Oxford is very hard, very tough. It's not like school, and the tutors aren't like our teachers who have known us for years. I lived in a cocoon and now I know what the real world is like. You understand that I couldn't tell Mum and Dad, don't you?'

'Poor Laura,' Mr Boothroyd said, still stroking her arm. 'And now you have your home breaking up too. Nowhere to turn. It doesn't seem fair, does it?'

The summer for Laura was one long purgatory from which, unlike the souls who, so legend says, ultimately ascend to heaven, she could see no escape. It was also the summer she turned twenty and became at the same time the mother of the family, fitting into her mother's role, taking her place almost instinctively: She rose early in the morning, took her father his tea, prepared her brothers' breakfasts, washed up, made the beds and left the house just before nine to go to the chemist, returning at five-thirty when she began the cooking and cleaning routine all over again.

It never occurred to the men to offer to help her and it never occurred to her to ask, which was strange for a seemingly liberated university-educated woman. But what applied to other people did not apply to her.

Her father, as if to prove that he really was ill, had what seemed to be a minor heart attack. He developed chest pains in the middle of the night and was taken to hospital, but released after a few days. The doctor seemed to think it was brought on by anxiety about the possibility that Laura might leave him. He was put on medication and Laura felt more imprisoned than ever.

Maybe she would never return to Oxford and would spend the rest of her days looking after her family, all of whom she now realised suffered from various degrees of selfishness, including her mother, whom she only saw when she visited her sister, and who had no regrets about what she had done.

Someone at least had achieved freedom.

She and Nick spoke on the phone regularly until he went to the family yacht in Monte after failing to get her to agree to join him. He tried to come up for her birthday, but she didn't want him to see where she lived, or how she lived. Above all, she didn't want him to meet her father. It was dreadful to be ashamed of her family, but she was. Her sense of low self-esteem was further enhanced by a feeling of disgust at her attitude; but then she thought of the house in St John's Wood, the Rolls in the garage, the yacht in Monte and the splendid youthful-looking parents, and she knew she couldn't help herself.

Laura remembered what Maggie had said about a year away from Nick doing her good, and she wondered if Maggie was right. It was, of course, not Nick's fault that she had fallen in love or failed her exams, but if he hadn't been there it wouldn't have happened. She would be going back to Oxford, some compensation for the wretched life she was leading.

Maybe, deep down, there was a core of resentment against him there.

Sometimes Nick would phone from the boat and he wrote regularly, but his letters were curiously passionless, as if he'd had second thoughts too, as if their love was finally dying.

Towards the end of August of that dreadful, endless summer, Laura was at the back of the shop checking in new stock that had been delivered earlier in the day when the bell that hung over the door jangled to announce the arrival of a customer. Mr Boothroyd called: 'Shop, Laura,' from the dispensary.

Laura, notepad and pencil in hand, went through the curtain into the shop and looked straight into the face smiling at her across the counter – that familiar, laid-back countenance. A great surge of unexpected joy rose up like a fountain inside her.

'Giles!' she cried, and she felt like rushing round and giving him a huge hug.

'Hey, Laura!' He seemed glad that she was so obviously pleased to see him, and held out his hand across the counter. 'How are you?'

She wanted to say something silly like, 'All the better for seeing you', but didn't, because at that moment Mr Boothroyd's face appeared round the dispensary door, his eyebrows raised in enquiry.

'It's alright, Mr Boothroyd. Just a friend.'

'Someone from the university?' Mr Boothroyd looked curiously at Giles.

'A friend of Nick's.'

'Ah!' Mr Boothroyd held out a hand across the counter. 'How do you do . . .'

'Giles Harvey,' Giles said jovially, clasping Mr Boothroyd's proffered hand. 'How do you do, sir?'

'I'm very well thank you, young man.' Laura could tell that Mr Boothroyd approved of Giles with his wide, friendly smile, superior accent and nice manners. 'Have you come from London just to see Laura?'

'Well, no. I had business in the area,' Giles explained, 'and I thought I'd look her up. Say,' he glanced at his watch, 'can we have lunch?'

Laura looked at Mr Boothroyd who nodded. 'It's not quite lunch time, Laura, but by all means go now.' And while Laura ran into the back to put a comb through her hair and get her cardigan she could hear Giles and Mr Boothroyd chatting amiably away in the shop.

'I'll be back in an hour,' she promised, and Giles, opening the door, stood back politely to let her pass.

'Now,' he said, following her, hands in his pockets, looking around, 'anywhere near here you can recommend?'

'I think it will have to be the pub,' she said. 'Unless we go into town, there's nothing much here.'

'Let it be the pub.' Giles fell in beside her with his easy stride.

The pub was on the other side of the street and, as usual, it was full of lunch-time drinkers.

They ordered a bar meal, cottage pie and chips, and Giles had a beer while Laura drank tonic water. The woman behind the bar said she would bring their food to them, and after Giles had paid they took their drinks to the far side of the dark saloon, as far away as possible from the jarring sound of the jukebox and the flashing lights of the garish slot machine. For a moment they sat staring at each other.

'Sure you didn't want anything stronger?' Giles asked, indicating her glass.

Laura shook her head and laughed. 'I have to work. Oh, Giles, it is *so* good to see you. You don't know how good.' She paused. 'How did you know where to find me?'

'I called at your home. Your father was there and he told me where you worked. I hope you don't mind?'

'No, I don't mind.' Laura shook her head but as she put her glass to her lips she knew she was blushing. 'I should actually go back and get my father some lunch.'

'I told him I'd be asking you out to lunch. He didn't seem to mind.'

'Seriously, Giles, what are you doing up here?'

'I came to see you,' he said, staring at her. 'Honestly.'

'Didn't you have business at the university?'

'No.'

'Oh!' She did not know what to say and felt hot again.

'I'm terribly sorry about your exams, Laura. Do you know that I haven't seen you since you left Oxford?'

'Yes, I know.'

'And you haven't seen Nick either?'

'No.' She bowed her head. 'I've hurt Nick. I'm aware of it and I'm sorry. He wanted to come up here but I told him not to. He wanted me to go on the yacht but I couldn't consider it. I find it hard to communicate and I don't think he understands, but it's been a very difficult time for me and it was hard for me to explain. I told you before that I think Nick's wealth comes between us. The wealth and the environment in which he lives. Nick is such a nice fellow and he would be horrified to know how I feel, so I can't tell him. I feel our lifestyles, our backgrounds, are so different. Honestly, I didn't even want you to see where I live. Now you have and I don't really care; but I've never seen your home or met your folks, so it doesn't bother me except that I don't feel the same differences with you that separate me from Nick. I can't explain that either.

'My mother left home recently, and I've had to look after the family, take her place. I didn't want to and I didn't mean to, but it was somehow forced on me. They were all so desolate without her, so lost. Then my father had a mild heart attack, and he needs extra special care.'

'Poor Laura.' Giles's hand closed tightly over hers. She

didn't say anything or try to remove her hand. 'Nick feels very cut up about all this.'

She nodded.

'How do you feel?'

'Cut up, too.' She raised her head and looked at him. 'How was the yacht?'

'We didn't go. My father's in a funny sort of mood and said he couldn't leave his work. I don't think things are too good, but I don't know why. Maybe it's money. My younger brother was going to Venice with the school, and my mother wanted to spend the summer at our house in Somerset. My parents are thinking of selling it.'

'Oh! Will you mind?'

Giles shrugged. 'I shan't mind at all. We hardly ever go there and it's falling to pieces. Look, Laura,' his hand tightened on hers, 'I've got a proposition to make to you. Oh . . .' seeing her expression, 'not *that* sort, well not yet, anyway. But I'm going to go abroad. I thought of going to Australia for six months, maybe a year, backpacking you know. I don't terribly want to go on my own and I wondered if you'd like to join me?'

'To Australia?' she gasped.

'Why not?'

'I couldn't possibly afford it. I haven't any money.'

'I've enough for the fare and a bit more, and then we can live cheaply. I've got some money left to me by my grandfather.'

'I couldn't. Nick wants me to live with him in Oxford. I couldn't even accept that. I'm not a concubine.'

Giles smiled at the old-fashioned word.

'I know you're not, and I don't regard you as one. But I guess you're depressed and I would like a companion for the journey. You can, if you like, regard the money as a loan and pay it back in future years as and when you like.'

'I want to go back to Oxford next year.'

182

'I know you do. No reason why you can't.'

'Did you talk to Nick?'

'Oh, no.' Giles gave a wry smile. 'Not yet. Not until I hear what you say.'

'But my father, my family . . .'

'Look, Laura, this is your life. You don't want to throw it away on them. They can look after themselves. If you went back to Oxford they'd have to.'

'They don't know that I'm not going back to Oxford. I could never pluck up the courage to tell them.'

'Well, then. This sounds just the thing to do. It's an opportunity you may never get again, Laura. Take a chance.'

Laura thought of the grim little terraced house, her father's insistent demands, the selfishness of her brothers. Who really cared anything about her? And the thought of going on like this, keeping house, working at the chemist for the next year, possibly longer, was unendurable. She would have a nervous breakdown, and who would look after *her*?

And if she regarded the money from Giles as a loan, why, it made her so much more independent. It altered the complexion of the whole thing.

She looked at Giles and her heart lifted.

'Seize the hour!' she said.

CHAPTER 11

Valerie opened the door of Edmund's study and stood looking in. He was sitting at his desk, working on some papers.

'Darling,' Valerie said, 'there's an odd bod waiting to see
you.'

Edmund turned and looked questioningly at her.

'What sort of "odd bod", dear?'

'Just odd. Hard to explain.' Valerie grimaced. 'I thought
at first he was a respectable tramp, you know. Someone
down on his luck. I was about to go and find some money
to give him and then turn him away when he stated his
business.'

She looked darkly at Edmund, and his heart plummeted.
All he could think of was a visit from the police. But surely
a member of the CID would never look like a tramp, even
a respectable one? Or would he? One never could tell with
the police, masters of disguise! He became anxious again.

'Can't you say I'm not in?'

'I have a feeling he'll stay here until you are. I mean, he
knows you live here.'

'How?'

'He asked for you by name.'

'Well, Valerie, go and ask him what he wants,' Edmund
said, impatiently turning back to his work.

Valerie folded her arms and leaned against the door. 'I
know what he wants, Ed.'

Fearful again, Edmund looked quickly round.

184

'What?'

'He's come about the girl Giles has gone to Australia with. He's her father. You better come and see him, Ed. I can't get rid of him. The poor man is obviously very upset.'

'But we don't know her.'

'I told him that, though I'm not sure he believes it.'

'Oh, well.' Impelled by a sense of relief, by acceptance of the inevitable, Edmund pushed back his chair and got to his feet. 'What's his name?'

'Mr Chase. Albert Chase. He was very polite. I think he's a bit frightened.'

'Good.' Edmund walked purposefully to the door. 'Then we'll soon get rid of him.'

When he got to the living room, Albert Chase was standing by the window looking into the garden, his back to the door. He turned as Edmund came into the room, and began nervously to twist his cap between his hands. Edmund could see why Valerie might have mistaken him for a gentleman of the road. As well as a tired, careworn expression on his not unhandsome face, his suit was maybe a size or two too large for him and looked as though it might have been bought from Montague Burton in the fifties and hardly worn since. The collar of his freshly-washed shirt stood out from his scrawny neck.

Edmund had decided that lashings of upper-class charm was what was required to deal with the working classes and advanced towards his clearly nervous and unwelcome guest, hand outstretched.

'How do you do, Mr Chase? I'm Edmund Harvey. Sorry to keep you waiting.'

Albert mumbled something inaudible and returned Edmund's clasp with a limp hand.

'Do sit down, Mr Chase.' Edmund pointed to a chair. 'Can I get you whisky?' he said, going to the drinks table.

'Or would you prefer coffee, or tea perhaps, Mr Chase?'

185

Valerie said from the background, remembering that tea was the favourite brew of people from up north.

Albert looked mulishly in front of him as though inclined neither to sit nor accept the offer of drinks. But he had come a long way and he was tired.

'A glass of whisky would be very nice thank you, Mr Harvey.' Albert looked behind him and sat down carefully.

'Are you staying long in town?' Edmund gave him his whisky, had one in his own hand and took a seat opposite him while Valerie also helped herself from the drinks table and sat on the sofa, between Albert and her husband.

'I'm going back tonight. There's a train from Euston at around midnight.'

'And how long have you been here?' Edmund raised his hand in the manner of one accustomed to asking questions.

'I arrived at three, sir.'

'Today, and you're going back *today*?'

'I came specifically to see you, Mr Harvey. I have never been to London before and I have no reason to stay here. It also took me some time to find you,' Albert dramatically clutched his chest, 'and I have a bad heart.'

'Oh, dear.' Valerie looked concerned. 'Of course we'll call you a taxi when you go.'

'The bus is quite alright for me thank you, Mrs Harvey. I don't like tube trains, they make me feel nervous, and I can't afford a taxi. I have been unemployed for a long time.'

Edmund wriggled uncomfortably and glanced at his wife.

'Would you like to come to the point, Mr Chase? We should hate you to miss your train as you have such a long way to go.'

Albert, sitting on the edge of his chair, one hand round his glass, the other on his knee, cleared his throat.

'It's about my daughter, Mr Harvey . . .'

'Mr Chase,' Edmund decided that domination must now replace charm and got to his feet, 'I'm afraid we do not know

186

your daughter. Neither my wife nor I have ever met her. We didn't know she existed until we had a letter from Giles which he posted from the airport shortly before he left for Australia. Giles did everything with the greatest secrecy apparently because this girl, your daughter – Laura is her name? – was practically engaged to Nick Constantine who was Giles's best friend. Now why Giles should have behaved in this wholly reprehensible manner I have no idea. I deprecate it, and so does my wife. The Constantines are friends of ours and I understand Nick is extremely upset. But it takes two to make a decision, you know, and Laura must have agreed to go of her own free will. I understand she is twenty, so she is of age. There is absolutely nothing I can do about it except to say that I'm sorry.'

'You must have known about it, Mr Harvey,' Albert insisted. 'You must have helped him, your son, to make off with my daughter.'

'I certainly did not help him . . .' Edmund began, but Albert was not to be stopped.

'Where did he get the money for the tickets? My daughter hadn't a penny. I consider that your son stole my daughter and he should pay for it, or you should.'

'Are you asking me for *money*, Mr Chase?' Edmund thundered, the veins bulging in his neck.

'I mean "pay" in the sense of being responsible for. No, I am not asking for money. But I want my daughter restored to me. I have not been well – I had a heart attack as a matter of fact – and she was looking after me. My wife left me and Laura replaced her. I need her and I want her back. It's all I have now. We still have a bit of pride in the community in which we live and we were proud of Laura. She was the first person in our family to get a place at Oxford and thanks to this Nick Constantine she lost that. Did you know that, Mr Harvey?' Albert stuck a finger out at him.

'Yes, I did. I mean I knew absolutely nothing about Laura

until this happened. Naturally the Constantines, who are friends, were upset on their son's behalf . . .'

'You said you'd never heard her name and yet you are their friend?'

'Well,' Edmund coughed, 'not *all* that friendly. I mean we don't socialise, though we used to. Our sons were at school together.'

'Oh, then you do know this Nick?'

'Oh, yes, we do know him. He's a nice boy.'

'Despite taking advantage of my daughter?'

'Really, Mr Chase. These days . . .' Edmund threw out his arms in a theatrical gesture. 'You don't think in those terms any more: seduction, all that sort of thing you know. It's what young people do. Standards which mattered to you and me when we were young matter no more. I do think however that my son's behaviour is inexcusable and I am very upset on your behalf.'

'Upset on *my* behalf. What a laugh.' Albert gave a wry chuckle. 'Until a year ago my daughter was a good, studious girl, of whom we were very proud. Now she goes down to this fancy university and runs amok. She gets seduced by a man and fails her exams – a fact I only learned from the chemist she worked for shortly after she left. She left without a word to him or a word to me. She did tell her mother, but her mother had no desire to help or assist me. She was aided and abetted by her mother and her sister.'

'But she left of her own accord?'

'Obviously she left of her own accord. She wasn't kidnapped if that's what you mean. But what has happened to my daughter that she goes to the bad in just over a year? Can you tell me that? Is your son going to marry her?'

'I have no idea.' Edmund sank back into his chair again. 'Frankly, as he explained it to us in his letter, she is a travelling companion. She was upset at failing her exams. She apparently didn't want to stay at home. She felt she couldn't tell you she had failed her exams and had to leave Oxford. I'm sure she'll write to you and explain. But as for romance,' Edmund shook his head, 'I don't think there is one. Young people these days do go off you know. It doesn't mean they're in love.'

Edmund looked abruptly at his watch and got to his feet. 'I will write and tell him of your concern when I have an address to which to write. They've gone off into the blue. I'll say we had this most interesting chat and ask him to get Laura to write to you.'

'I want her to come home,' Albert said stubbornly, also rising to his feet, clutching his cloth cap close to his body as though it were a sporran. 'I want Laura to come back.' He advanced a step or two towards Edmund, who began to feel threatened and put up a hand.

'My dear man, there is absolutely nothing I can do to bring your daughter back if she doesn't wish to come back. I have no power at all. Look, as soon as I hear, as soon as I have an address I'll let you know and you can write.'

Suddenly Albert's right hand shot out and he seized a fistful of Edmund's clothing, the sweater he was wearing, part of his shirt. He tried to pull Edmund towards him but lacked the strength. He was not as fit as Edmund, and in the end it was Edmund who was doing the pulling while Albert, clinging on to his clothes as though he was taking part in a tug of war, resisted him all he could.

It was a farcical sight and Valerie, while registering horror, couldn't resist seeing the comical side to the whole affair and had to stifle a giggle.

'Stop, stop,' she cried, holding up a hand. 'This is too dreadful, too absurd,' and she caught at Albert's jacket and tried to pull him away. The harder she tugged, the harder Albert resisted, and the more he pulled at Edmund's pullover until his shirt burst out of his trousers. Albert fell backwards on top of Valerie who tumbled onto the sofa, Albert on top of her, finally letting go of Edmund's shirt.

Edmund was now able to gain control of the situation and, stuffing his shirt back into his trousers and pulling his sweater firmly over his hips, he bounded over to the sofa, dragged Albert away from his wife and pushed him towards the door.

'Get out of here,' he cried. 'Get out and don't *ever* let me see or hear from you again, do you understand? I don't want to *see* you or *hear* from you ever again, and if I do I shall call the police. I'm a lawyer you know, and I could charge you with assault, coming into my house and creating mayhem.'

Still with his hand firmly on Albert's shoulder he led him into the hall and opened the front door, practically throwing him down the steps. Then, without seeing what happened, he shut the door and turned round to see if Valerie was alright.

He found her sitting on the side of the sofa tugging her jersey back into shape, convulsed now in helpless giggles.

'Are you alright?' he asked, sitting down beside her and looking anxiously into her face. 'What's so funny?'

'My dear,' she gasped, pushing her hair back from her face with both hands, 'what a terrible experience. But I can't help seeing the funny side.'

'I don't think it was funny at all.' Edmund didn't try to conceal his irritation. 'It *was* a terrible experience. And it calls for another whisky,' and rising, he poured them two stiff measures and downed his in a gulp.

'I mean, what on earth . . . Is he alright, Ed?' Her hand still on her brow, Valerie looked anxiously at her husband.

'How do you mean, is *he* alright?'

'Well, he said he had a bad heart. I hope he hasn't collapsed in a heap outside our front door.'

With an exclamation Edmund got up, glass still in his hand, went back into the hall and opened the front door. The path to the gate was clear, but the gate swung open. He went along the path looking to right and left, did the same on the

190

pavement, and then shutting the gate after him returned to the house.

'Not a sign of him.'

'Poor man,' she said, shaking her head.

'What on earth do you mean "poor man"?' Edmund poured himself another drink. 'The fellow invades our house and then launches an attack on me.'

'I feel just a bit sorry for him, coming after his daughter. It was rather pathetic. You can hardly call it an invasion. Besides, you're much bigger and stronger than he is, darling.'

'It still doesn't give him the right to assault me in my own house.'

'Oh, basically I agree. I do.' Valerie hauled herself out of the couch, and still stroking back her hair, looked out of the window. 'I still feel vaguely sorry for him, vaguely uncomfortable. Thinking of him finding his way back to the station, no money.' She hitched her trousers up and sighed deeply then, rather shakily, poured herself a fresh drink. 'Still, it's a bad situation and, frankly, I can't help blaming Giles.'

'If I could get my hands on him I'd murder him,' Edmund said, screwing up his fist and looking darkly into his glass.

Andreas Constantine stood in the lobby of the club in St James's and raised his eyes to the high ornate ceiling decorated with intricate plasterwork: quatrefoils, rectangles, lozenges, rosettes, fleurs-de-lis and various heraldic devices of the aristocratic family to whom, many years ago, this town house had belonged. From the ceiling his eyes travelled along the walls, lingering on the portraits of the august members of the family who for centuries had helped govern England. Also hanging were portraits of distinguished former members of the club who had served in many of the outposts of the British Empire, and had in some cases given their lives for it.

Andreas would have liked to belong to a club like this, but he didn't know how to go about it. Unlike Edmund Harvey, who, doubtless, was born to it. He had no connections with the world of gentlemen's clubs, nor did any member of his family. Most of his friends were like him: thrusting entrepreneurs of the second or third generation whose forebears had been born abroad.

Andreas reckoned he despised snobs, yet he was in his own way snobbish. He had sent his children to public school, not only to get a good education but to mingle with the sort of people whose fathers, by right, belonged to clubs like this.

And he had been successful. Nick had made a best friend of Giles Harvey, and Edmund Harvey was the reason why Andreas was here.

The invitation had come, via secretaries, a few days beforehand. Would Andreas dine with him at his club? No reason given. As Lydia had not been invited and, Andreas gathered, nor would Valerie, it must be something to do with men's affairs. Andreas suspected business, unless it was the matter between Giles and that girl, in which case he thought the women would have been invited too.

There were a few men in the lobby presumably, like Andreas, waiting to meet a club member. The members were quite obvious because of the way they sauntered past, perfectly at home in their patch. The guests, on the other hand, looked slightly nervous, more humble, more in awe at being in a famous club in the centre of clubland.

It was ridiculous to feel awed, but Andreas did. He shuffled his feet impatiently and looked at his watch. Harvey was already ten minutes late. Was he trying to tell Andreas something? Demonstrate his superiority? Lydia would have assumed that he was, and would have started to talk about insults and so on. 'Shall we leave?' and that kind of thing.

Andreas didn't quite feel as Lydia did about the Harveys, never had. But men tended not to, especially if they felt, as

Andreas did, that they had their place in the world, had it made in fact. He was an extremely wealthy man with a son at Oxford and a Rolls Royce parked round the corner.

But still there was something missing. He was not quite sure what it was, but he would like to belong to a club like this.

'Ah, there you are!' Both hands extended in greeting, Edmund entered the lobby with confidence, smiled at the porter, affably hailed one or two members he knew: a chap comfortable and at home in his own territory. Both hands clasped Andreas's, who felt rather confused by the warmth of the welcome and wondered what he had done to deserve it.

'I'm so glad you could make it,' Edmund said, leading his guest into the bar. 'Lydia well?'

'Very well, thank you.' Andreas looked keenly at Edmund. 'And Valerie?'

'Yes, very well, thanks. Now what will you have to drink?'

Drinks in hand they stood in the bar chatting, Edmund occasionally exchanging a word with other members, all of whom he introduced to his guest. They kept the conversation general: politics, the weather, the economic situation (grim but improving) and what a pity it was that the Harveys had been unable to join the Constantines on the yacht.

'Did you have a good time?'

'Yes, excellent. The Thompsons wished to be remembered to you.'

'Oh, they were there again?'

'Never miss. I hope you'll come next year?'

'Well . . .' Edmund looked meaningfully at Andreas and then gestured towards the door. 'Shall we dine?'

The dining room was large, elegant, with a view of a walled garden adjoining the backs of houses on the other side of the street. These had probably been turned into clubs, flats or offices at about the same time that the noble family had

193

left the present building for, doubtless, a humbler dwelling. This would mean restricted space, fewer servants or none at all, and therefore easier and less costly to maintain. The new rich now were the Constantines of this world, not that even they could have afforded a place like this, or necessarily wanted one. Their wealth was probably comparable to that of the former inhabitants when they lived here, but these days money had different values and was spent on different things. It was a changed world from the last decade of the nineteenth century, a hundred years ago.

New money had now superseded the old.

'I've ordered us a very nice wine,' Edmund said, bending enthusiastically towards Andreas as the waiter seated them at the table and handed them each a menu. 'I think you'll approve. It's a Haut-Brion 1980, just ready for drinking, isn't it, Mathieu?' He turned to the wine waiter who was hovering respectfully by his elbow clutching a basket which contained a bottle, as though he had just discovered the Holy Grail. He placed it reverentially on the table and handed Edmund the cork. 'I think you will find it perfect, Mr Harvey. One of the finest first growths in our cellars and also,' he hung his head sadly, 'alas, one of the last. Would you like to taste it, Mr Harvey?'

'I can't resist it, Mathieu, but I think we're having a bottle of Montrachet to start?'

''85 Mr Harvey. I've had it on ice for an hour.'

'Just a drop of the claret then.' Edmund leaned forward with the eagerness of a greedy schoolboy and watched the wine waiter as he poured a little of the purple liquid into his glass. Edmund raised the glass towards the light, scrutinised it, held it away again, brought it to his nose and sniffed it, twirled it between his fingers, sniffed it again and, applying it to his lips, gulped down the drop in the glass.

'Wonderful stuff,' he said, looking enthusiastically at his guest. 'Would you like to try it, Andy?'

'I'm no connoisseur.' Andreas diffidently put forward his glass and, as the wine waiter poured an amount that hardly covered the bottom, lifted the glass without any of the elaborate ritual that Edmund had performed and swallowed the lot.

'Very nice,' he said, putting the glass down. 'Excellent.'

'Beats all that Australian muck,' Edmund said with a conspiratorial glance at the waiter. 'Now bring on the Montrachet, Mathieu, and let's try that.'

'Certainly, Mr Harvey.' The man withdrew as Edmund began enthusiastically to study the menu.

Andreas, recalling all the Chardonnay and Shiraz they had drunk on board the yacht in the summer, and served to the Harveys the summer before, wondered if Edmund's remark about Australian wine had been intended as a snub. But, looking at him covertly from behind his own menu, he decided it wasn't. There was no malice in the man, no deliberate intention to offend, or at least he didn't think so. Surely someone as well-bred as Edmund Harvey would have considered such a remark, if made intentionally, bad form?

He good-naturedly fell in with his suggestions for food to accompany the wine – a plate of smoked Scottish salmon followed by fillet of beef – and approved of the Montrachet when that was brought forward for tasting.

'How do you become a member of a place like this?' Andreas asked, looking round. 'Do you have to be proposed?'

The question seemed to surprise Edmund. 'Of course.' Then, 'Why, would you like to join?'

'Well . . .' Andreas self-consciously rearranged the army of knives and forks in front of him. 'Am I eligible?'

'Of course you're eligible. You can pay the membership fee, can't you?'

'I hope so. I suppose so. But everyone seems well . . . top drawer, you know what I mean.'

'My dear Andreas, there is no such thing as *class* these

days. Thank heavens for it too. Don't you agree?'

'Not really. There aren't many people here who would seem to me to have grandfathers who were Greek peasants.'

'But you don't *know*, do you, Andreas? You go by appearances. No, as long as you're proposed and seconded by members in good standing – and accepted by the committee, that goes without saying – and you can pay the entrance fee and the annual sub, you'd be welcome as a member. The next time I'm in I'll have a word with the club secretary.'

'That's very good of you.'

There was a pause while Edmund too started to rearrange his knives and forks. Obviously they were approaching the reason for the meeting.

'How's Nick?' he said looking up.

'Well . . .' Andreas studied the tablecloth, 'I think he's thrown himself into his work.'

'I can't say how sorry . . . it was *nothing* to do with us.'

'We realised that.'

'We didn't even know the girl. We never met her.'

'It's not your fault. Don't think that. Actually, we weren't really sorry, but it was hard on Nick.'

'Didn't like her then?' Edmund looked curious.

'Nothing to like or dislike. Not quite the sort of girl we hoped Nick would choose?'

'Working class?'

'I thought there was no such thing as class any more? You just said . . .'

'You know what I *mean*.' Edmund loftily wafted a hand in the air. 'You see, we had a very unpleasant encounter with the girl's father and we know what sort of man *he* was.'

'With Laura's father?' Andreas looked astonished. 'How did you come to meet him?'

'He came to see us. Just appeared on the doorstep. No "May I" or "By your leave". He said he wanted his daughter back and blamed us for what had happened to her. We were extremely civil to him and gave him a drink – Valerie was actually quite sorry for the man – but in the end he went for me and I had to throw him out.'

'Went . . . you mean he *attacked* you?'

'Pushed me, shoved me, that sort of thing. There was an unholy fracas.'

'Well, I'm terribly sorry . . .'

'My dear Andreas, I'm not telling you this because I in any way blame you. On the contrary. I blame my son and I intend to have it out with him when I see him again as I undoubtedly shall, as sooner or later he is going to run out of money. Giles behaved very badly, to us, to Nick who was his best friend, to the girl, though I suppose she is responsible for her own actions. Is Nick very cut up?'

'Nick doesn't say very much. He was very quiet during the vacation and he didn't tell us that she'd been sent down. Of course when they went away we were still on the yacht. We went to Greece and Turkey this year. He only found out when we got back. He took it very much with a stiff upper lip I must say. Then he went back to Oxford early. Frankly, Edmund, Lydia and I were quite relieved.'

'Is she pretty, is she . . .'

'She is not exactly pretty, but she is what I suppose you'd call striking. Her features are bold, very pronounced. She is very tall, but rather blunt and down to earth. No dress sense at all. Not a "womanly" woman, if you know what I mean. I think, yes, we were a little disappointed in her and are not sorry that she and Nick are no longer together. We certainly think Nick could do better.'

'Giles says they are just good friends, no intention of marrying.'

'Do you hear from him often?'

'No. And we don't write often either. All we want to know is whether or not he's alright and apparently he is. I only hope that when he comes back this friendship can revive.'

Edmund looked at Andreas who didn't reply. The excellent salmon, accompanied by the Montrachet, was finished, and a waiter removed the empty plates replacing them with warm ones on which was served succulent looking portions of best fillet of beef. The sacred Haut-Brion was reverentially poured by the wine waiter, was admired all over again, like a libation to the gods, and the waiters retired to let the two men proceed with their meal.

There were no more references to Nick, Giles and Laura and the conversation reverted to politics, the state of the nation and the global economic situation. Edmund was relieved to discover that he and Andreas were at least united on one thing: they were still Tories to the core.

After dinner they repaired to the lounge where, ensconced in deep armchairs, cigars in their hands and a fine old Cognac and coffee on the table in front of them Edmund, having tested the waters, got down to the real purpose of the meeting.

'Andreas, I'm wondering whether you would be interested in a little business proposition.'

'Oh?' Andreas felt immediately on the alert. 'Of what nature?'

'Well,' Edmund took a few deep puffs, swallowed some more Cognac and proceeded. 'I am, as you know, a solicitor specialising in corporate finance. I have a number of clients with large funds to invest and others in need of capital.'

'And which category do I come into?' Andreas, unaccustomed to a large amount of wine, was feeling slightly drunk.

'Of course I don't suppose you need money, but if you do . . .'

'No, just joking.' Andreas waved a hand dismissively.

'I try and marry the needs of one with the capacity of another. Of course there's some risk, there always is, but on the whole I think I can say I have a list of satisfied clients.'

Andreas, no slouch when it came to matters of business,

even if he had had too much to drink, looked sharply at his companion.

'Is all this perfectly legit?'

'My dear Andreas,' Edmund appeared deeply affronted by the question, 'do you think I could possibly discuss anything with you that wasn't? After all, we have known each other many years and our sons have been best friends. No, the fact is,' he studied the tip of his cigar, 'no, it is simply that I know you to be a man of means and . . . well . . . if you've funds at your disposal . . .'

'I'm *quite* interested,' Andreas said cautiously, 'but I'd be happier if you could give me examples of people, companies you've had dealings with, naming names of course.'

'Ah . . .' Edmund put his head on one side in imitation of a wise old bird. 'You wouldn't like *me* to give people details about *you*, would you?'

'Well, then, examples, but leave out the names . . .'

'Right.' Edmund took a deep breath and, for the next twenty minutes or so, took Andreas through a number of cases involving many companies and substantial sums of money. All the time Andreas watched Edmund carefully. He was an astute man of business and always believed he could tell when someone wasn't straight. He didn't particularly trust lawyers, but it was hard to credit that, in the circumstances, and considering all that was at stake, Harvey would set him up. As he listened, his eyes roved from time to time towards the members, some of them somnolent by now, in their deep comfortable armchairs: the backbone of the nation, pillars of the community. For generations, Harveys had been members of clubs like these, clubs that had their own codes of honour that few would dare offend.

Yes, it would be very nice, very satisfying if one day he, like them, could also consider himself well and truly to have arrived, no longer a third generation Greek immigrant, nouveau riche to boot, but a member of the Establishment, just like the Harveys.

At the end of the recital, which was impressive, he nodded and, after a brief pause, said: 'How much are we talking about?'

Edmund appeared to consider, looked at the ceiling, at the man beside him and, finally, lowering his voice: 'In the first instance? A million?'

Then, glancing at the tip of his cigar, he noted that by now it had gone quite cold.

CHAPTER 12

The garish lights from the amusement arcade opposite combined with the noise from the disco next door, to say nothing of the heat and Giles's restlessness in bed, contrived to give Laura another sleepless night. There had been too many of these since they arrived in Sydney, having abandoned their plans for further travel in Australia due to lack of money. The dingy hotel in the Kings Cross area of Sydney had been their home for almost a month, although it was the last place in the world you could call 'home'. Home it was not.

Laura abandoned her frantic attempts to sleep, banged the pillow into a ball and lay on her back staring at the kaleidoscopic effects of the strobe lights dancing upon the ceiling. She recalled with a pang then, as she so often did these days, lying awake in the morning at home listening to the distant thunder of traffic up the motorway. She also remembered, more vividly and with a terrible feeling of loss and yearning, lying in her bed at Oxford; sometimes with Nick by her side, sometimes not, aware of the peace surrounding her, the great and beautiful silence. Then the nostalgia overwhelmed her and she wept silently into her pillow, so as not to disturb Giles.

She wondered how anyone could sleep in this town where there was no demarcation between night and day. Only sometimes, when dawn appeared on the horizon and the rubbish carts started their early morning clear-up and began a different kind of noise, did there seem a lull and one's eyelids began to close, but not for long. She began work at eleven and had to be on her feet by ten.

It had all been very different when, six months before, they had landed in Sydney, stayed at the Park Hyatt, ate at the Rockpool, attended a concert in the spectacular Opera House on the Harbour and seen all the sights of Sydney and beyond: the Blue Mountains, Ku-ring-gai Chase National Park, Berrima in the Southern Highlands – an almost perfectly preserved Georgian settlement – and Lake Illawarra, south of Wollongong.

Sydney was an enchanting city, or so it seemed on that first visit, and its environs equally varied, beautiful and spectacular.

Still on a high and, more importantly, still in funds, they flew to Darwin in the Northern Territory, hired a car and drove along the Stuart Highway through hundreds of miles of arid scrub and huge termite mounds to Alice Springs and Ayers Rock, known nowadays as Uluru, on the way catching their first sight of kangaroos. It was still the dry season but after that the weather turned and so, in a way, did their fortunes.

Money didn't exactly run out but became scarcer, and they began backpacking in earnest, hitching lifts and staying in cheap lodgings. They went into Western Australia, the original first home of the Aborigines, touching the deserted and the beautiful Kimberley coastline with its scattered tropical islands and sandy beaches, crossing the Bungle Bungle Range of sandstone mountains in a jeep with some more affluent tourists they fell in with. Then, saying goodbye to their friends, hitching more lifts and travelling via the Canning Stock Route, skirting the Gibson Desert and the Great Victoria Nature Reserve, into South Australia, where Giles would have liked to make for the wine areas of the Coonawarra and the Barossa Valley in search of work. But Australia was a huge continent, its distances compared to England immeasurable, and what looked a short distance on the map was proving the opposite. They wanted to get to Sydney before the Australian winter came, and Laura in particular was tired of travelling and longing for home.

So instead of proceeding south towards Adelaide, they hugged the northern extremities of the State; on past Lake Eyre and the Simpson Desert, via the Oodnadatta and Birdsville Tracks, into Queensland where they made straight for Brisbane, the state capital, and stayed at the YHA hostel in the hope of finding work.

That was really when the fun stopped and life began in earnest. Giles did a variety of jobs, none of which paid well, and Laura found work where she could in bars and cafés. They made their way down the Gold Coast with a brief stop and more work at Surfers Paradise, a glitzy, tatty resort, until they reached Sydney just as summer was ending. But this time they stayed not at the Hyatt or the Regent but found a room in a backpacker's lodge in the Kings Cross area whose seedy atmosphere resembled its London namesake, housing pimps, prostitutes, drug addicts, down-and-outs and the general flotsam and jetsam of social derelicts and misfits.

By this time Giles and Laura were totally out of funds. Giles, who once had a rather glamorised vision of working on a sheep farm or a vineyard, found himself cleaning cars at a taxi firm in nearby Darlinghurst while Laura got a job in a bar/restaurant on Bondi Beach. At least she was away from the clammy heat of the city and within sight of the ocean though Bondi, apart from its famous crescent-shaped sandy beach, had little of the glamour she had expected, being flanked by tacky bars and eating places and third-rate shops catering mainly for tourists.

Giles stirred but did not wake, he lay on his back with one hand flung sideways away from him. His mouth hung open and he had a few days' growth of beard. Laura looked at him with distaste and began to get gingerly out of bed so that she would not wake him.

They had become lovers by accident, and not because they had fallen in love or were ever likely to, at least not from Laura's side. She supposed that with Giles it was lust, the normal male desire to copulate with a woman he found sexually attractive. With her it was because she felt she owed him so much. Their relationship moved from a platonic to a physical level because during their travels they were forced to share a room. The step from sharing a bed to sex was almost inevitable.

They had never had a great rapport as lovers. Laura found Giles clumsy and inexpert, insensitive too after Nick. She thought that Giles might never have heard of the female orgasm because he was strangely indifferent to her feelings. Consequently, for her, it was mainly sex without pleasure and from that grew dislike.

This was a pity because, for a long time, they had a good relationship as companions and friends. They enjoyed travelling, and the sights and sounds of that glorious country to which, she felt, one day she would certainly return. The relationship also began to deteriorate because of over-familiarity, being together all the time, petty squabbles. Giles had never really known poverty. She remembered how he sometimes stayed at the Randolph when he came to Oxford. He basically didn't like travelling rough and staying in flea pits, and it made him disagreeable and morose.

Yes, one day she would like to return to Australia, but not with Giles. Maybe with Nick.

Laura knew it was futile to speculate about that. She had not written to him to explain her rather thoughtless and disgraceful conduct – she had not dared – and she had not heard from him; but she still loved him and the part of her that had broken away from him still cried out, in self-reproach, daily.

Laura threw on some clothes and then went down the corridor to wash and do her teeth in the grotty shower room that served the whole floor. Later she'd have a swim, which was the main way of keeping clean. She crept back to their room, and was about to slide her washing kit and towel through the door when Giles called out: 'Laura!'

'Yes?'

'What the devil are you up to?'

'Going to work, mate,' she said, preparing to close the door.

'What time is it, Laura?' Giles was shaking his head in an attempt to waken himself up.

'It's gone ten.'

'Christ, Laura, why didn't you wake me? I'll get the sack.'

'You didn't ask me to wake you,' she said sulkily, preparing to leave again.

'Don't be such a little shit, Laura. You want me to lose this job?'

Laura leaned against the wall and gazed at him. He'd been out drinking the night before, without her, and he looked a mess. She realised that she really despised Giles. Once she had admired him, looked up to him, found him dashing, unusual, different from Nick. There had been something rather wicked about Giles whereas there was nothing wicked at all about Nick. On the contrary: Nick was good, he was reliable, he was faithful, loving. Was it that she had in a very short time found Nick just a bit dull? Had he seemed dull, or was it really only his money that had come between them? Or was it that she still blamed Nick for being rusticated?

Giles appeared to have dozed off to sleep again and Laura quietly took up the canvas bag in which she kept her things, slid out of the room and flew down the corridor.

As soon as the door closed Giles was immediately wide awake. He jumped out of bed and rushed to the door flinging it open.

'Hi, Laura!' he called, but she'd gone. He was naked, so instead of running along the corridor, and the chance of bumping into someone, he went back into the room and arrived at the window just in time to see her crossing the street and head in the direction of the bus stop. A man on the pavement glanced behind him as she passed and, stopping, stood watching her. She was a tall, striking girl who moved easily and confidently, her bronze curly hair billowing out behind her. The bloke seemed in half a mind whether or not to follow her. Laura created that kind of reaction. Men were always looking at her. He supposed he should feel jealous but he didn't. Frankly if someone had taken her off his hands he wouldn't have minded at all; but until someone did he felt a responsibility for her.

Giles remained at the window until Laura was out of sight. Then he turned and went back to bed. He felt depressed and he felt hung over. He sat on the bed and looked round the dismal room, which had the bare essentials to conform to Government tourist standards. It was a very far cry from the Hyatt where they'd stayed when they'd first arrived. In fact, Giles had never stayed in a place like it until he'd come to Australia.

He lay down on the bed and closed his eyes. His head ached and his mouth was dry. He'd had much too much beer the night before, going from bar to bar with a few cronies from work, hoping that he might hear of better jobs, maybe something in the wineries in the Hunter Valley about a hundred miles from Sydney. All he heard about were other badly-paid jobs locally, and he got propositioned by a couple of gays.

His relationship with Laura had been disastrous. He had been so keen to go away with her, but he thought guilt about Nick prevented him loving her. All the time he was aware of Nick's hurt and how he would face him when he got home. He, Giles, had offended against the sacred trust that bound men of their sort together: the old school tie.

Or maybe the truth was that, although sexy, Laura wasn't his type. Truth to tell he thought he preferred those clean-cut, well-reared young women, like the sisters of his friends who, in their middle age, would eventually resemble his mother.

He had been clumsy with Laura. He knew very little about sex, and hadn't wanted her to know that she was his first woman. She wasn't very expert either, and neither of them knew anything more than the basics about contraception. He was left to fumble about with condoms which he found messy and vaguely disgusting.

Though at times exhilarating, the whole Australian experience had frightened him. He hated not having money, being down on his luck, being with a woman he was not in love with, with whom sex was difficult and unsatisfactory. He longed, now, to go home.

Depressed with his thoughts, Giles decided he would go back to sleep rather than go to work, and that when he woke he would spend the day on the Rocks, the rocky promontory opposite the Opera House where the original convict tents were pitched in 1788. There he and Laura had had some of their best days when they first arrived in Sydney, exploring the place and the old eighteenth-century buildings – the first fort, hospital, bakery – that still remained. There, full of energy, hope and enthusiasm, they had dreamed of the adventures that lay ahead of them. Today he would really make an effort to revive those dreams and in the evening he would take Laura out to dinner and try and devise some more positive plan for the future to make up to her for the pig he knew he'd been.

Laura sat on top of the double-decker bus taking her to Bondi Beach and her destination at Leo's Bar/Restaurant in the Bondi Pavilion. As she had no work permit, the job was poorly paid, but any money was better than none and they were skint. What had once seemed glamorous had become a tedious chore, and she longed to throw it all in and go home. Sometimes on impulse she had thought of telephoning Nick and asking for some money; but right now she couldn't bring herself to do it. To go begging to Nick would be a complete capitulation, and she still had too much pride to admit defeat.

The bus came in sight of the sea and she prepared to descend, jumping off at the stop and making her way swiftly through the crowds drifting down to the beach, to the bar. The Australians really did say 'g'day'. They said it all the time and after saying 'g'day' to her boss she got on with her work, which was to prepare the tables for lunch.

Leo had come as a baby to Australia with his parents. When he was a teenager they had decided to return to Italy. Leo had stayed behind and, in due course, opened the bar which bore his name. It was a clean, well-run establishment with a smarter clientele than some of the other places around. This was reflected in the prices he charged, which were designed to keep away the druggies and the dropouts who were common in the area. When trade was slack Laura sometimes chatted to Leo, who was about thirty-five, married with children, and who lived in the fashionable suburb of Kirribilli, north of the Harbour Bridge. She wondered today if she might take him to one side and explore the possibility of a loan. On the other hand, if she did, he might be eager to replace her once he knew that she wasn't going to stay. Then she'd be without a job altogether.

At about three o'clock Laura was sitting in the kitchen having a cool drink when Leo came to the door and beckoned to her. She finished her fruit squash, jumped up and followed him to his office next to the kitchen, where he invited her to sit down. She was immediately apprehensive and wondered if it was something about her lack of a work permit.

208

'Laura,' Leo said, taking his seat behind the desk, 'this is very difficult for me to say because I'm very pleased with your work. But I know that you're backpacking and, well, I have an Australian girl interested in this job and . . .'

'But, Leo, I want to stay on.' Laura, suddenly panic-stricken, leaned forward. 'I like it here. We have no intention of leaving yet.'

'Come off it, Laura,' Leo said in a tone that was not quite as friendly as the one she was used to. 'You know you're not going to stay, and with winter approaching, I'm having to reduce staff anyway.' He stood up. 'Sorry, Laura.'

'You don't mean goodbye *now*?' she said, aghast.

'Yes, why don't you take the rest of the day off?' He looked at the clock on the wall. 'I'll pay you off and you can go right now. Spend some time on the beach.'

'Leo, have I done anything wrong?' Laura felt close to tears.

'On the contrary, Laura. You've been first class, and I like you. But I'm always worried in case the authorities check up on me. I have a good place here and I want to stay on the right side of the law.' He handed her an envelope. 'I've put a few extra dollars in the packet, Laura, and I do wish you every luck. Come back and have a drink with us before you go.' He reached out to shake her hand, but she withheld hers.

'I think you've behaved very shabbily, Leo. I've given you all I've got, worked late whenever you wanted me to and now I'm dismissed without notice.'

Leo put his head on one side. 'That's the way of the world, Laura. If you come and work without a permit you're taking a risk, and your employer is taking a risk too. I wish you luck, Laura. Goodbye.' And he turned his back, signifying that the interview was at an end.

Laura picked up her bag and went into the kitchen to say goodbye to the rest of the staff. She had only been there a few weeks and she didn't know them very well, but there had been something about the place and she was sorry to leave. Now that the summer was ending she knew it would be very hard to find a job and a feeling of complete despair suddenly overwhelmed her.

She left the bar and walked towards the beach, not wanting to go back to the hotel. She sat there for a long time letting the sand run through her fingers, watching the bathers in the sea and the surfers riding the waves.

She'd brought her bathing costume and towel with her, thinking that after work she'd have a swim. Now she changed rapidly, and leaving her things in a neat bundle – she had carried no money with her except the bus fare and some loose coins – she coiled her hair above her head and walked towards the waves, flinging herself in, relishing the sensation of the cold clear water on her skin. She was a strong swimmer and she struck out away from the shore, the sound of the surf drowning the warning that was being shouted at her by one of the lifeguards who had started to run in her direction.

Laura felt liberated by the sea and headed firmly towards the horizon. Maybe it would be nice to go on swimming until she was too tired to go back, let herself float on a tide of oblivion? To fade away on a sea of forgetfulness. She swam and swam, riding with the waves and being tossed back by them. Suddenly a huge wave rose towards her, she braced herself to withstand it and, too late, saw the surfer coming over on the crest above her. She dived to avoid it but she didn't stand a chance. The last thing she heard before darkness claimed her was an awful drumming in her head, which felt as though it had split open.

By ten o'clock Giles decided to go to Leo's and find out what had happened to Laura. All his plans for a nice evening had evaporated and he felt intensely irritated and annoyed and, just slightly, worried. He felt that if she was working late, as she sometimes did, the least she could have done was telephone. On the other hand, she'd been annoyed with him in the morning; he'd been rude to her and this maybe was her way of paying him back.

When Giles got to the bar it was full of people, sitting outside as well as in. It was a balmy evening with a warm breeze and the gentle sound of the surf breaking on the shore. Giles stood around for some time looking for Laura but there was no sign of her. The barman polishing glasses behind the bar knew him and kept looking in his direction. Finally Giles went up to him and said: 'Is Laura around?'

The barman shook his head and then from around the corner of the bar Leo appeared. He seemed surprised to see Giles.

'Hi, Giles!' he said, looking slightly nervous.

'Hi!'

'Something wrong?' Leo spoke again.

'I'm looking for Laura.'

'Laura's not here.'

'She hasn't come home.'

Leo shrugged in an offhand way and was about to turn his back when Giles said: 'What time did she leave?'

'About three.'

'*Three*!' Giles gasped. 'Three o'clock this afternoon?'

'That's what I said.' Leo looked around and beckoned to Giles. 'Say, Giles, come into my office for a moment,' and Leo lifted the bar and pointed towards the door, standing to one side as Giles preceded him. Leo didn't ask him to come in but spoke standing up, just outside the door.

'Giles, I gave Laura notice to quit this afternoon. Nothing wrong with her, she's very good, but I need permanent staff. I know you're going back to England.'

'Well, not right away . . .'

'I know, but eventually. Also, I get nervous employing people without a permit.'

211

'Was Laura upset?'

Leo looked at the floor. 'Well, she wasn't exactly pleased. I gave her some extra cash and off she went.'

'You've no idea where she went?'

'Well, no. I guess she's at home by now and when you get back you'll find her there. No hard feelings, Giles? I mean Laura is a great girl . . .'

One of the waiters en route from the kitchen with a tray balanced on one hand stopped to get past and glanced at Giles.

'Did I hear someone say that Laura was not at home?'

'Yes. Were you on this afternoon?'

The waiter shook his head. 'But I did hear there was an accident on the beach. Maybe you should . . .'

Laura looked very peaceful, a little smile on her face as though in her dreams she had found some happiness. If he hadn't been told differently, Giles would have thought she was dead.

'Is she still unconscious?' he whispered to the young doctor standing next to him, who shook his head.

'She's sleeping, heavily sedated. She had a nasty bump.' He pointed to her skull which was swathed in bandages. 'She was very lucky not to have been killed or severely brain-damaged.'

'How did it happen?'

'There was some surfing championship and the area where she was swimming was out of bounds. She either failed to see or observe the warnings and the lifeguard was too late to save her. She was knocked unconscious by the surfboard, but luckily the guard who had seen her, and tried to warn her, pulled her from the water and resuscitated her. She is very lucky to be alive.'

'And she's OK?' Giles looked at him anxiously.

'As far as we can tell. We did a brain scan and there is no

apparent damage. We'll keep her in here for a few days just to be sure. She'll probably feel very woozy anyway with that wound.' The doctor paused and looked closely at Giles. 'I don't suppose it could have been deliberate?'

'Deliberate?' Giles didn't appear to understand.

'You know, tried to do herself in. It seemed such a very dangerous thing to do, unless she was desperate about something. If you think it might be so, I'll have the psychiatrist come along and have a chat with her.'

'Oh, no.' Giles shook his head vigorously. 'I don't think she'd try anything like that. She's not that sort.'

'Oh, good.' The young man seemed reassured. 'Just thought I'd check.' He shook his head. 'It really was a stupid thing to do.'

Giles sat by Laura's side throughout the night, and wondered. *Was* it possible that she had indeed intended to kill herself? Everyone knew the beaches were dangerous, and when there were surfing championships they kept well away. Laura knew that as well as anybody. Yet she'd just had the sack. She'd had a row with him. They'd both been low for ages. He began to feel terribly responsible for what had happened to her.

Once in the small hours she looked as though she was about to wake. Her eyelids flickered but didn't open. Regularly throughout the night the nurses monitored her blood pressure and temperature, and in the morning another doctor came to supervise a change of dressing and inspect her wound.

Giles nearly fainted himself when he saw the gash on her temple, and how her head had been shaved when they stitched the wound, which was about four inches long.

Laura opened her eyes when they were changing the dressing and for a long time she gazed at Giles. He looked at her sadly, wanting to reach out and hold her hand.

'Hi!' she said eventually.

'Hi!' He gave a sheepish grin. 'Glad you're alright.'

'God, my head.' Laura lifted a hand gingerly to feel the wound but the nurse gently stopped her. 'Does it hurt, dearie?' she enquired and, when Laura nodded, 'we'll give you something to make you go to sleep again.'

'How did it happen, Laura?' When the dressing was finished Giles bent forward so that only she could hear.

'I can't remember a thing . . .' Laura's limpid eyes suddenly filled with tears and she stretched out a hand towards him. 'Let's go home, Giles. *Please* let's go home.'

Back at the hotel Giles shaved, had a shower, changed his clothes and went out to a bar down the road where he had coffee and a sandwich. It was nearly noon but at home it would be two in the morning. The earliest he could ring would be five o'clock New South Wales time. Giles tried to compose himself but it was very difficult. He felt in a turmoil. It was going to be hard enough to admit defeat and failure, and that they'd had a bad time. But worst of all he felt that he hadn't taken sufficient care of Laura and that her accident was really his fault.

If it *was* an accident. He couldn't rule out the possibility that, as the hospital doctor had suggested, what Laura had done might have been deliberate. The sacking, on top of everything else that had gone wrong, might have been the last straw.

Giles finished his food, paid for it, and then set off in the direction of the hospital on Macquarie Street, but when he came to the Victorian sandstone building he walked past it and continued towards the harbour in the direction of the Rocks. Reaching Sydney Cove he found a bar and had a beer, sitting for a long time looking towards the Opera House and the bridge and watching the busy ferries as they plied industriously to and from the wharves.

He thought Sydney was a place he would like to return to. Maybe one could start a new life here, begin again. Or would it have too many unhappy memories of fear and failure?

Maybe one day, armed with a work permit, he would make it to the wineries of the Barossa or Hunter Valleys. As it struck five, Giles finished his beer and went to the telephone at the back of the bar. He had plenty of change and he put the coins in the telephone, dialled several numbers and listened to the telephone ringing thousands of miles away. He realised his heart was thumping and he prayed that his mother would answer rather than his father.

But then the ringing stopped and that familiar, well-modulated voice said: 'Hello?'

'Mum, is that you?'

'Giles, darling, where are you?' Valerie sounded pleased but, as always, controlled.

'I'm still in Sydney, Mum. Did you get my cards?'

'A letter *would* have been nice.' The voice now sounded rather reproachful. 'Giles, why . . .'

'Mum, I can't talk. I'm at a call box. Look, Mum, Laura's had a terrible accident. She's OK, but as soon as we can we'll be on our way home.'

PART IV

The Silver Spoon: Emma

CHAPTER 13

Giles stood for some time looking round the room trying to acclimatise himself to the gloom and the noise. He did not really know why he'd come; driven, he supposed, by boredom. He'd found his old membership card in a drawer in his bedroom and decided to use it to get in, though he hadn't visited the place for at least a couple of years.

He'd explained at the door that he'd been in Australia and they gave him an updated membership card on payment of the required fee. He thought the last time he'd been here had been with a group of friends during the Christmas break while he was still at university.

Having accustomed himself to his environment, Giles strolled across to the bar and ordered a beer. Then, glass in hand, he went over to a corner where he found himself a table and sat down, surveying the scene. Couples gyrated in time to the beat of the music, some dancing closely, some doing their own thing, touching occasionally, joining hands briefly from time to time. As well as mixed couples, men were dancing with men and women with women. Anything went. In some ways it reminded him of Australia, though really the scene could be universal.

Giles sat sipping his beer and gradually the figures on the floor became more discernible. He could pick out faces, although it was not always easy to distinguish men from women. He was quite enjoying the atmosphere, the fact that he could be here on his own and no one took any notice of him or bothered him. It might have been nicer to have brought a few mates or a girl, but it didn't matter. Giles finished his beer, rose to get another and, bumping into a couple who had come careering across the floor towards him, politely stood to one side and said: 'I'm sorry.' Though, in fact, it wasn't his fault. The couple seemed to have difficulty regaining their balance and Giles reached out to help pull the woman to her feet, realising they were both probably very drunk, or stoned, or both. He took hold of both the woman's hands and gently pulled her up, and as he did the strobe pinpointed them and he could see her face quite clearly, head back, eyes closed, mouth a little open.

'Emma!' he cried. But the woman didn't register and Giles, looking down, saw that her partner had passed out on the floor at his feet. It seemed to him that Emma was semi-conscious and he tried to sit her down in the chair he'd been occupying, but as soon as he did she slipped sideways.

As no one else was taking any notice of his predicament, and he supposed it was one that was not uncommon in a joint like this, he hauled Emma to her feet and, half lifting, half dragging, got her to a side door on which were the bold letters EMERGENCY EXIT. He pushed the bar and almost collapsed outside, where he propped Emma against the wall while he recovered, breathing heavily. Now what to do? Maybe he should have left her where she was. There was surely some kind of provision for people who collapsed in a club where drink and drugs were freely available. Maybe he should take her back and leave her inside the door? But he knew he couldn't. If anything were to happen to Emma he would never be able to forgive himself.

Giles was now in a quandary. Having gone to a Soho club for a few beers and a bit of relaxation, he now found himself in an unexpected predicament, due purely to an act of kindness. He was saddled with the sister of his former best friend who was drunk and helpless in a dark narrow alley off

Gerrard Street. It was nearly midnight, it was January and bitterly cold and Giles did the only thing he could do. Leaving Emma, who had started to slide down the wall where she stood, he went out into Gerrard Street to look for a taxi. He soon found one and, giving the driver instructions and asking him to wait, he went back to get Emma, who seemed to be reviving, maybe due to the cold air, and actually walked the last few steps to the cab.

The driver looked dubiously at Giles and his charge.

'I hope she's not going to be sick in my cab, guv.'

'I hope so too,' Giles said grimly, and slipped the driver a ten-pound note through the window. 'There'll be another one when we get to Lamb's Conduit Street.'

The driver pocketed the note and, without a word, set his cab in a westerly direction.

Emma Constantine woke in a strange place in a strange bed. She guessed from the faint aura round the curtained window that it might be dawn, or maybe a bit later. She had no idea where she was or how she'd got here. She had no clothes on except for her pants; she hadn't worn a bra but she could see in the gloom that her clothes were draped neatly over a chair next to the bed. She reached out an arm, fumbled about a bit, found a light and put it on. It was rather a nice room, well and tastefully furnished, definitely masculine with ties round the mirror of the dressing table and a suit hanging on the outside of the wardrobe.

She felt, as usual, dreadful, with a raging thirst and a terrible head. She wondered where on earth Philip had got to and who this place belonged to.

She staggered out of bed, sat on the side for a moment to overcome a feeling of nausea, and then made for a door opposite, which was ajar. She groped for a switch, found one and, as she'd hoped, lit up the bathroom. She was immediately sick down the lavatory and remained on her knees for several minutes gazing into the bowl. Then she staggered to her feet, swayed, caught hold of the towel rail and, balancing herself carefully, got to the washbasin, sluiced her face in cold water and took a long long drink.

She grabbed a towel, wiped her face and, feeling marginally better, went back into the bedroom and climbed thankfully into bed, drawing the duvet right up to her chin. The door immediately in front of her opened slowly and a face peered round. She looked at it with curiosity, without fear but also without recognition. The door opened wider and a man dressed in a bathrobe came into the room carrying something and stood looking down at her.

Emma couldn't believe what or, rather, who, she saw and felt she should pinch herself to see if he was real.

'Giles?' she said tremulously, almost in a tone of enquiry.

'Giles it is,' he said smiling. 'Would you like a cup of tea?' And he held out his hand and placed a cup and saucer on the table by her bed.

'But how, where?' Emma looked round shaking her head. 'I have no idea how I got here.'

Giles sat on the side of her bed.

'I guess you remember the club?'

'Oh, I remember we were at the club. But where's Philip?'

'Well, I left the bloke you were with on the floor, I'm afraid. I could only cope with one.'

'Oh!' Emma looked crestfallen. 'It was that bad, eh?'

'It was bad. I had to bribe the taxi driver to bring you home.'

'And this is *home*? Gosh your mum and dad . . .' Emma looked at him aghast.

'This is *my* home, not theirs. I rented a flat near the law courts and the school where I'm studying law.'

'Ah!' she nodded. 'It's nice.'

'I like it.' Giles rose. 'Hang on and I'll fetch myself some tea.' He stopped and looked at her. 'If you don't mind?'

'Of course I don't mind. Golly, I just don't quite know where I'd be without you.'

Giles went over to the wardrobe and, taking a light dressing gown from it, tossed it to her. 'You might like this to keep you decent.'

'Thanks.' She grinned rather shamefacedly, and after he'd left the room shrugged it on. When he returned she had snuggled back against the pillows, teacup in hand. This time he didn't sit on the bed but in the chair, on the back of which were her clothes.

'I don't suppose you've got any Paracetamol?' she said.

'That bad, eh?' He got up.

'Terrible.'

Giles went into the bathroom and came back with a glass in which two tablets were fizzing.

'You'd make someone a lovely wife,' Emma said, taking the glass from him. 'Tea in bed, headache remedies . . .' She drank the liquid, put the glass by the bed and snuggled down again. 'What were *you* doing at Mephistos?'

'Well, I was there by myself, believe it or not. I'd had a hard day. I remembered I used to belong to it and renewed my membership. I'd just been there about half an hour and was about to get another beer when you came literally crashing back into my life.'

'Oh, gosh!' Emma put a hand to her mouth, half amused, half contrite.

'It was the most extraordinary coincidence.'

'I'll say.'

'Emma,' Giles wriggled in his seat, 'if I hadn't been there . . .'

'They've got a room where you can chill off. It's called "The Cooler". They'd have thrown us in there until one of us was fit to make the journey.'

From what she was saying, Giles gathered that this wasn't the first time Emma had found herself in such a situation.

He also thought that, in the circumstances, she didn't seem to mind very much. If this was regular behaviour he wondered what her parents thought about it.

He could see Emma was staring at him as if she could read his mind. 'You're wondering how often?'

'Kind of,' he nodded.

'Quite often. And now you're wondering what my parents say?'

Again Giles nodded.

'I think they're worried, but they put it down to youthful high spirits. Usually I go home anyway, or back to Phil's. Last night was an exception. We both went over the top. Phil had lost his job and most of his trouble was drink. He doesn't usually pass out.'

'Is Phil,' Giles paused, 'the boyfriend?'

Emma screwed up her nose. 'He's *a* friend. A good friend. He is a very good friend as a matter of fact.'

'Won't he be worried?'

'He may be. I'll phone him later. He was told to clear his desk and leave, just like that, so he won't be at work. Maybe we'll meet for lunch if I can get myself out of bed.' She groaned and lay back on the pillows again.

'And your mother?'

'I'll call her. I've got a very good friend, Sue, and I always say I'm with Sue.' She looked at him defensively. 'This doesn't happen *a lot*, Giles. It happens *sometimes*. I'm a big girl now. I'm twenty-one.'

'Emma, what do you do with yourself?' Giles asked, putting down his cup.

'How do you mean? *Do* with myself?'

'Do you work? Do you have a job?'

Emma shook her head. 'Uh, uh.'

'Don't you want a job, don't you want to do anything? Go to college maybe?'

'Giles, you know I'm not academic.' Emma began to look

224

restlessly about. 'And please don't give me the third degree. After all, from what I hear you haven't done so brilliantly yourself, messed up poor Nick's love life, to say nothing of what happened to Laura. She nearly died I understand.'

Giles rose and, going over to the dressing table, began to sort through one of the drawers. Finally he took out a pair of socks and what were obviously clean underpants.

'That's a part of my life over which I'd prefer to draw a veil,' he said. 'It's not something I'm proud of especially.'

'I should think it isn't. Well, then that's what I feel too. I am not particularly proud of this lifestyle either. But for the moment and until something better turns up it's how I live.'

'Sorry.' Giles turned to gaze down at her and thought how vulnerable she looked. Tired, drawn, older than her years. She stared back at him rather defensively as though daring him to say more. 'I did screw things up,' he said. 'And you're right. Laura nearly lost her life. But that was nothing to do with me. It was an accident that could have happened to anyone.'

'If it *was* an accident.' Emma looked at him oddly. 'Nick said . . .'

'Nick knew absolutely nothing about what happened. He has not talked to me about it because we haven't seen each other, and I don't think he's seen Laura either.'

'No, he hasn't.'

'So how does he know?'

'I guess he's hurt. He loved her very much.'

'I know.' Giles turned away. 'And now two friendships are smashed up. His and mine, his and Laura's, and throw in a third and you can say Laura and mine too. I did her no favours, and it's an episode of my life I very much regret. But now I'm trying to make up for it. I'm taking the law seriously. I'm working hard and maybe one day I can make things up with Laura and Nick too. My parents have been brilliant. After an initial rocket from my dad there were no more recriminations. They're paying for my course, they give me an allowance, and they didn't even mind when I left home.'

Emma, sitting up in bed, her arms round her knees, rested her chin against them.

'Parents are great,' she said. 'Mine are great too. Say, Giles, thanks for the rescue. Maybe we can see each other again?'

'I'll give you a call,' Giles said, looking at his watch. 'Meanwhile I have to run. My first class is at nine.' And he went into the bathroom, shutting the door behind him, while Emma lay back listening to the swishing sounds made by the shower.

After Giles had gone, Emma got unsteadily out of bed and, with a hand that was beginning to tremble, hurried over to her bag which she opened. She only hoped that Giles hadn't inspected the contents, but being a gentleman she didn't think he had. Snooping into people's bags wasn't the sort of thing that a gentleman would do.

She took from it a hypodermic syringe, a small silver teaspoon and a tiny packet of fine white powder, which she spread out on the table by the side of the bed. This she mixed on a teaspoon with a little water from a glass by her bed and carefully fed into the syringe. With the aid of a silk scarf that she'd worn the night before, she assembled a tourniquet round her arm and spent some time selecting a vein into which she then plunged the syringe, leaning forward tensely for a moment while she waited for the blessed feeling of relief and elation slowly to surge through her, and the trembling to cease. She packed away her kit and lay down on the bed letting her mind drift pleasantly towards oblivion, wondering what dear old Giles would say if he knew.

During that day and the ones that followed, Giles found himself preoccupied with thoughts of Emma. He knew he had always rather liked her, in a way fancied her. Maybe, because she was Nick's twin, there was something incestuous about his feelings for her. She and Nick hardly resembled each other, but there was something about them that indicated their closeness.

Of course, too, in a way Emma had always been a mate. He had known her since she was thirteen when he and Nick had established a rapport on their first day at school. There was a cosy, casual informality about his relationship with her, but that morning he had been particularly aware that they were alone together in a bedroom, and that when he had put her to bed the night before he had removed most of her clothes.

Was that the first time he had been conscious of an erotic sensation about Emma? He wasn't sure. He thought maybe not. During the holiday on the yacht, he had been very aware of her as a woman rather than a chum, had been interested when she sunbathed topless on the boat as it ploughed through the warm Mediterranean waters.

In a way she would have been a better companion for his Australian trip than Laura; but at that time it was Laura who obsessed him, not Emma. Now, Laura no longer interested him at all. And Emma was beginning to.

It was a chastened and much wiser Giles who had returned nine months before from Australia, as soon as Laura had recovered. They had parted immediately on their return despite the invitation to Laura by his mother, who met them at the airport, to spend a few days in London. Since then they had hardly communicated, though he rang her every now and then to see how she was. She reported no ill effects from the accident and that she was now back working in the chemist's shop, looking after her father and studying hard for her exams to return to Oxford.

It was as though Australia had never been, but it had. It was an experience Giles couldn't get out of his mind. There, for the first time, he had been at his worst and most vulnerable. There was a lot about Giles Harvey he had discovered he didn't like. Nick didn't like him either. There was no forgiveness there, no willingness to re-establish their old and long friendship, no invitation to the yacht the previous summer.

And now Emma and the Constantines had come back into his life again in the most unexpected of ways.

Giles waited a week or two before he telephoned Emma. He was rather nervous about ringing the house, but to his relief the phone was answered by Maria, the domestic who was still with the family, and Emma was in. They saw each other that night. They went to a film in Swiss Cottage and then to Lemonia, the fabulous Greek-Cypriot restaurant in Regent's Park Road. It had been a good evening and there were many others like it. They slipped into the easy-going camaraderie of their adolescence and enjoyed each other's company.

Then one night there was sex, back in Giles's flat. It was impetuous, passionate and very good. There was a harmony between their bodies he had never known with Laura. He couldn't believe it, nor could Emma. Neither could believe that at last they had found someone with whom they could be happy.

Yet there was something about Emma that worried Giles. She was so moody, at times distant, at times loving, at times she was offhand and rude. He didn't quite know what to make of her.

Another complication was that the affair was a secret both from Emma's parents and Giles's. Giles was still considered to have betrayed his best friend, to have behaved shamefully and, well, the Harveys would not have been delighted by the news either. This added spice to the relationship, a touch of the Romeo and Juliet scenario enacted in the unlikely setting of London of the nineteen-nineties.

One day, when the relationship was about four months'

old, Giles returned to the flat to pick up a file for one of his lectures that he had forgotten. As usual, he had left Emma in bed in the morning and they did not expect to meet again until that evening.

It was about eleven, and at first the silence was so profound that he thought Emma must have left. But when he pushed open the bedroom door he heard sounds from the bathroom, Emma singing, and he smiled to himself, relieved that all was well because the night before she had been in one of her moods, as though she had formed a barrier between them he had been unable to penetrate. At times like this he began to despair, and to wonder if they would ever be able to form the strong and enduring relationship that he was hoping for. Because, finally, he realised that he was in love. That Emma, mysterious Emma, was the one for him. Giles was about to go back into the living room to collect his file, and leave Emma to her ablutions, when a metallic gleam by the side of the bed caught his attention. It was a dark room and the bedside lamp was usually left on, and it was this light that illuminated an elongated object lying by its side.

Giles went over and, as he stooped to examine it, he was aware of a faint smell in the air; as he sat down heavily on the bed, he knew.

He thought perhaps he had always suspected, ever since they met, and that her preferring to make love in the dark was so that he would not see the tell-tale pinpricks on her arms. It also did much to explain her moods.

Giles sank his head in his hands just as Emma, wrapped in a towel, came out of the bathroom, her hair wet, still singing, and then stopped when she saw him. She put her hand to her mouth and gazed at him.

'Golly!' she said, and came and sat down beside him, putting an arm round his waist as if trying to comfort him. She leaned her head on his shoulder and for some time they sat like that in silence.

'Why did you come back?' she said at last. 'Did you guess?'

'I wanted a file for a lecture I have at twelve.'

'In that case you'd better go,' she said, glancing at the clock, 'or you'll be late.'

'I can't go now.'

'Didn't you guess? I was sure you knew and didn't say. I can give it up, you know, any time.'

'Then give it up.'

'I don't want to. I like the highs. I need them to stop me feeling so bloody miserable. That's why the sex is so good. That's why when I'm on a high everything is so good.'

'I thought you were only E-ing.' Occasionally they bought Ecstasy tablets at the club, or smoked a joint together. 'When did you start with heroin?'

'Well, Philip was into heroin, that's why he could never hold down a job. I just tried it for a lark. We smoked it to begin with, then we started to jag.' She looked at the syringe beside the bed. 'You get more of a high with the needle.'

Giles turned and seized her roughly by the arm. 'Then give it up for Christ's sake. Give it up *now*. Don't you realise, Emma, what it will do to you? Give it up and I'll help you. I love you. Oh, Emma, I love you so much, I need you so much, and the last thing in the world I want you to be is a junkie. Give it up for my sake, *please*.'

And he held her tightly in his arms and wept, because of all the pain of finding someone he realised he loved so much so deeply flawed.

Mary said: 'I thought you'd be so happy, Ed, that Adam passed the Common Entrance.'

'I am happy,' Edmund said woodenly.

'You don't sound happy.'

'Well, I am.'

'Trevor, the Head, said he's got a great future.'

'You call him Trevor now?'

230

Mary tried to hide the fact that she was blushing by taking a step back and walking behind him as they circled the pond in Regent's Park while Adam had a piano lesson in Camden Town. It was a chilly summer's day, below average temperature, with a steady drizzle, and they looked a miserable pair; a pair completely out of sorts and out of love with each other.

'Well, of course Trevor has been of enormous help to Adam. But for him he would never have passed Common Entrance and got into a good school. We owe Trevor a very great debt indeed.'

Edmund stopped and looked behind at her, waiting for her to catch up with him.

'Mary, about the school . . .'

'What about the school, Ed?' she said sharply, always on the defensive, alert for some underhand trick of Edmund's, something devious at the back of his crafty mind.

'Does it operate the Assisted Places scheme?'

'How do you mean does it operate the Assisted Places scheme?' She reddened again, but this time from anger rather than coyness. 'You're not suggesting that we should *demean* ourselves by applying for government help with all the disadvantages that would have for Adam?'

'I don't see why not. It's a perfectly respectable thing.'

'Is Paul on an Assisted Places scheme? Is Alice?'

'You know they're not.'

'Well, then.'

'Mary . . .' Edmund paused and breathed deeply several times. 'You know that, for my children, my income is assessed. For Adam, *your* income is assessed and I should have thought you were qualified to receive support which as far as I'm concerned,' he held up a hand as she tried to intervene. 'No, let me speak, let me finish what I have to say. Don't be so impetuous, Mary. As far as *I* am concerned, such help would be very welcome. I have the entire burden to bear of Adam's fees which I understand will amount to some nine thousand a year, and that's just for starters. In addition, I am supporting all my children, including Giles, and frankly the strain is wearing me down.' Edmund got out a handkerchief and mopped his brow. 'Sometimes I don't know how I can go on and that's a fact. The worry, the strain, is enormous. There is no shame in Assisted Places, no disgrace, none whatsoever.'

'I would feel ashamed,' Mary said, flopping suddenly on a dry patch of grass by the side of the lake. 'I would feel deeply humiliated. Just because poor Adam has not the advantages of your other children . . .'

'Mary,' Edmund flopped down beside her, 'how often have I heard this in the last few years? It's like a never-ending litany of whining and complaining. I have done all I can for Adam and for you. You know that. I think in the circumstances I have been a good father. I have done my best. But recently things have been very difficult financially and, frankly, you don't seem to care. You've become very hard, Mary, and since we're no longer lovers I feel I don't understand you.'

'Maybe you'd rather not see me again?' Mary said.

'I didn't say that. I want to see you and I want to see Adam, but I also want you to apply for the Assisted Places scheme because, if you don't, I don't think I can afford the fees for the school, the very expensive school you have chosen for Adam.'

Edmund was about to rise, but Mary made a grab for his coat and pulled him towards her. He felt so angry he almost struck out and hit her, but the curious gazes of the passers-by stopped him. They were almost eyeball to eyeball, Mary still clinging fiercely onto the lapels of his jacket.

'Listen, Ed,' she said in a tone of voice he had never heard before, 'you pay that money, and you be sure you pay it and on time. I have fooled around with you for too many years solely because of my son. The only good thing that came out of my relationship with you *has* been my son. I am not going to have him, already disadvantaged, going around a pauper, dependent on the state. I have often threatened to disclose Adam's existence to Valerie and, believe me, if I hear any more nonsense about Assisted Places, this time I bloody well shall!'

Edmund wondered just how much a man could take as he drove shakily home, leaving Mary to pick up Adam on her own. One part of him thought that maybe to unburden himself to Valerie would be the best thing. Tell her the truth, all of it. But the other part knew that he couldn't risk it. If he told Valerie that he had been deceiving her for so many years, that he had a son she knew nothing about and, not only that, but he was in deep financial trouble because he was also cheating on his clients and could possibly go to prison ... Well, it was a bit much to suppose, certainly to hope that she would take it all on the chin. He knew he couldn't do it. The only chance he had now was to try and prolong the bluster. After all, it had gone on for a long time already, and there was always the possibility that one day everything he had gambled on would come good, that the tide would turn in his favour.

At last he was free of Mary. Their relationship had ended some time ago now. It had simply petered out. He nearly always saw her together with Adam. He was quite sure she was involved with someone else, maybe the Headmaster, and he didn't care. Sometimes he entertained a fantasy that one day he would simply pack up his gear and disappear and leave the rest of the world to get on with things without him.

Valerie wasn't at home when he got in. She was on one of her 'do good' missions among the hapless poor of East London, or some disadvantaged community or other north of the city, and had left him a cold meal in the fridge. Alice was with one of her friends, and Valerie said in her note that she would pick her up on the way home.

Edmund had a few whiskies, watched the news and then had his meal in the kitchen with half a bottle of wine.

Afterwards he climbed a little unsteadily to his study and, unlocking the drawer of his desk, got out the notebook in which he kept details of all his secret transactions. Finally he poured a fresh whisky from the bottle he kept in his study and put the telephone receiver to his ear, punched in a number and listened. He realised he was sweating heavily and the handset was sticky in the palm of his hand.

'Hello?' a voice said at the other end just as Edmund was about to put the phone down.'

'Andy?' Edmund boomed with false joviality. 'Is that you?'

'Yes.' The tone of voice was chilly. 'I was about to ring you, Edmund.'

'Oh, were you? Good. Well I have good news for you.'

'Oh!' The voice at the other end became more amiable. 'Were you? That's great.'

'I have found a seconder, at last, who is willing, despite the fact that he doesn't know you – he goes on my recommendation of course – and your adoption as a member will go up at the next selection meeting of the club.'

'It's taken a long time, Edmund.'

'It has and I'm sorry. But these things do.'

'But what I was going to telephone you about,' Andy's tone of voice was more assured, 'well, that little financial matter between us.'

'Yes?'

'How's it going?'

'It's going fine. Nothing to worry about . . .'

'I'm not exactly worried . . .'

'These things take time . . .'

'I know they do. But . . .'

'Another half a million would speed things up . . .'

'A *what*?'

'Half a million. My client is on the brink of great things. Look, maybe I can come round and show you the preliminary results?'

'That would be *very* good of you.' Andreas didn't attempt to hide his sarcasm. 'After all, I have expended a lot of money on vague promises. Some people might doubt my business acumen. I am regarded, I know, as a pretty tough customer to deal with, but you seem to have taken me for a patsy.'

'I say.' On the other end of the line, Edmund was visibly sweating. 'I do object to that.'

Andreas's tone grew more heated. 'I've trusted you because we have known each other a very long time. Our boys were at school together. Maybe I've let myself be taken in. A million quid is a lot of money, and now you're telling me you want more . . .'

'Look,' Edmund made a great effort to keep his tone soothing, moderate. 'This can easily be sorted out over lunch. At the club? I'll explain everything in detail then. Would Wednesday suit you. Say one o'clock?'

After agreeing, Andreas put down the phone and remained where he was for a few seconds, his head bent in thought. He had a profound feeling that his wish for social acceptance had overcome his sound business instincts. Yet, this was different from the usual cut and thrust of the marketplace he was used to. It was difficult to know just how to deal with a man, a respected solicitor of many years standing, who was about to propose you for a pukka London club. The last thing you wanted to do was insult him.

'Who was that, dear?' Lydia, passing in the hallway with a huge vase of freshly arranged flowers, paused and looked at her husband.

'Edmund.'

'Edmund Harvey?' She seemed surprised.

'Yes.'

'Haven't heard from them for ages, thank God. What on earth did he want?'

Lydia's love affair with the Harveys and her desire to emulate them and be approved of by them was long since over, and her tone was censorious.

'He wants money,' Andreas said with a sigh, following her into the drawing room.

'Money!' She swung round, nearly dropping the vase.

'It's a business matter. I should have told you about it but I didn't. It was after that trouble with Nick and I knew you'd be unhappy about it. Some time ago I let him have quite a considerable sum for investment. His projects sounded promising. I have yet to see a penny back and he wants more.'

'How much more, dear?' Lydia put down the vase and, sitting on the sofa, helped herself to a cigarette from an onyx box. Andreas leaned over and lit it for her with a matching lighter in the form of a dragon, the flame leaping from its mouth.

'Half a million. I let him have a million in the first place.'

'You must be joking!'

'I'm not. He took me to his club and set up the deal. It all seemed OK. I trusted him – after all, he *is* a Harvey – and I'm still not sure that it isn't all kosher. He wants to have lunch with me. I shan't give him a penny until I know more.'

Lydia leaned back in her chair and blew a long stream of smoke in the air.

'I never trusted that man, you know. I wouldn't have lent him a penny.'

'It wasn't a loan exactly. It was an investment.'

'Same thing. I wouldn't have invested in him either.'

'Why not?' Andreas looked at her uncomfortably.

'Well, look how Giles behaved, running off with that girl and then leaving her in the lurch, to say nothing about deceiving his best friend. Oh, I know they think they're better than the rest of us, and they certainly act like it, but, if you ask me, Andy, there are bad genes in that family.'

And through a cloud of tobacco smoke she gave her husband a knowing smile. 'You should have consulted *me*, dear, before you gave any money to Edmund Harvey.'

CHAPTER 14

As Laura came through the door Maggie looked up, a wide smile on her face.

'Greetings,' she said, rising to welcome her and, to Laura's embarrassment, kissed her on the cheek. 'And congratulations.' She pointed to a chair and Laura sat down, feeling almost overwhelmed by her tutor's reception.

Maggie had gone over to the kettle which she plugged in, and then fiddled around with mugs and coffee, chatting animatedly over her shoulder.

'You must have worked really hard. What sort of year did you have at home? How was Australia?'

Laura laughed.

'What will I answer first?'

'Whichever one you like.' Maggie brought the mugs over and set Laura's down in front of her. Then she squatted on a cushion on the floor and lit a cigarette. Laura thought it was very good to see Maggie, who hadn't changed a scrap in the past two years, and it was very good, very good indeed to be back in Oxford.

Laura had heard in July that she'd passed the exam and would be readmitted to the second year. It had enabled her to survive the summer, as working for the exam had helped her through the difficult time since her return from Australia. It had been hard to get away, to say goodbye to Mr Boothroyd, who had enjoyed having her work for him. It was harder still to say goodbye to her father who, she realised, was a sick man and who now only had his teenage son Gordon to look after him, and that wouldn't be for long as Gordon was ambitious and would follow his sister into higher education.

'Australia was a long time ago.' Laura tossed back her hair and paused to sip her coffee. 'It was an experience, but it wasn't a very happy time. Things with Giles didn't work out. We grated upon each other. We ran out of money and had to work. Giles wasn't used to roughing it. We had to do menial jobs as we hadn't a work permit. Giles didn't like the hardship.' Laura delicately fingered her brow, where Maggie could see a slight scar which disappeared into her hair. 'Then I had an accident swimming in the sea at Bondi, and we decided immediately to come home. In a way the accident was a blessing in disguise. Giles had some crazy idea I'd tried to kill myself, but I hadn't, although, to be honest, as I swam towards the horizon I remember thinking how nice it would be to get away from it all, a kind of natural reaction I guess to all that was going on.'

Maggie nodded sympathetically.

'And did you see Giles again?'

Laura shook her head. 'He telephoned a few times to keep in touch. I promised I'd pay him back the money for the fare, but when that will be I don't know. Not for a while.'

'And Nick?' Maggie lowered her eyes.

'I haven't seen Nick. I hear he got a very good degree?'

Maggie nodded. 'He also got his fellowship. But he's working on some project at the LSE. The future looks very bright for him.'

When she saw Laura's downcast expression she reached up and patted her on the knee. '*And* it's very bright for you. Your exam papers justified all the faith I had in you and, you know, I think your experiences these past two years have helped you to mature. They've broadened your mind.

You're not quite the girl you were when you left here. No experience you know, Laura, is ever wasted.'

No indeed. No experience was ever wasted but it was a pity, Laura thought, as she walked along the High swinging her bag, that one had to discover things the hard way, at so much personal cost. She felt wiser, more mature as Maggie had pointed out, but she felt older too, much much older than her fellow students in the second year, most of whom were nineteen whereas she had turned twenty-two in August. There seemed a big gap between nineteen and twenty-two.

Despite her joy at being back in Oxford, she also felt rootless, lost and a little depressed. Being there reminded her of Nick and the brief, beautiful doomed months of their love affair. It had undoubtedly been the best time of her life, but it also contained all the seeds of a Hardy novel; that such a love would inevitably founder because of the violent opposing forces of a savage and unrelenting destiny. Nick was rich, gifted, dedicated. She was poor, not nearly as gifted and lacking his dedication and self-control. And in the end it was she, the less gifted one, who had hurt him and, by betraying their love, destroyed any chance they might have had of being happy together.

Obsessed with these gloomy thoughts, Laura realised she had come to the café where she and Nick had first met, and she slowed down and found herself gazing through the great pane of plate glass at the table where he'd asked if he could join her, as if hoping, in some miraculous way, to see him there now. But another couple sat there, hands joined across the formica, gazing into each other's eyes.

What did the future hold for them? They suddenly looked up and saw her staring so intensely at them, and she gave them a little self-conscious wave and walked on back to college.

At the gate the porter stopped her.

'Oh, Miss Chase. I've let a gentleman into your room. He said you knew him very well. He didn't want to give me his name. He said it was a surprise.' The porter looked at her anxiously. 'I hope I did the right thing?'

'Yes, that's OK,' Laura said thoughtfully, wondering who of her past acquaintances would want to surprise her in this fashion. She supposed she could immediately eliminate Giles or Nick, the names that first sprang to mind.

'Shall I come with you, Miss Chase?'

'No, no, I'll be fine.' She smiled reassuringly at him and swiftly crossed the quad looking up at her window as she did, but seeing no one there. Maybe she *should* have asked the porter to chaperone her?

She smiled at the thought and sped up the stairs, standing outside her room for a moment listening. She turned the handle and pushed open the door, and for what seemed like a long time she stared at the still figure sitting in the chair by the window, head bent over a book. She realised that she had been hoping all the time it was him and her heart, literally, missed a beat.

Nick looked up at her and, for several seconds, they gazed at each other. It was such a long time since they had parted, but nothing had changed, physically at least. They looked the same; but did they still feel the same?

'Hi!' she said shyly, closing the door behind her and slowly entering into the room.

'Hi!' He stood up, also shy, and put down the book. Then, awkwardly, he approached her and kissed her on the cheek. For a moment they clung to each other and then they separated.

'I heard you were in Oxford?' Nick cleared his throat.

'I heard you got a very good degree,' she said. 'Congratulations.'

'Thanks.'

Awkward pause. Then: 'Would you like a coffee?'

241

'I thought we might have a bite to eat in the pub?' He looked at his watch. 'Nearly time for lunch.'

'That would be nice.'

The conversation was stilted, awkward. Of course that was natural, given what had happened and the time that had passed. They walked almost in silence to the pub. When they entered, Laura discovered it had the same air of nostalgia as the coffee bar. It even had the same barman, who recognised them, and they chatted to him as Nick ordered a beer for himself and a white wine for Laura, just as he used to, without consulting her, a fact she rather liked.

They even went over to the table they used to sit at in a corner and Nick raised his glass and turned to her. 'Cheers!'

'Cheers!' she said, raising hers.

'This is like old times.'

'It certainly is.'

'Why didn't you ever get in touch with me, Laura?' Nick said quietly after the barman had brought over their sandwiches. Laura looked at them, feeling around in her mind for the right reply.

'I guess I felt ashamed,' she said at last. 'I behaved terribly badly.' She raised her eyes and studied his face. 'After all we'd been to each other I didn't have to treat you like that.'

'It must have been partly my fault,' he said.

'How do you mean?' That searching look again.

'There was something I didn't understand. Something I didn't do right.'

'I was very hurt at fluffing my exams, hurt and humiliated. I think I blamed you which was stupid.'

'Blamed me?' Now Nick looked confused.

'You know, falling in love, all that crap. I thought you could take it in your stride and I couldn't. It mattered terribly to me letting my folks down.'

'I'm sorry.' His hand closed over hers, but she thought it felt like the clasp of a brother rather than a lover. There was

242

no electricity there. She realised then that too much had happened for them to resume their relationship, as though time had not intervened.

'I know. I'm awfully confused, Nick,' Laura's eyes were swimming with tears, 'and I don't know why I did what I did.'

'You fancied Giles more.' His tone hardened and he removed his hand which had comforted her a little.

'No, I didn't fancy Giles; but he offered an escape.'

'I offered you a home with me in Oxford. We might have been married now, or on the verge. Something like that. Losing you was bad enough, but going off with Giles . . . I nearly had a breakdown. For weeks I simply couldn't concentrate on anything. I don't know what kept me going.'

She reached for his hand and ran her thumb up and down along the back.

'I lost a friend and a lover . . . Don't,' tears sprang to her eyes again, 'please don't reproach me. I simply can't bear it. I had a lousy two years. My mum left my dad. My dad, who we always thought was a hypochondriac, turned out to have real heart disease. He went off by himself, after I'd gone, to remonstrate with Giles's parents and they kicked him out of the house, and when he got home he collapsed again and this time the heart attack was worse than the one he'd had before.'

'Giles's parents kicked him out of the house?' Nick looked aghast.

'Pushed him into the street, but he was a silly old bugger to have gone. He'd never even been to London before. It was all too much for him, but he felt so angry. He was angry really at losing a nurse, not at my morals. As for Australia,' Laura paused and sniffed, 'that was a disaster. It was not "the experience of a lifetime" I can assure you.'

'But you and Giles were lovers?' The bitter tone had entered Nick's voice again.

Laura sighed. 'Well, we fucked, yes. I wouldn't call it love. It was nothing like what happened between you and me. Giles felt guilty too about you.'

'Oh, tough.'

'I know you're hurt, Nick. That it's difficult to understand. I can't understand it myself. Last year I paid for it dearly, working in the chemist's shop, looking after my dad. All I did was work, studying at night. It was the most dreary, awful year of my life and if there is ever retribution in this world, I paid it.'

Nick and Laura left the pub at about three and he took her back to college as far as the porter's lodge. The porter seeing him smiled, rather conspiratorially, and Nick winked as though they shared some secret.

Nick stood watching Laura cross the quad and then he turned and walked to where he'd left his car to drive back to London. The compulsion to see Laura had been overwhelming. He'd felt there was something he needed to settle before he could move on. And even now he was not sure that he'd settled it, that he'd got Laura out of his system.

And that was what he wanted to do. He didn't want to begin an affair with her again although he knew he still loved her. But it was the sort of irrational, obsessional love he despised. To love someone who had hurt you as badly as she had was absurd. Having done it once she would do it again. She had the power.

A woman like Laura was a very dangerous person to have under your skin.

When Nick realised he would be spending most of his time in London rather than Oxford he decided to move out of his parents' house and rented a flat in Covent Garden, a short walk from the LSE.

The LSE had grown from small beginnings at the end of the nineteenth century into a huge institution housed in a hybrid collection of buildings in the Aldwych, which formed what must have been one of the ugliest campus sites in the country. It was part of a dense jungle of buildings, somewhat randomly constructed, and a bridge ran over the narrow street which connected one part of the school with another. Round it was a warren of smaller houses and buildings, even a converted pub, that now contributed to the amorphous whole that was one of the greatest and most prestigious academic centres in the world.

Nick was very proud to have been given a research job in government at the LSE which enabled him to combine work with research for his doctorate. Eventually he hoped this would land him a lectureship at Oxford, LSE or some other comparable seat of learning.

Nick arrived home shortly after six, put his car in a mews garage which he rented at great expense, Covent Garden's parking restrictions being punitive. He occupied the second floor of an eighteenth century house that had been converted into flats, and although it could be noisy at times, due to the perpetual congestion in the streets around, he loved his flat and thought he was lucky to have acquired it in such a central and atmospheric location.

It was near the school and within walking distance of the West End. It was surrounded by nice pubs, some of the best restaurants in London and, of course, was a stone's throw from not one opera house but two, where he could indulge his favourite form of entertainment. Nick saw his parents at least once a week, sometimes twice. He usually dined with them on a Friday, though he didn't stick to the day because it was dangerous and also tedious to get into a routine.

Occasionally he had them to dinner or took them out and Emma was usually there too. She wanted her own flat and would quite like, he thought, to have moved in with him. But he thought Emma, with her love of a good time, involving late nights, would be too much of a liability when he wanted to apply himself to serious study. Nick rather liked his lifestyle and he felt that if only Laura hadn't deserted him he would have been the happiest man in the world; but now it was too late, far too late, to turn back the clock.

After his meeting with Laura, Nick flung himself into his work more than ever in an effort to forget her. Laura was no use to him; there was no point in being haunted by her, in craving her presence. He had a good life and career ahead of him and Laura would only mean trouble. Apart from that, he had seen nothing in her attitude to make him think she wanted to start up again.

He would never be able to trust her again.

One day, having sat in on a seminar on the European Union at the LSE, Nick was making his way from the new building to the old when, passing the porter's lodge, he noticed a tall familiar figure seemingly in consultation with one of the staff who, seeing Nick, suddenly hailed him.

'Mr Constantine! You've got a visitor. Someone asking for you.'

Giles turned in surprise and saw Nick just about to mount the steps to one of the lifts. Nick stopped and looked at him.

'Oh, hi!' he said, with little enthusiasm in his voice.

Nick saw the porter watching him with interest. To refuse Giles's outstretched hand would be churlish, so he took it and shook it.

'I was just passing,' Giles said, feeling awkward and thinking that, maybe, this chance encounter was not such a good idea. 'You know my law tutorial college is just round the corner in Lincoln's Inn Fields?'

'No, I didn't know.' Nick's tone was cool, indifferent.

'Well, it is. Look, Nick . . .' Giles's manner changed and he looked urgently at his former friend. 'I need to talk to you.'

'Well . . .' Nick looked as though he was going to refuse, but Giles caught hold of his arm. The porter turned and pretended to be busy with something else.

'It is something quite urgent, quite personal, and it concerns you.'

'Really?' Nick's expression was puzzled.

'Yes, really.'

'You'd better come to my room then.'

Nick rang for the lift and Giles stood beside him waiting for it.

'It's not exactly Oxford, is it?' he said, looking around.

'No. It's not. I think maybe it's what's meant by a blackboard jungle.' In fact, almost to prove the point, in the entrance hall were blackboards on which were scribbled in chalk a number of announcements and messages.

The lift came and they got in. A number of others piled in too. They got out at the third floor and Nick led Giles along the corridor, up a small flight of stairs, and opened the door of a room at the top. It was a room without charm or beauty, a functional room, very small and crammed with books, papers and on the desk, a computer. The narrow window looked onto the roof garden which, in summer, was one of the few places where the thousands of students and staff could get an unrestricted view of the sun. Now, on a cold November day with a keen wind blowing, it was deserted.

No, squashed in a corner of the Aldwych, opposite Bush House, the LSE was certainly not Oxford. That wonderful city with its quads filled with trees and flowers, its huge stretch of central meadowland and its ancient buildings hallowed by time.

'This is home, is it?' Hands in his pockets, Giles looked around, and Nick was reminded of that slight air of arrogance that his mother always hated and resented so much.

'It's not home,' Nick answered brusquely, 'it's merely where I work.'

'I hear you got a very good degree.'

'Thanks.'

'And a fellowship?'

'Can you come to the point, Giles?' Nick perched on the end of his desk and pointed to one of the two chairs in the room.

'I realise this is very difficult, for both of us.' Giles paused to clear his throat. 'And it's no use saying "I'm sorry".'

'Too late to say you're sorry.' Nick folded his arms and gazed out of the window. 'In fact, I can't think why you even considered coming to see me. What happened was a long time ago. It's over,' he turned and looked at Giles, 'but it is not forgotten, either for what you did to me or for what you did to Laura. Laura is deeply scarred by her experience, and I can't say that I'm unmoved either.'

'Laura was a free agent you know,' Giles said quietly. 'She wasn't kidnapped, or even coerced.'

'That's what you say. You paid her fare. It must have been tempting.'

'Laura insisted that the fare was a loan, and I agreed. If one day she can pay it back I'll accept it. There was more to it than that, Nick. I'll agree that the issue was complicated, and Laura is a complicated human being, maybe far more than you, or I, realise. Basically, she was upset by your wealth, or rather the fact that your dad was so wealthy: the yacht, the Rolls. She never felt happy about it or being your "concubine", as she called it, if she returned to Oxford to live with you.'

'My concubine!' Nick exploded angrily.

'Her very word. I swear I didn't make it up.' Giles gestured helplessly. 'But what is the point of raking over the past, Nick? It happened, and I'm very sorry. It didn't work out for Laura and me. It was not a happy time for either of us. If you like we were both punished. You and I had a great friendship which I thought would last all our lives and that has gone too. You are right to be angry and upset, but I have come to you not to rake over the past. I've come to tell you something else which I'm afraid is also going to upset you a great deal. However I feel I need your help.'

Nick looked puzzled and started to fiddle with some things on his desk.

'Go on,' he said at last.

'Nick, I have been seeing Emma for nearly a year.'

'*Emma*!' Nick bawled. 'My sister?'

Giles nodded. 'That may sound horrifying enough, which is the reason we kept it a secret.'

'But how . . .'

Giles raised a hand. 'I'll come to that in a minute. What I want to tell you, which is why I need help, is that Emma is a drug addict. She's addicted to heroin and I can't handle it alone any more.'

Nick buried his face in his hands and stood there for some time saying nothing. Then he slumped into the chair behind his desk and sat there staring at the blank computer screen.

'This needs a hell of a lot of explanation,' he said.

'I can't think how no one else in your family seems to have noticed. She leads a completely wild life and no one seems to try to rein her in – except me.'

'My parents are very worried about Emma,' Nick nodded slowly in agreement. 'But she is over twenty-one. If they ask her where she's been or what she's doing she flies off the handle. My mother finds she can't speak to her. I've tried . . . but heroin,' he put his hands over his face again. 'I can't believe it.'

'When I met her she already had the habit. It was just under a year ago. January this year in fact, and I didn't know for some time. She was very moody, either up or down, and this I realised, when I knew, was according to whether she'd had a fix or not. She had ample funds of course, well supplied by your father. She could get the finest heroin, only the best. When I first got to know about it she claimed she could give it up any time; but she can't. She's hooked and she's getting worse. She craves it more frequently in bigger quantities as her tolerance rises. Luckily, because she has money and is an intelligent woman, she knows the ropes. She would never, for instance, share a needle. She doesn't mix with the riffraff on the streets because she doesn't have to. But I have found it increasingly difficult to control her, and now I know she needs, and must have, professional help. If not, before she's thirty she'll be dead.'

Nick rose and, finger on his chin, went to stand at the window.

'What on earth can I do?'

'You'll have to speak to your father.' Giles's tone was firm. 'He'll have to cut off the money, cut off the supply and then, so as not to drive her underground, try and persuade her to have the best treatment. I will do all I can because I love her. I know this will not be good news to you or your family; but I think my love is strong enough to help and support her.'

'I don't suppose it will be good news to yours either.' Nick gave an ironic chuckle. 'Do they know?' He turned and looked at Giles, his expression somehow softened. He could feel that, imperceptibly, the tension between them was breaking down.

Giles shook his head.

'No, they don't know anything about me and Emma. I met her by accident at Mephistos, the nightclub. I was a bit lonely, at a loose end, and I went there alone one night for a few beers. I just bumped into Emma.' Giles thought he would leave out the rather sordid details of that occasion. 'We kind of hit it off.'

'You always liked each other.' Nick, to his surprise, felt himself warming once again to his old friend.

'Yes, we did. Well we started to meet and the friendship grew.'

250

'And you had no idea about the . . .' Nick could hardly bring himself to say the dreaded word.

'No. I mean we used to smoke hash and take Es at various clubs and parties – I mean everyone does, don't they? – but I didn't realise she was on a steady diet of heroin until I came back to my flat unexpectedly one day and found all the paraphernalia. Ever since then I've been trying to control it, but now,' Giles despairingly flung his arms in the air, 'I've had to confess to failure.'

'God knows what Dad will say.' Nick again slumped in his chair. 'He'll hit the roof. Yet in a way he has himself to blame. They've always spoiled Emma. She was born with a silver spoon in her mouth and has led a privileged lifestyle. She has a good brain but was never encouraged to work or to use it. It's their fault, as much as hers, that she turned to drugs. What else is there to do when you have everything? Dad, like Mum, had his ideas still anchored in the past. Women are not expected to work or have a career. Dad just wanted her to be decorative, happy, spend as much money as she liked on nice clothes, and marry well. They're worried that she hasn't already. Heavens, she's twenty-*two*.' Nick's expression mocked the amazement and concern of his parents. 'But then there was a man, Philip, she saw a lot of and they didn't like him either. No one is quite good enough for their princess.'

'I think Philip introduced her to H,' Giles said. 'I met him and I didn't care for him at all.'

'He was always losing his job. They were relieved when she seemed to have stopped seeing him.'

'Well, at least I'm not heavily into the drug scene, even if I am a Harvey.' Giles gave a rueful, self-deprecating smile. He went over to his old friend and put a hand on his shoulder. 'Perhaps this will help us to patch things up between ourselves, Nick? I'd like it more than anything, because maybe one day we'll be brothers-in-law.'

'You'd really do that?' Nick looked at him incredulously. 'You'd marry a junkie, with all the trouble and difficulty that entails?'

'I wouldn't marry a junkie, but I'll marry Emma when she's free from dope. If she'll have me.'

And at that moment Nick felt a resurgence of love for his old mate, companion in arms, friend of his youth.

Impulsively, he stood up and flung out his arms and embraced him.

CHAPTER 15

'You won't see a return on your investment overnight,' Edmund said with a trace of impatience in his voice. 'I think I've told you that before. Be reasonable, Andy.'

'I think I'm being very reasonable,' Andreas replied, gripping the receiver tightly in his hand. 'A million and a half is a lot of money.'

'I agree. It is a lot of money. But when this product comes on the market and you see your dividends, you will be thanking me for the rest of your life.'

'Well, let's hope so.' Andreas glanced round to be sure Lydia was not within earshot. 'Any news about the other matter?'

'What other matter?'

'The club.'

'Oh, the club. Yes, that's going through.'

'When?'

'Well, again, it's a matter of time.'

'But my name has gone forward?'

'Oh, definitely.'

'And I will be elected?'

'Don't see why not.'

'Well, I'll wait to hear about both matters.' Andreas felt a curious and untypical sense of defeat. It was not a sensation he was at all accustomed to. ''Bye, then,' he said, and replaced the receiver.

There was something about Edmund and his tactics that,

to an experienced man of business, smelt of rank dishonesty. Yet Andreas still couldn't bring himself to believe that someone of Harvey's background, with family traditions rooted deep in English soil, could deceive him. If he was engaged in some tricky transaction, Andreas was quite sure that Valerie knew nothing about it.

'Was that Emma?' Lydia asked, coming to the door of the dining room from where Andreas had been phoning.

'No.'

'I'm very worried about her.'

Andreas consulted his watch.

'It's only ten.'

'Last night she didn't come home at all.'

'You know she stays with Sue.' Andreas, still with a worried frown on his brow, followed his wife from the room.

'But *is* she with Sue?' Lydia turned anxiously towards him as they reached the drawing room.

'Why shouldn't she be? Look, darling, she's not a child.'

Andreas switched on the ten o'clock news. After watching it for a few moments he impatiently flicked off the remote control and, flopping into a chair, took up the *Evening Standard*.

'Andreas.' Looking tense, ill at ease, Lydia sat opposite him, perched on the edge of her chair. 'I do wish you'd take this seriously.'

'My dear, I am taking it seriously.' Andreas allowed the paper to fall to the floor. 'But Emma will soon be twenty-three.'

'She seems to have no permanent boyfriend, so where does she go? What does she do?'

'Do you want me to talk to her?'

Lydia clasped her hands together. 'Oh, Andy, I wish you would.'

'What shall I say?'

'Well, say we're a bit worried, concerned at the unusual

hours she keeps. She's also getting through a tremendous amount of money and I don't see it reflected in the clothes she buys.'

'She doesn't buy clothes?' Andreas looked surprised.

'Not with me any more.'

'Then what does she do with the money?'

'You'll have to ask her, Andy. You'll have to find out what's going on.'

They both listened at the sound of the front door closing.

'Oh, there she is,' Lydia said, relief in her voice.

'I shan't talk to her tonight,' Andreas murmured, rising to his feet. 'It's much too late.'

'Oh, no. Try to get her when she's fresh, not tired out. Take her to lunch or something. She'd like that. Lorenzo's, somewhere smart.'

'Hi, Mum. Hi, Dad!' Nick came into the room and both his parents stared at him in surprise.

'Where did you spring from?'

'Sorry, is it too late?'

'Is Emma with you?'

'No.'

Nick looked uncomfortable. He stooped to the floor for the paper his father had thrown down and stared at the front page for a few moments.

'Well, to what do we owe the pleasure, darling?' Lydia watched him a little anxiously. 'Is anything wrong?'

Nick put down the paper again and looked from one parent to the other.

'I don't really know where to start,' he said.

Andreas came downstairs into the living room, quietly closing the door behind him.

'Is she OK?' Nick asked.

'She's taken a sleeping tablet. She'll soon go off.' With an air of profound exhaustion Andreas sank into a chair

255

opposite his son. 'I do wish you could have found another way to tell us all this.'

'I tried, Dad, but I could think of no other way. I thought I'd just tell you alone, but I knew Mum would have to know. I decided it was better to see you together.'

'It's had a terrible effect on your mother.' Andreas paused and looked at the floor. 'It's had a terrible effect on me.'

'And me,' Nick said. 'Don't forget, I heard it first.'

'And Giles Harvey of *all* people.' Andreas savagely banged his fist into the palm of his hand. 'I blame him for a lot of this.'

'I don't think you can blame him for any of it. He said that when he met up with her again she was already an addict.'

'And that was almost a year ago! Why couldn't he have told us then?'

'Well . . . he fell in love. He was in a quandary. Knowing how you felt about him, Emma didn't want you to know she was seeing him. He tried to get her off the habit himself. Frankly, I don't think his influence has been anything but good.'

'Rubbish!' Andreas snarled. 'He was probably after her money, just as his wretched father has been after mine.'

'I beg your pardon?' Nick looked up startled. 'I thought the Harveys were very well off, thank you.'

'Some time ago I let Edmund have some money towards a so-called investment. At the time it sounded promising, but I have yet to see a penny of my money back.'

'Well, I'm sure Edmund is a very straight guy. And Giles is very straight too.'

'You call him straight?' Andreas looked incredulously at his son. 'After what he did to you? He went off with your girl and you call that straight?'

'It's all over and forgotten now. I don't want to talk about it again.'

'Look how he treated her? Don't you think that might be relevant to how he might treat your sister? Has treated her, for all we know.'

'No, I don't and he is very supportive of her. He has tried desperately to get her off. He came to me as a last resort.'

'I don't believe a word of it. I don't like young Harvey and I don't like his father and, like your mother, who has shown much wisdom in all this, I bitterly regret that our paths ever crossed. To think of my daughter being involved with them is almost more than I can bear.'

'Dad,' Nick sat down next to his father and grabbed his hand urgently. 'You've got to think of Emma's welfare. We've got to see her together, and we've got to get her to agree to treatment.'

'However, I must insist,' Andreas said firmly, 'that she gives up seeing Harvey. It's got to be a clean break.'

'I don't think you can insist on that, Dad.'

'I can and I do. I will not tolerate Giles Harvey sniffing around my daughter.'

Andreas came out of the Greek Orthodox Church in Camden Town, went to his car which he had parked at a meter round the corner, and sat for a long time in the driver's seat staring in front of him. He felt like a man who had been crucified, and not even God could help him.

Andreas was not religious, didn't even go to church on holy days. But his children had been baptised into the Orthodox faith and he contributed to church charities and helped to support the priest.

The previous day, he and Nick had taken Emma to a clinic in rural Hampshire, to try and cure her of her addiction. It was costing him nearly two thousand pounds a week, but he didn't care about the money. He cared about his daughter who, the doctors had assured him, he would lose at an early age if she wasn't cured.

257

It had been a ghastly time with Emma. Once confronted, she had denied it and then she had tried to disappear, run away. Giles brought her back and was asked immediately to leave by Andreas, who still could not believe that she could have got into this condition without his help. Emma promptly had, or manufactured, a sort of fit and Giles was asked to come back.

Inevitably the Harvey family became aware of what was going on and they too tried to intervene, with all sorts of theories and good advice that Emma's increasingly tense and irritated parents could have done without.

They took Emma on a cruise in the yacht round the coast of North Africa, the only place to be sure of the sun, but they had to make an emergency run to Alexandria for her to see a doctor. Without her fix she was hallucinating and having fits. Finally she became frightened and consented to enter the clinic.

Giles assured her parents that, in the interests of her well-being and recovery, he would not see her unless they asked him to. By this time Emma hardly knew what was going on.

And now it was spring, but that didn't seem to help. Andreas had always felt a lift with the arrival of the season, the glimpse of leaves on the trees in the park, the blossom on the streets in the Wood. He was a naturally cheerful and buoyant man, his outlook on life one of optimism rather than pessimism. He could never in his life recall having felt so low; so low and depressed that he had driven to the Orthodox church to seek the help of one of the priests who listened to him most sympathetically and then invited him to come into the church with him and pray before the icon of the crucified Christ.

He had asked the Father what had he done to deserve this? He had always been a faithful husband and loving father. He had made money, but by honest means, never cheated; and had paid his taxes. God what a lot of those there were. He knew he liked nice things, expensive things like the boat and the Rolls, but was this wrong, was it a sin? He had not, he thought, been overly greedy, he gave generously to church funds and helped numerous other good causes. He had never stolen money or cheated people. He had never had a mistress.

He had, he thought, been vain in wanting so desperately to belong to a gentleman's club in St James's, a club that admitted people only from the very top drawer; but surely that was a weakness rather than a sin?

What, then, had he done to deserve that his beautiful, well-educated, well brought-up daughter, the light of his life, who should have everything to live for, should turn out to be a junkie. One so bad that the doctors gave her a limited lifespan of a few years maximum, unless she was cured?

The Father told him how difficult it was to explain or understand these things, said he would pray for him and his wife and their daughter and asked him to trust in God.

Father Spiros's final words had been ones of comfort and hope, but Andreas felt no hope, only a bleakness of spirit. And, as he started his car the tears that had lurked for so long began to roll slowly down his cheeks.

But, by the time he arrived at the West End offices of Frank Thompson, the tears had dried and, greeting Frank, it would have been hard to tell that here was a man who, half an hour earlier, had been in the grips of despair.

Frank greeted him warmly, and enquired after his family.

'Fine, fine,' Andreas replied.

'We're looking forward to our trip on the yacht this year.' Frank sat himself behind his enormous desk and, leaning towards Andreas, offered him a cigar. Andreas shook his head. 'It is on, isn't it?' Frank began the ritual of cigar lighting, removing the band, inspecting the tip, taking a cutter from a tray on the desk and puncturing the end. Then he looked at Andreas. 'Will the Harveys be there?'

Andreas appeared taken aback by the question: 'I don't expect so. Why do you ask?'

'Just wondered.' Frank began thoughtfully to examine the burning tip of his Havana. 'Now to business, Andy.' He reached over for a folder which he opened, and started going through the documents inside. 'We have a very large consignment of the finest pure virgin olive oil. It's not cheap, but all the best places will take it: Harrods, Fortnums. Guaranteed . . .'

'I just wondered why you asked about Harvey?' Andreas interrupted him.

'Well . . .' Frank, who was a bulky man, leaned forward and joined his hands on his desk. 'I have come across him again in a rather strange way.'

'Really?'

'Coincidence is a very funny thing.' Frank wriggled his bulk in his chair. 'Well, it's like this, Andy. I won't beat about the bush. I have been looking for money to expand. As you know, interest rates are competitive and the banks are tight. We're already over-geared. A friend of mine, Arnold Smart, who is in the fruit business, knew through a friend of a friend a lawyer able to lend money on favourable terms. I realised I knew him. We'd met on your yacht.'

'Edmund Harvey.' Andreas nodded.

'Oh, you know he does this sort of thing?'

'I certainly do.'

'Oh, that's a relief.' Frank sat back as if Andreas had taken a weight off his mind.

'Well, I don't know that it should be a relief. Harvey has taken a considerable amount of money off me and I have yet to see any return on investment.'

'Well, he is offering to advance me a million.'

'That's probably the money he took off me.'

'Thing is, I haven't had it and he wants twenty thousand pounds upfront.'

'For what?' Andreas looked amazed.

'Security.'

'And have you given it to him?'

'I was about to.'

'And in exchange for twenty thousand pounds he is going to let you have a million?'

'Approximately, at fifteen per cent over base.'

'Over what period of time?'

'Five years.'

'At fifteen per cent over base?'

Frank nodded. He suddenly looked a crumpled individual, rather than a giant of a man.

'And you haven't seen any of it yet?'

Frank shook his head.

'Why didn't you ask *me* for the money, Frank?' Andreas leaned forward and looked at him earnestly.

Thompson put his head on one side, studied his nails. 'You know how it is with friends. Doing business is one thing, but asking favours, borrowing money, is another. It may have made you doubt us financially and, commercially speaking, the business is extremely viable. We just have to pay more upfront for goods before receipt. You know how it is . . .'

He looked ruefully at Andreas, who slowly shook his head.

'It doesn't really work out, does it?' Andreas asked. 'The terms are ridiculous. In the meantime he's getting other loans while you and others repay theirs. It seems to me a highly risky, dubious enterprise. From what you tell me, I definitely think I'm going to have to make some enquiries into the business dealings of Mr Edmund Harvey.'

'Look, don't get me wrong.' Frank nervously held up his hands. 'I mean, I don't want to get the guy into trouble. He's a family friend of yours I know. The boys were at school together. I'm sure he's legit.' A look of disbelief spread over his homely features. 'He must be. He took me to lunch at his club. His grandfather was on the committee of the MCC.'

'Why do we trust these people?' Andreas said in a despairing voice. 'Is it because we think they're better than we are? It's nothing to do with brains or money, is it, Frank? It's to do with class. Something you can't buy, no matter how you try. Do you remember the way they behaved on the boat? Didn't bring the right clothes, tried to put us down at every turn, criticised the wine. Patronising. Acted as if they owned it. In a sense you'd think *we* were their guests. Lydia took to her bed because of the nervous strain of trying to entertain them. Now I've parted with a million and a half, and you have nearly parted with twenty thousand for nothing, just because he took us to dine at his club and his grandfather was on the committee of the MCC. Doubtless another grandfather was a High Court judge and an uncle or two an Admiral of the Fleet and a General in the British Army.'

Andreas, slightly frenzied by now, agitatedly stabbed the air with his finger. 'Do you know that his son lured my son's girlfriend to Australia, thus breaking up her relationship with Nick, and abandoned her after she nearly died in a swimming accident? Do you know that I have discovered that this very same son has been having an affair with *my* daughter and has introduced her to drugs? Emma is in a clinic at this moment in an effort to rehabilitate. That's the sort of people we're dealing with, Frank,' Andy continued, his voice finally breaking. 'If you ask *me*, they're the scum of the earth.'

When Andreas reached home later that same day, he ran his car into the garage beside the Rolls. He seldom used it for business in the city; it was too big, and too precious, to risk damaging in the narrow streets of London, the chances of a collision, or an act of vandalism were too great.

He got out of the Jag, locked it and then ran his hands lightly along the side of the Rolls. It was pale blue and it was very beautiful, over one hundred thousand pounds' worth of top-rate car. Not just a miracle of modern engineering and design, but a work of art. More importantly; it was a symbol of success.

And there was the yacht, *The Lydia*, at anchor in the port of Monaco, waiting the next trip. Its crew were fully paid throughout the year, ready to cast off at a moment's notice, on the whim of the boss: him, Andreas Michael Constantine.

He left the garage, closed it with a flip of the remote control, and stood for a few moments looking up at the house. His house, bought with his money. No mortgage, and now worth in today's inflated prices three and a half to four million. Inside it had several good paintings, many antiques, bought with taste and care by his wife, who kept a lovely home, a fitting place for a successful man. Not a greedy man, not an outrageous, bullying man, not a boastful, arrogant man, but a successful one. And what was wrong with success? Why, nothing, unless it meant that, perhaps, it had contributed to the loss of a daughter.

Andreas punched in the numbers at the door that gained him admission to his high-security home, vigilance that was important and necessary in these days when there were so many villains about. He had no doubt that Edmund Harvey and his ilk would have been outraged at the thought of breaking into someone's house and stealing their possessions, yet what they were doing was no less harmful, no less destructive.

There remained however a part of Andreas that found it difficult to believe that Edmund Harvey was a crooked lawyer, a con man who could end up behind bars, investing money he didn't have, offering to lend clients spurious loans. There were all sorts of things in business that were marginal. Maybe he should give Edmund the benefit of the doubt. Confront and warn him? Maybe that would be the decent, honourable thing to do.

Hadn't their sons gone to the same public school? Yet, when you thought about it, that being the case, didn't you

263

deserve to be better treated by that self-same friend?

Inside, the house was quiet. Andreas guessed Lydia would be upstairs resting. She was still on tranquillisers and had been absolutely unable to face the journey to the clinic with Emma. It was almost five and, after depositing his briefcase in the hall, Andreas went into the kitchen, which was empty. This was the time of day that Maria and her husband usually had off. By six she would be back on duty again preparing the dinner. When Andreas used the Rolls, or had a particularly busy day with a round of engagements, Marco acted as chauffeur. Today had probably been spent doing jobs around the house or in the garden.

Andreas got a bottle of mineral water out of the fridge, poured some into a glass and drank it. Then with the glass still in his hand he went back to the drawing room and, after consulting the telephone directory, punched in a number.

'Good afternoon,' he said after asking for the club secretary, 'this is Andreas Constantine speaking.'

Polite pause.

'Does my name ring a bell?'

'I don't think so, Mr Constantine,' the plummy-toned voice replied. 'Are you a member of the club?'

'I was hoping to be elected,' Andreas replied. 'I understood my name had gone before the club committee. Some time ago, as a matter of fact.'

'Ah! In that case just let me look at my records. I'm afraid these things do take time.' The voice sounded regretful. 'May I ask the name of your proposer, Mr Constantine?'

'Mr Harvey. Edmund Harvey.'

'Edmund Harvey . . .' The voice went on repeating 'Harvey, Harvey' and then, finally, 'I'm afraid I have no record of a person with your name being proposed by Mr Harvey, Mr Constantine. I'm so sorry. I feel there must be some mistake.'

'But I think *you* must be mistaken,' Andreas insisted.

'Could you consult your records again, please?'

The plummy tone became less friendly.

'I have, sir, I assure you. Now that we are computerised, everything is here before me on the screen, and I'm afraid there is no one answering to the name of Constantine. My advice is that you should consult Mr Harvey again. Good day to you, sir.' The voice sounded very final.

Upstairs, when Andreas put his head round the door of their bedroom, he found Lydia still asleep. The curtains were drawn and it was so cool and peaceful that for a moment his terrible feeling of tension seemed to evaporate and he longed to throw himself by the side of his wife and go to sleep too. Instead, he sat by her side, still with the glass of water in his hand, and looked at her.

How she'd suffered. She didn't deserve it. She had been everything a man could ask for and more. Not only a good wife, but a good mother, too. A loyal companion and friend.

Yet in some way both of them had failed Emma. Had they been too indulgent? Demanding in one way, but not demanding enough in another? They had given her freedom, but should they really have been asking more questions?

In this day and age it was so hard to know the answer.

They had treated both their children the same, and yet no one could fault Nick, who had turned into a splendid specimen of humanity. A true Renaissance man: academically brilliant, cultured, good and kind.

Lydia's eyelids fluttered, and when she opened them and saw Andreas beside her, she reached out and took his hand.

'Is anything wrong, Andy?'

These days she was so nervous and anxious, fearful about everything, that it seemed that for her nothing could go right. Well at last something would go right.

'I've got Harvey,' he said, clutching her hand hard.

'You've got *what*, Andy?' Still frightened, she half-sat up

265

in bed, running a hand nervously through her hair.

'Harvey's a crook. Edmund. Though the son's a crook too.'

She lay back on the bed, an expression of triumph on her pale, ill-looking face.

'I told you he was no good.'

'He's been defrauding people of thousands, perhaps millions. I've spent part of the day doing some checking and I am absolutely sure of my facts. Frank Thompson is one he nearly got, but I think I saved him. Alas, I also think I can kiss goodbye to my million and a half.' He squeezed her hand more tightly. 'My father and brothers won't be pleased.'

'Oh, Andy, it wasn't money from the business . . .'

'No, no. It was mine. But it was almost all the spare cash I'd got.'

'But *why* did you let him have it, Andy?'

'I guess I was stupid. Vain. I wanted to show off, impress him. I shall have to tell Father that I'll need a float for a while just to make it up. I'm afraid the yacht will have to go.'

'Well, I shan't miss *that*,' she said firmly.

'Maybe the Rolls.'

Silence. Like him, Lydia loved the beautiful car.

'Well, it may not be necessary. It's up to Father and the boys. They may let me keep it. They may want me to sell. Things are quite good business-wise, but they might want to teach me a lesson. I was taken in by Harvey. I let him blind me. I thought he was going to put me up for his club and even that was a lie. He made a fool of me. He had no intention of it. Nouveau riche, I guess. Not good enough. Now I'm going to shop him. I'm going to turn him in. Notify the police.'

Lydia put a hand to her mouth.

'Oh, *Andy*,' she said, 'do you think you should?'

'Yes,' Andreas said firmly, going over to the window and gazing out on to the tree-lined streets of St John's Wood.

Beautiful St John's Wood. The best part of London. *His* part of London. Turning to Lydia he nodded vigorously.

'Yes, I most certainly do. Edmund Harvey and his like have had this coming to them for a very long time.'

CHAPTER 16

Dr Pascoe had a youthful, unlined face, clear blue eyes and a sunny expression, which was remarkable, because his entire time was spent trying to solve the heart-rending problems of others. He looked not much older than Emma, but in fact he was nearly forty, had been married fifteen years and had three children.

It was not so much that David Pascoe was young, but that Emma had aged. She looked about thirty-five, and for a young woman of twenty-three who should have been on the brink of life, this was a terrible thing.

David, during the months he had been treating her, had become fond of Emma. He, too, thought it was a very terrible thing, even though for most of his medical career he had specialised in drugs and addiction. No matter how experienced you were, you never really became used to the effect drugs had on people. When they were young, beautiful, rich and had everything going for them, it was almost impossible to understand.

But perhaps that was the key to it. Emma *had* everything. She had only to ask, and her merest whim was satisfied by doting parents. It was not only the deprived and the disadvantaged who took to drugs; the clinics were unfortunately full of rich, beautiful and talented people, too.

Even though Emma looked much older than her years, she was still beautiful. Added to which, she had a nobility of expression and a serenity that was probably due to the suffering she had endured. For she had suffered, but she had overcome. She was cured of her heroin addiction, but remained on prescribed drugs and would be for some time.

But what to do with Emma now? She was ready to leave the clinic; but was it wise to allow her to go home, back to the environment that had been the cause of the whole thing in the first place? That was the question.

Emma and David sat in his pleasant office, facing each other. They were both smoking. Smoking tobacco was permitted. Though bad for you, it was better than smoking dope. It was the one concession the clinic made to those of its patients who were victims of addiction.

Emma had on jeans and a T-shirt. It was a long time since she had worn designer clothes. She didn't use make-up. She was the sort of girl who would have made a fabulous model. Now she was probably too old.

'What to do with you, Emma?' David murmured, tapping his pencil on the table. 'What to do?'

Emma had just been told she was free to leave, and she didn't seem too pleased. Here she felt safe, in an attractive environment, surrounded by helpful people, people who cared. It was not that her parents didn't care; but she knew that when she went home they would scarcely let her out of their sight. Her father could be bad-tempered and her mother was prone to hysterics.

But she knew she had to go because the expense of the clinic was causing difficulties. Six months in a place that cost two thousand pounds a week was a lot of money, even for her father. He had recently experienced some business reverses and had to get rid of the yacht and the Rolls. That much she knew, no more.

In the safe confines of the clinic, Emma had been protected from the harsh realities of life outside.

Emma watched David cogitating. She felt very peaceful. Away from the pressures of life, she had tried to come to

269

terms with herself. The treatment in the clinic was a mixture of drug therapy, psychotherapy, healthy eating, exercise, and early nights. It had suited her. She didn't want to leave.

'What about this boyfriend of yours?' David asked, as he shifted through her notes. He looked up. 'Giles. Have you missed him?'

Emma wasn't quite sure whether she'd missed Giles or not. At the beginning she had been so ill that she didn't remember much about anyone; but now she thought about Giles quite a lot and where their relationship would be at when she got out. In a way it was a bit like getting out of prison after being deprived of sex and normal companionship for six months.

'Daddy made Giles promise not to contact me.'

'Ah, Daddy again!' David nodded and wrote something down on a notepad in front of him.

'Daddy's lovely,' Emma said defensively.

'I'm sure he is.'

'He just thinks Giles had something to do with my addiction. He hadn't, but Daddy has convinced himself of this, and nothing anyone can say or do will change his mind.'

'Why is this?' David looked interested.

'He doesn't like Giles's family. They're rather snobby, upper class. Toffee-nosed, you know the type. Giles and my brother Nick were at school together and the Harveys, Giles's family, always had a bad effect on my mother.'

'What kind of effect?'

'She kind of went to pieces. Freaked out.' Emma smiled at the recollection. 'Poor Mum. She was so anxious to please despite the fact that we'd pots more money than they had. They *were* kind of arrogant.'

'But Giles is not like that?'

'Not at all. Unfortunately he also went off with Nick's girlfriend, and although Daddy didn't like her either, he thought Giles didn't behave very well.' Emma grimaced and shook another cigarette from the pack. 'Well, frankly, he didn't, did he?'

'I don't know the circumstances.' David scribbled something more. 'I can't judge.'

'You're being very tactful, David.'

'Tact is my business,' David said with a smile.

'I shall miss you.' Emma looked at him rather wistfully.

'And I, believe it or not, shall miss you. But I'm always here, on the end of the telephone line.' David tapped the desk again with his pencil, still looking pensive.

'I would somehow rather you didn't go straight home when you left here, Emma. Is there a relation, a friend you can stay with?'

Emma looked doubtful. 'But what will Daddy say?'

'I'll speak to Daddy if you like. You have to stand on your own feet, and I feel that if you go home you'll be Daddy's little girl again, and Mummy's. You'll be smothered all over with parental love. Not good for you. You've got to be Emma: a person in her own right.'

'I can always stay with my brother.'

'Where does he live?'

'In London. He has a flat in Covent Garden. I don't think he'll mind for a time. As long as it's not too long.'

'I think Nick is a good idea.' David put down his pencil and stood up. 'Time to make some phone calls, Emma.'

They sat opposite each other, conscious of a feeling, now that they were alone, of strangeness, unease. It was the first time they'd seen each other since Emma entered the clinic. Giles had kept his word, anxious to do nothing that might impede Emma's recovery. He felt in a way that he'd been in rehabilitation too.

Giles had chosen the restaurant with care: Hampstead, classy, expensive. Afterwards, if all went well, they could go for a stroll on the Heath.

271

They each had a glass of wine while they studied the menu. Emma sipped hers nervously, as though it was a long time since she'd had a drink. She looked very pale and she was still underweight but, as he gazed at her furtively round the menu, almost drinking in her beauty, Giles knew he was as much in love with her as ever. More so, in fact.

Absence had driven the heart to desperation.

Much to his relief, Giles had picked her up at Nick's, with whom she was staying after being discharged from the clinic. He didn't think he could have faced Andreas and Lydia.

They hadn't spoken much in the car as they drove through Covent Garden, except for Giles to ask her approval of the restaurant.

When they stopped outside, he had reached out and tentatively taken her hand. Her responding squeeze was encouraging.

The waiter, pad in hand, approached, and they ordered. Emma said she wouldn't drink any more wine, so Giles only ordered half a bottle. The waiter whisked their menus away and again they were alone, staring at each other.

It was Emma who broke the silence.

'It seems like years,' she said, her features suddenly relaxing, breaking into a smile.

'A lifetime,' Giles replied.

Avoiding his eyes, she gazed at the tablecloth. 'I guess it's as well I'm staying at Nick's.'

'You mean to avoid me meeting your mum and dad?'

'It's an awful situation. I wasn't sure you'd want to see me.'

'Don't be silly.' His hand closed over hers. 'I've thought of nothing else. It wasn't your fault.'

She raised her eyes and stared into his. 'I want you to know neither Nick nor I approve of what Dad did. Going to the police. We think he should have discussed it with your father first. After all, they were old family friends. We think

272

he had some sort of brainstorm, you know, a kind of mini-breakdown. He was full of so much anger that your father had deceived him, about the money, that stupid club.'

'And he always thought I was responsible for your addiction.' Giles looked rueful. 'I guess he boiled over.'

'That was rubbish, as I told him.' Emma frenziedly crumbled the bread roll on her plate. 'What . . . what's happening with your father now?'

'He's on bail, following the hearing at the magistrates' court. He is to be sent for trial, charged with conspiracy to defraud, false accounting. He will almost certainly go to prison.'

'It must be terrible for you.'

'It is terrible. It has thrown the family all over the place; but above all it means the end of Dad's career, his livelihood. He admits he was foolish, that he did wrong. He says, and I believe him, that he didn't mean to defraud, not at the beginning, anyway. He thought he could control it. He just found himself in a jam, lots of expense, things getting out of hand. Panic. We've never been really wealthy, though Mum has money of her own. She says she wishes like anything he'd told her, but he couldn't talk to Mum, couldn't talk to anyone. I feel so desperately sad that he felt he couldn't confide in the family, but we've all rallied round now. We're closer. Mum has been terrific even though she was as shocked as we were to learn that he had a mistress.'

'A mistress!' Emma gasped, putting down her glass.

'He'd had her for years, apparently. That was part of his financial problem. We knew her. She used to be his secretary. The worst part was learning they had a son, Adam. He's about twelve. Obviously we were upset, but somehow we also felt sorry for the woman, Mary, and the poor kid.'

'Have you met him?'

'Who? Adam. Not yet. It's a difficult sort of thing to arrange, and Mary is very uncooperative. I mean with Dad.'

'He's very lucky that you are all so understanding.'

'Well, we love him. He's a good father, a kind man. This is where it pays off, even if you find he has been dishonest and deceitful. We all have lots of happy childhood memories, and in a way we helped to get him into this mess. We've had a very expensive education. We were very selfish. I guess we thought money was like a bottomless well.'

'It makes me feel worse for what my father did.' Emma looked close to tears and Giles reached out and clasped her hand.

'It had *nothing* to do with you. Sooner or later Dad would have been found out. He was an idiot. He was the one who had the nervous breakdown. Must have. He lost millions of pounds. He could never have concealed it forever. Darling, Emma, it must not make any difference to us. We have our lives too. We've weathered this separation. We can weather anything.' He looked at her intensely. 'Do you feel as I do? Still?'

She nodded, eyes now blurred by tears. They were in a corner of the dimly-lit restaurant and Giles, rising, went round to her, bent and kissed her, indifferent to the surreptitious glances of their fellow diners.

'Darling,' Giles impulsively pulled his chair closer to her and took her hand. 'We shall have to go away.'

'Go away?'

'If we want to be together, we shall have to go away. Eventually, that is. I mean, I want to support Dad when he comes up for trial, but he's going to plead guilty to save embarrassing the family. Even so, I think he'll go away for quite a long time. After I'm certain that Mum and Paul and Alice are settled and OK, I want to start a new life, and if you and I are to be together, and want to avoid the press, we'll have to get away.'

'I think David would like that.'

'David?'

'My therapist at the clinic.'

'Oh, you think he'd like it.' Giles seemed amused. 'Good.'

'Daddy's girl. He helped me discover a lot about myself.' Suddenly she looked excited. 'But where shall we go?'

'How about Australia?'

'Australia?'

'It's a great place, a young place. It really is a new country, hot, alive.' He gazed thoughtfully at the wine in his glass. 'I'd like to go into the wine business. I know I've made a few false starts, but I'm pretty sure about this. There's so much opportunity with Australian wines.'

'I'd love to go to Australia.' All at once Emma looked better, happy, a changed person.

Giles realised at that moment that her whole wellbeing, as well as their future, depended on him. He might have failed his father, but he could help now to rebuild Emma's life. He felt a new, welcome but altogether strange feeling of responsibility and saw how, after a long period of darkness, could come the light.

Once again Nick found himself the bearer of bad tidings. He looked from one parent to the other, wishing these awful jobs didn't always fall on him.

Whichever way you looked at it, things were in a terrible mess. Not only had Edmund Harvey suffered, the Constantines had suffered too.

The trial at the Old Bailey had been reported in the papers, but it had not made national headlines. In view of the sum of money he'd lost and the people he'd involved, some of them well-known names, and many respectable companies, Edmund's case might have produced a bigger stir. The recession, however, had produced a number of crooked lawyers, and one who pleaded guilty had not as much interest for the media as a long, juicy, bitter fight with as much scandal as possible thrown in. The only real interest in Edmund was from the *Financial Times* and his local paper, both of which were read, unfortunately, by too many people who knew both families.

Oddly enough, there was a lot of sympathy for the Harveys, and it was the Constantines who seemed to have to bear the brunt of ostracism by local people and some who remembered them from the school. Moreover, Andreas's family had acted with incredulity. His father and brothers came down on him particularly hard for bad judgement; an abandonment of good business principles. The loss of money seemed second place.

They helped him out, of course, but the yacht had had to go; the Rolls, naturally, a particular wrench. At least they still had the house. Andy's family had wanted them to sacrifice that and move into something smaller to release capital, but so far so good. Andy had eaten humble pie, and they held on.

Visiting her parents since Emma had come out of the clinic had been a particular ordeal. Andreas, especially, resented the fact that she had moved in with Nick instead of returning to the nest. He felt that she would resume her old, bad habits away from the protective eyes of her parents. He didn't seem to realise that the combination of their adulation together with too much money had probably brought on and encouraged her addiction in the first place.

Daddy's little girl no longer.

Emma usually accompanied Nick to dinner, but tonight he came alone, mumbling some excuse. He felt unhappy and ill at ease, and knew that this transmitted itself to his parents. His mother was particularly jumpy, her wine disappearing very rapidly from her glass.

During the meal, Nick tried to keep the conversation more or less neutral. He told them about his course, enlivened with tales of mutual friends. But all the time the real reason for his visit weighed heavily upon him, like a lodestone, and frequently his words faltered.

After dinner they moved into the drawing room. Marco brought coffee and closed the door quietly behind him. Lydia helped herself to a brandy while Andreas, watching her anxiously, gnawed at a fingernail, noting the level in her glass, frowning at her as she sat down as though to say that one addict in the family was enough.

'Emma's where?' he asked at last.

His parents gazing at him expectantly, Nick cleared his throat.

'Look, I've got something to tell you. Well . . . Emma and Giles have been seeing each other. They want to go to Australia together.' He finished in a rush and waited for his mother to burst into tears and his father to start performing.

'Now I've heard everything,' Andreas said. 'But this I can't believe. Can you believe it, Lydia?' He stared at his wife who, as Nick had foreseen, was having trouble controlling her emotions. Lydia wordlessly shook her head.

'I'd instructed him not to see my daughter,' Andreas went on.

'That was while she was in the clinic, Dad.'

'I forbade him ever to see her.'

'Then I'm afraid you can't do that. You can't behave like a Victorian father. He obeyed your wishes while Emma was in the clinic because he loved her, and he desperately wanted her to get better. He didn't want you to blame him if she didn't.'

'And now, as soon as she gets out, round he trots . . .'

'That is not the case.'

'I don't know why you're so nice to Giles,' Andreas said peevishly, shaking his head. 'I can't fathom it out. It just doesn't seem natural to me. This is a man who pinches your girl, leaves her in the lurch and now runs off with your sister. Who knows that he won't do it again?'

'I know he won't do it again. He loves Emma, he's proved that. And if he does do it again, he will have me to reckon with.'

'You didn't reckon with him before.'

'Because I don't think he loved Laura, and she didn't love him. There were all sorts of complex reasons for what happened. It wasn't a straightforward situation. She had a hang-up about me having money; she was desperately insecure. Giles wanted a travelling companion and, finally, you keep on saying he left her in the lurch, but he did not. She wanted to come home and he brought her back. He kept in touch to see if she was OK. Alright, at the time I was confused, I was hurt, but now I think I understand. Besides, a lot of water has flown under the bridge and we are all older. Perhaps a little wiser.'

'You are too nice, Nick.' Lydia began with a wail, but Andreas, clearly still angry and unconvinced by Nick's defence of his friend, butted in.

'That clinic cost me an absolute fortune, coming on top of everything else. I had to sell the yacht.'

'And the Rolls.' Lydia's tone was aggrieved.

'Emma has a lot to answer for,' Andreas mumbled and, looking across at his wife, got up to help himself to a brandy, pointedly not inviting Nick to have one as if he too shared some of the blame.

'Dad, it wasn't just Emma's fault,' Nick crossed one leg over the other, and calmly regarded his father. 'It was also your fault for lending over a million quid to Edmund Harvey.'

As his wife and son turned their reproachful eyes on him, Andreas resumed his seat.

'I think it was the only bad business mistake I ever made in my life. I shan't make one like it again; but I am hurt, Nick, and I emphasise "hurt" rather than "annoyed" that Emma chooses to live with you rather than us, now that she's out of the clinic. Here she has her own room, her

278

mother and father who love her very much, her freedom . . .'

'It wasn't really Emma's choice, Dad.'

'I know, and the psychiatrist spoke to me trying to explain
the reasons. I'm not saying that I agree with all this mumbo
jumbo these people talk. Basically, the medication cured
Emma, I'm convinced of that. And I hope she doesn't remain
under his influence now that she *is* cured.'

'Dad!' Nick looked angrily at his father. 'Emma can relapse
any time. This is the trouble with addiction.'

'But if she stays on the medication?'

'Well, she doesn't want to stay on it forever. She wants to
be permanently cured. She took the advice of Dr Pascoe and
moved in with me. But that's not the issue, is it? We've
moved on from there. It's what happens now, between her
and Giles.'

'Australia . . .' Lydia murmured, raising her eyes to the
ceiling and, finally, burst into tears. Her husband ignored her
while Nick rose and, crossing the room, gazed helplessly
down at her, simply not knowing what to do.

'You'd think that with all the harm Giles's family has done
to mine . . .'

'And you have done to him, Dad. Don't forget that.' Nick
turned savagely towards Andreas, beginning to feel that he
was entitled to lose his temper too.

'What harm have *I* done to his family?'

'You reported him to the police.'

'Because he was a crook.'

'He'd hoped to get out of his difficulties. He had enormous
financial problems he felt he couldn't tell anyone about. He
did not intend to steal or dishonestly defraud anyone. OK,
he knew what he was doing was risky, but he hoped and
wanted to pay it all back.'

'Huh. That's what they all say. He must have known he
could never pay it back. He owed millions.'

'He was in a jam. You could have gone to him, talked to him, warned him. You chose not to.'

'Because I knew he was dishonest.'

'Because,' Nick answered hotly, 'you didn't get into some stupid gentleman's club he'd put you up for.'

'He never put me up for it.'

'He did.'

'He did not.' The two men were now bawling across the room at each other, while Lydia, still ignored, quietly went on weeping.

'He put you up and you were blackballed. He didn't know how to tell you.'

'Blackballed?' Andreas gazed incredulously at Nick. 'Did you say blackballed?'

'They didn't want you. Sorry, Dad, you're not the right type. Surely you must have realised that these gentleman's clubs in St James's are full of assholes? Of course they wouldn't want you, a third generation immigrant from a Greek peasant family. They'd hardly want the Royal Family because they came from Hanover, and that was over two hundred years ago. There's nothing so rotten as the entrenched ruling classes in this country.'

Andreas leaned back in his chair, his mouth hanging open like a fish gasping for air.

'But I rang the secretary. He said he'd never heard of me.'

'Probably being tactful. They don't like to admit to that kind of thing. You were blackballed, Dad, and that's the truth.'

Whether it was the truth or not, Andreas was certain he would never know.

A month or so later, Giles and Emma flew to Sydney with Emma's parents' blessing, but without them to see her off. There was a loving farewell at the house, and they even shook Giles warmly by the hand. They were too afraid of meeting the Harveys, who also stayed away from the airport. They, too, were afraid of meeting the Constantines.

Nick alone, prey to many conflicting emotions, stood waving at the huge plane as it lifted into the air, en route for a new life for at least two of the people on board. As for him, he had his own life to get on with. Not quite the one he had perhaps at one time wished for, or·expected, but a good life nevertheless.

And, in time, there would be other Lauras, other loves.

CHAPTER 17

Alice, Edmund's darling, was nearly sixteen. She was a tall, rangy, good-looking girl with long straight fair hair and a rather superior expression that she had inherited from her mother. It seemed to go with the breed. She was very casual and laid-back like most of her generation, but maybe she'd miss Whiteboys more than anybody, Valerie thought, watching her from her bedroom window as she took her horse Tuppence through his paces in the paddock.

But Alice was a sensible, self-contained young person who, in common with the rest of the family, could see nothing so dreadfully wrong in what poor Ed had done. It was an awful pity, and quite unfair, that he'd landed up in prison. They all went to see him as often as they could to cheer him up and bring him nice treats like cigars from Dunhills and chocolates from Bendicks in Wigmore Street.

Edmund had got seven years, but with remission for good behaviour he would be out after four.

The house, just outside the pretty village of Montacute, a few miles from Yeovil, belonged to Ed, so it had to go on the instructions of his trustees in bankruptcy. Fortunately the London house was Valerie's outright. The estate agents were due any moment to give a valuation before putting it on the market. It was ridiculous really, because what it would fetch in its dilapidated state would hardly pay legal fees and certainly not a penny would go to the people to whom he owed so much money.

Nothing to the wretched Andreas. Valerie, who was not a very vindictive woman, was glad of that. She *was* vindictive, though, in her feelings towards Andreas Constantine. It just showed how little breeding the man had, that instead of coming round to see Ed and discussing the problem like a gentleman, he'd gone to the police and poor Ed never stood a chance. After all, they were supposed to be *friends*. Their sons had gone to the same school. They'd socialised together and spent a holiday on that horribly vulgar yacht.

Valerie turned away from the window and pulled the duvet and sheets off the bed, dumping them violently on the floor as though it was the sort of thing she'd like to do to Andreas. Yes, *and* she'd stamp all over him, too.

The blasted Constantines seemed to have dogged their lives, Valerie thought, as she gathered up the bedclothes and threw them into the landing, where they joined another lot from the room next door. And now it looked as though one day they might be united by marriage, Giles being clearly in love with Emma and she with him.

Everything had to be reasonably tidy for the estate agents, not that she cared much because they wouldn't see any of the money. There was five bedrooms in the house and, frankly, she'd be quite glad to see the back of it. It was a lot of work when they were there, a constant worry when they were not, and they had thought for some time of putting it on the market. However, the children, who had happy childhood memories of it, resisted.

Valerie went back to the window and, waving her arms about to get her attention, called out to Alice indicating that she wanted her back in the house.

The summer holidays had just begun. Normally the whole family would have descended on the house and done the jolly, sporty, horsey things they invariably did when they spent time there. Alice was mad about horses. Paul and Giles not so much. To everyone's astonishment, after he left school

Paul had settled down and got a menial job in the futures department of a City merchant bank, starting in quite a humble capacity as a runner; but he had learned fast and was doing well. He was quick and agile and quite bright, and it seemed that soon he might start to deal and perhaps, eventually, he'd help to revive the family fortunes again.

Valerie went downstairs to make a cup of coffee, and then walked to the door to see if Alice had done as she'd asked. Yes, there was no sign of her in the paddock, and then she could see her making her way slowly round from the stables towards the house, her fair hair glistening in the sun.

The odd thing was that Giles, who had appeared so bright, so gifted, was the one who kept on changing his mind about his vocation. Paul, on the other hand, who had always been considered a bit dim and unreliable, now seemed so single-minded. Of course he had made a lot of valuable contacts at his expensive school (not public, but for the intellectually challenged sons of the wealthy and well connected) which had got him into the bank in the first place.

Maybe it was the example of his brother and father that had helped to give him a sense of direction. Giles had given up psychology, then law, and was now working at a winery near Adelaide in South Australia with the hope of making it a career.

Alice came into the kitchen and threw herself into a chair by the table, saying how tired she was and just how much she would love a cup of coffee.

'Coming up,' Valerie said and pushed a mug towards her. 'I could do with a bit of help in the house, darling.'

'Of course, Mum.' Alice glanced across at her mother as she seated herself opposite her. 'You look tired.'

'A bit tired,' Valerie acknowledged, pushing her hair back from her forehead. Alice thought her mother had been magnificent, stoical and stalwart, and had made the very best of a bad situation. But Alice knew that, beneath the sang-froid, the stiff upper lip, it had taken a lot out of her.

Apart from the trial itself, which wasn't quite as bad as they'd expected because Dad had pleaded guilty so it was short, the worst part in a way was discovering that Dad had a mistress and there was a half-brother, none of them had known anything about. Mum had been absolutely amazing about that.

'How are you *really* feeling, Mum?' Alice insisted. 'I think you bottle it all up.'

Valerie sat opposite her daughter, drew her mug of coffee towards her, suddenly, completely unexpectedly, feeling too overcome by emotion to trust herself to speak. Darling Alice. She was such a comfort, a caring, helpful companion despite her youth. A real little trouper. Yet Valerie had been brought up not to show feelings, except those of pleasure or satisfaction, never grief or, horror of horrors, despair. These virtues, if they could be called virtues, and in another era they had been, were inculcated in her from a young age, from the nursery and a series of strict, disciplined, nannies; through her girls' boarding school with its thick serge uniforms and grey felt hats, its motto of '*Labor omnia vincit* – work conquers all', and is certainly better than making an ass of yourself in public, it seemed to imply.

In its philosophy, its emphasis on hard work and games, it aped the better known public schools for boys. Emotions were to be firmly hidden, kept under control.

In many ways Valerie knew now, too late, that this had been responsible for the way she and Ed conducted their marriage. She was so awkward about sex that he had turned to someone else for pleasure. Yet when they were engaged she had found it all rather thrilling and exciting, perhaps because it was dangerous and, by implication, forbidden. After marriage and especially after children, all the pleasure went, and it became a duty.

Then there was their inability to talk, to confide in each

285

other, and Ed had kept all his terrible problems from her because he felt she would not understand, would disapprove.

At that moment another awful thing happened: tears began to roll down her cheeks and, as astonished as her mother, Alice urgently whispered: 'Mum?'

'Pretty terrible,' Valerie said at last, hastily producing a handkerchief and wiping her eyes. 'I feel pretty terrible really, darling.'

'Oh, *Mum*,' Alice swiftly rounded the table and flung both arms around her mother, pressing her cheek close to hers. This was a mother she didn't know, but nevertheless was glad to see. This was a mother with the raw, human emotions of everyone else, not someone whom nothing ever seemed to move very much. For instance, it was very seldom that they hugged, or touched as closely as they were now.

'Oh, Mum, have a good cry, let it all hang out.'

'You're such an angel.' Valerie put her arms more closely round her daughter's body and pressed it to hers. It was so warm, vibrant and alive; so comforting. 'I was always brought up, you know, darling, to hold things back, to be in control. It was considered a weakness to cry or show emotion. I felt when it all came out about Daddy . . . and Mary, and the boy, my whole world had collapsed. But all I knew how to do, had been taught to do, was to carry on as though nothing had happened. Then Giles going to Australia so soon after the trial . . .'

'Because he thought you were alright.' Alice brushed the hair back from her mother's damp forehead. 'You *told* him you were perfectly alright.'

'I know. I *was* alright. I am alright, but sometimes I think, darling, it doesn't do to be too strong, keep things back. People value your weaknesses. I'm glad I didn't send you to boarding school. You're a kind, sweet, understanding girl, older than your years. You're a great support to me and I'm sure you will never make the mistakes in your marriage I made in mine. Now then.'

Valerie made a visible effort to pull herself together, reverting to type. She released Alice, blew her nose several times and drew a crumpled letter from the pocket of her jeans. 'Enough of this nonsense. Look, I heard from Giles today. He wants to go into the wine business seriously.'

'That means he'll stay in Australia.'

'I suppose so.' Valerie pushed her untidy mop of hair away from her face again. 'Maybe it's just as well. Start a new life. I mean it's not the end of the world, though it does seem so far away.'

Alice reached for the letter and opened it. 'Does he say anything about Emma?'

'Emma *loves* it. She likes the wine business too, the people they're staying with, and she seems like a new person.'

Alice swiftly scanned the airmail letter and nodded, tossing it back to her mother. 'I always liked Emma.'

Valerie seemed to agree. 'Emma was the last person I thought would go off the rails.' She stuffed the letter back in her pocket. 'She seemed so sensible, not like her mother who was an hysteric. So detached.'

'Maybe that's why she went off the rails.' Alice assumed an expression of wisdom that made her look older than her years.

'You mean it was because of her parents?'

'Probably.'

Valerie sniffed. 'Emma and Nick were certainly *most* unfortunate in their parents. They simply had no breeding, no manners. I liked Nick too, frankly, but this whole ghastly business would never have happened if Andreas had had the decency to talk to Daddy.' She paused and sighed deeply. 'Or if he, Daddy, that is, had talked to *me*. I could have gone to Grandpa, who I'm sure would have helped, not only with money but with good advice. What Daddy did was stupid, not criminal. He never meant to steal, but to pay it all back. As if a person like him would *steal*! But I blame myself that he felt he couldn't talk to me. He must have suffered such agonies, poor lamb, deeply in debt, that accursed woman round his neck sponging off him.'

'Oh, Mum, you *are* a brick.' Impulsively Alice reached out and seized hold of her hand. 'I do so love you.'

'Don't be *silly*, darling,' Valerie said in a wobbly voice, taking a hankie from her pocket and blowing her nose really hard. 'We Harveys must stick together. Show a united front. Noblesse oblige, and all that, you know.'

Edmund leaned on his spade, got out a large handkerchief from his pocket and mopped his brow. Digging was hard work but it was very satisfying. Curious that, because he had never taken much interest in gardening before; woman's work he called it, and now he was in charge of the open prison's kitchen garden. Winter was coming on and he was preparing the ground for the planting of next year's crop of potatoes.

He was very into gardening catalogues, and the tomatoes he'd produced in the summer had been judged by his fellow inmates, some of whom had been there for years, as the very best.

In so far as he could say he was happy, Edmund *was* happy, perhaps really happy for the first time, or one of the few times, in his life.

There was this glorious freedom, a complete absence of responsibility. He had to make no decisions for himself or anyone else except what seed potatoes to plant, and what fertiliser to use. He was strongly in favour of organic garden-ing, so that was the difficult choice: how to produce spuds that were free from pests without the use of pesticides? Ah, that was the question. But there was no sweating and no sleepless nights about that, as had been the case in the bad old days. He slept like a baby, dreaming about seed potatoes and ripe plum tomatoes, organic fertilisers, mulch and manure.

Everything was ritualised from morning until he retired to bed at night to sleep the sleep of the just. No decisions. No worry. No fevered schemes for robbing Peter to pay Paul. No demanding mistress with ideas far above her station. No fear of discovery, because now all was out in the open. It was wonderful. He'd gained half a stone in weight.

Edmund tucked his handkerchief back in his pocket and bent his back over the spade thinking of the lucky break that had landed him here. At the time he hadn't called it luck. It had seemed like disaster, the end of the world.

But then the unexpected happened. He found he could talk to his wife, unburden himself, tell her about Mary, about Adam, about all the hideous deceit of the years gone by; the increasing demands, growing financial difficulties, the fall in property prices, the decline in the market. And while Val had been wonderful he'd had nothing but trouble from Mary who, of course in her awful lower-middle class way, was deeply ashamed of him. He was terribly fond of Adam, dear little boy, but there was now no question of him paying private school fees. So sucks to you, greedy Mary!

It was beginning to get dark and Edmund decided to finish his digging. A fellow inmate passed and he waved to him, had a word. It was really like being at school again, he thought, looking towards the large ivy-clad country house as, spade over his shoulder, he made his way through the fields and across smooth lawns, past well-filled herbaceous borders, round the back to the prisoners' entrance. Ah well, one couldn't have everything. The main entrance was reserved for people who were not detained at the pleasure of Her Majesty.

There was a stimulating atmosphere about the place with lots of good conversation. Doubtless, over the time he'd be here he'd make a number of valuable contacts for the future, though whether he'd be allowed to practise again was another matter. Doubtful. Perhaps he could act as a consultant? Consultancies were highly profitable. You didn't actually have to know much except your way about and, of course, the right people.

Edmund shook his head thoughtfully, went into the cloakroom and began removing his muddy boots, shaking out the soil and putting on clean socks. He would go upstairs and have a shower and then go to the common room for a jaw with fellow guests of the Queen.

If you looked carefully you found a lot of kindred spirits in an open prison. There were, inevitably, thick-necked brutes and hardened felons such as he'd encountered in Wormwood Scrubs. After all, in a democracy you had to give everyone an equal chance; you couldn't just have an open prison for gentlemen, nice as that would be. But it was quite easy to make one's way around the riffraff, because they enjoyed one another's company just as much as he did people of his own kind.

No, here, one also found lawyers, accountants – quite a lot of these – income tax inspectors, barristers, of course, plenty of ex-senior policemen, a few doctors, a surprising number of teachers, even a former High Court judge who had been at school with his uncle.

People of one's own kind. People like him.

In a way, when the time came, Edmund Harvey thought, he would be sorry to leave this sanctuary and return to the battles that, inevitably, he'd find in the real world.

There would be the struggle for existence, trying to make a living, patching up his marriage, dealing with Mary, facing old friends. Naturally he'd already resigned from the club. That club, the source of so much trouble.

Dear, oh dear, Edmund thought, shaking his head as he made his way along the corridor. Better not even to think about what lay ahead, but make the best of the present good times. And who'd have thought he, a man of the law, would ever say that about prison?

As for Laura Chase, she too was a survivor, discovering things about herself in the past few years every bit as profound as had someone she'd never known, never met, Edmund Harvey.

She'd read that he'd been sent to prison, but not about the involvement of Andreas Constantine, because the trial was a short affair, mostly ignored by the press.

She didn't write to Giles. 'Sorry your dad was sent to prison.' Somehow it sounded false. Also, she'd been quite glad. What she knew of Mr Harvey she hadn't liked. It seemed such a long time ago, and it was.

She had worked very hard at Oxford and gratified her tutor with a 2:1. But getting a job had been less easy. Even Oxbridge graduates were not wanted, and she'd had little alternative but to work at Mr Boothroyd's while endlessly applying for jobs.

Finally, persistence paid off. She was about to start as a trainee reporter on a local newspaper. She'd been one of three successful applicants out of over a thousand. The bottom rung of the ladder, but a ladder nevertheless.

It was very sad to say goodbye to Mr Boothroyd. He'd become like a second father, and the last day had been almost painful. He was a good and kind man, and in a way she loved him like she now loved her dad, although there was a distance between them and always would be. She would never, for instance, have dreamt of using his Christian name, Cecil, even in these days of easy familiarity.

There was something old worldly about Cecil Boothroyd, just as there was about his shop, and Laura, who in many ways was old worldly too, preferred it like that.

She took a long time getting her coat, her bag, the carrier

with the usual provisions for the evening meal. Early in the day she'd taken flowers to Mrs Boothroyd who was going into hospital in the near future for a hysterectomy and spent a great deal of time resting.

Laura never thought of Mrs Boothroyd as a second mother. In fact, she scarcely ever saw her and she sometimes wondered if she was not, in fact, jealous of Laura's relationship with her husband. It was absurd, of course, but there was always a funny air, a distance about Mrs Boothroyd that was hard to fathom. And as Laura handed her the flowers, had she perhaps discerned a gleam of pleasure, of relief in Mrs Boothroyd's eyes?

Finally it was time to go. Mr Boothroyd, in paying her her wages had added a generous sum of money, two hundred pounds, to help her, he told her, through the first few weeks until she drew her pay. She'd almost kissed him, but no, it would not do, even if there was no Mrs Boothroyd nursing her diseased womb upstairs. Besides, it would have embarrassed Mr Boothroyd who was not a demonstrative man.

Mr Boothroyd came to the door to see her off, held out his hand and shook hers.

'This isn't goodbye, Laura.'

'Of course not, Mr Boothroyd. Who knows, I might be back?'

Mr Boothroyd smiled and shook his head.

'No, young woman, I think you're on the up and up. But good luck.'

'Maybe I'll come and help out on my days off?'

'That would be great.'

Now that she was leaving, she didn't really want to go. The great, frantic, outside world of newspapers seemed a frightening place.

Laura had always liked writing. She had won an essay prize at school and her name was on a scroll in the school hall. 'The Deirdre Simpson Essay Prize' it was called, though everyone had long forgotten who Deirdre Simpson was. But writing an essay with loads of time in which to do it was very different from the succinct hack work required by a daily newspaper.

It was very cold, mid-winter. The wind blew in from the Pennines and people scurried, heads bent, along the street, as Laura, her head also down, hurried home.

Inside the house her father was waiting for her, looking expectantly towards the door, his face lighting up as she came in. Some days he never left his room, but others he came down and lit a fire and made tea for her. His isolation and dependence on his daughter had revealed a kindness neither he nor she knew he possessed.

Laura, who had once despised him, now loved her dad. They lived alone, her brothers having left home. They hardly saw Gary, or his wife and baby, who now lived in another town. Gordon hadn't made it to Academe, but had joined the regular army instead and was stationed somewhere abroad.

Occasionally Laura went to see her mother who still lived with her sister, a council flat having not yet materialised. They never visited her or her father, who thus far was entirely dependent on Laura.

Her father was excited about her job, which was starting the next day, but he was fearful too.

'I'm sure one of these days you'll leave me, love,' he said over tea, which they had sitting close to the fire. One of these days too, when Laura was a wealthy, successful journalist she told herself, she'd have central heating installed.

She smiled at her father and spread butter on her cake. Butter on a piece of fruitcake was a lovely indulgence.

'If I go, I'll take you with me, Dad.'

'Promise.'

'Promise.'

'Excited, Laura?'

She popped the piece of cake into her mouth.

'I'm excited,' she said, 'and a bit scared.'

She'd done a computer course, she'd done shorthand. She was well prepared. She didn't know why she was scared, but she was.

Little Laura going out into the big world. Well, not so little, she was speaking figuratively but, really, all she had behind her was her Oxford degree and her father, no rich powerful friends like Giles and Nick.

After tea, she washed up and they sat watching television. This was the ritual every night. She hardly ever went out and she had few friends. Her time was given to her father, and her dreams. She daydreamed a great deal.

But all this would change. Inevitably, it would change. She was ambitious and she would climb. She would go to London, maybe abroad; but not while her father was alive. The doctor had told her in confidence that he didn't think he'd last long. One more heart attack . . .

She kissed him fondly after taking his milk to him in bed, chatting for a while before saying good night.

Laura went to her room and, for a long time, remained standing by the window looking out on the sleeping city: ugly, ramshackle, a huge mixed conurbation yet exciting too – the place of her birth.

She knew for sure that however far she travelled from Salford, Manchester, she would always retain her regional accent, her forthright, uncompromising manner, and be at one with the people among whom she'd been born. She would always return home again, back to her roots.

But nothing ventured, nothing gained.

Then her thoughts went back, as they often did, to Nick and Giles. To her brief ecstatic love affair with one, her travels and not so ecstatic love affair with the other.

The trouble was that she had never really fitted in with either, with their manners, their outlook, their lifestyle or their folks.

Look at the way Edmund Harvey had treated her father; thrown him out into the street like a tramp. No respect, no dignity for the father of a girl they also doubtless thought of as a tramp. She'd only met Giles's mother at the airport on their return from Australia. She'd fallen over herself to be nice to Laura in a patronising kind of way. But how relieved she must have been when she knew the romance was over.

Despite what was said about modern times, democracy, equality, the rest, there was still class distinction about, and it mattered. You spoke differently, you behaved differently, you held your knife differently, your values and expectations were different. If you wanted to move up to the middle classes from the working class, you had to unlearn everything you already knew.

Some people said that you were born into a class, just as you inherited your genes. It was not something you could acquire.

But others said that you could change class if you were rich enough. Or maybe some people would say she had changed it by being educated, having an Oxford degree and aspiring to a profession like journalism.

Class mattered with the Constantines. They had looked down on her and she was aware of it. Never mind that the grandfather had been a Greek peasant; huge wealth had changed all that. The recollection of that overpowering visit to the house in St John's Wood still made her uncomfortable: the exquisite furnishings, the trappings of power, the high security with little screens and cameras all over the house showing you this section and that, the butler and maid, the Rolls in the garage. And the yacht ... the yacht she had never seen and now never would.

Sometimes she thought she would write to Nick, tell him about her change of fortune. But then she knew she wouldn't. Nick and Giles were strangers to her now, alien. There were some barriers that could never be overcome.

Or was it, simply, that you moved on?

Laura knew then that, for the rest of her life, somewhere beneath the surface, no matter what happened to her, however much she changed or altered her views, she would be imprinted with the memory of that strange encounter in her youth with the children of the rich.